Praise for *The Summer of Skinny Dipping*

"A deep, realistic exploration into first love and, yes, even loss."
—*RT Book Reviews (4 out of 5 stars)*

"Looking for a book that you can lose yourself in this summer? Pick up *The Summer of Skinny Dipping*." —CosmoGirl.com

"Tailor-made for Sarah Dessen's fans, this novel mingles family drama and teen relationships...With a lyrical yet straightforward voice and a layered plot, this novel will live on for more than a summer." —*School Library Journal*

"[A] realistic and satisfying chick-lit debut." —*Kirkus*

"First-time novelist Howells's teen and adult characters are well-developed, and Mia's growth and new perspective on her own good fortune are satisfying." —*Publishers Weekly*

"Readers will appreciate the departure from the run-of-the mill girl meets boy on the beach story. *The Summer of Skinny Dipping* is a perfect fit for fans of Sarah Dessen."
—*Elizabeth Duffy, CATS Meow*

"Many teens will appreciate this first novel for how the dialogue not only captures the dynamics of Mia's standoffs with her peers but also reveals her surprising discoveries about adults."　　　　　　　　　　　　*—Booklist*

"Howells has created a touching love story and an inspirational self-discovery story all in one book. I highly recommended it to anyone who wants to be truly moved."　　*—Charleston Gazette*

"I don't want to compare *The Summer of Skinny Dipping* to anything else, because it's very unique, but I just have to say: it was better than a Sarah Dessen novel. I know, I know. That's saying a lot, but really, Amanda Howells's writing is just as great."　　　　　　　　*—The Naughty Book Kitties*

"This is a touching novel about falling in love, being independent, and learning to believe in yourself…a terrific summer read!"
—Teens Read Too

"I pretty much devoured this book in one sitting."
—Cindy's Love of Books

"A solid stand-alone novel that will hook readers any time of year. Hand this one over to your Dessen, Han, and Ockler fans without hesitation."　　　　　　　　　　　　*—Stacked*

"Mia's voice grabbed me. And the rest is history."

—*The Story Siren*

"*The Summer of Skinny Dipping* will make you wish for days with nothing to do but lie on the beach and read."

—*Mother-Daughter Book Club*

"An exceptional debut that had me crying, laughing, shouting, and smiling." —*The Book Scout*

"The realism of *The Summer of Skinny Dipping* makes for an excellent summer read that I devoured in one sitting."

—*Writing from the Tub*

"Perfect for Sarah Dessen fans…readers (primarily girls) will gobble up this nostalgic, breezy tale of adventure, family secrets, first love, and loss." —*Bookworm Readers*

"Highly recommended." —*Pudgy Penguin Perusals*

"Sad and happy, dangerous and free spirited, angry and loving, and so much more. A most definite read for anyone this summer and one that should be on high school reading requirements nationwide." —*Yankee Romance Reviewers*

"*The Summer of Skinny Dipping* is an emotional roller coaster, one you would ride again and again." —*A Journey of Books*

"Breathtaking." —*Chick Lit Reviews*

"Perfect for the beach if you want that 'fun summer romance' book, but the depth and realism make it so much more." —*Bookmac*

"The writing is so beautiful that I had to reread many passages out loud because I loved it so much." —*Enchanted by Books*

"You'll want to read this book over and over and over." —*Paranormal Obsession*

the summer *of* skinny dipping

a novel by amanda howells

sourcebooks
fire

Published by Sourcebooks Fire, an imprint of Sourcebooks, Inc.
P.O. Box 4410, Naperville, Illinois 60567-4410
(630) 961-3900
Fax: (630) 961-2168
teenfire.sourcebooks.com

Library of Congress Cataloging-in-Publication Data.

Howells, Amanda.
   The summer of skinny dipping / by Amanda Howells.
      p. cm.
   Summary: While spending the summer in the Hamptons, sixteen-year-old Mia is disap-
pointed that her cousin Corinne has grown so distant, but when she meets the irresistible
and adventurous boy next door, everything changes for the better.
   (pbk. : alk. paper) [1. Cousins—Fiction. 2. Family problems—Fiction. 3. Love—Fiction.
4. Ocean—Fiction. 5. Swimming—Fiction. 6. Death—Fiction. 7. Hamptons (N.Y.)—
Fiction.] I. Title.
   PZ7.H8388Sum 2010
   [Fic]—dc22
                                  2009049926

Printed and bound in the United States of America.
VP 10 9 8 7 6 5

There are summers you'll always remember and summers you've forgotten even before they're through. It's never an in-between season. Whole months can slip by, and you don't know what you did or where you were. June, July, August, they're all the same.

This is the other kind.

Long after that summer ended, I stayed stuck inside it, reliving that night, over and over, and everything that led up to it. Sometimes I still wake up shivering in the early hours of the morning, drowning in dreams of being out there in the ocean, of looking up at the moon and feeling as invisible and free as a fish.

I know I am different, and yet also, in a way, I'm still the same, only more myself now, because that's what happens when your life changes so completely. It takes pieces of you that you kept deeply hidden, even from yourself, and forces them to the surface like splinters working their way out of your skin.

But I'm jumping ahead, and to tell the story right, I have to go back to the very beginning. To a place called Indigo Beach. To a boy with pale skin that glowed against the dark waves. To the start of something neither of us could have predicted, and which would mark us forever, making everything that came after and before seem like it belonged to another life.

My name is Mia Gordon: I was sixteen years old, and I remember everything.

SOUTHAMPTON

chapter one

his is terrible," Mom moaned, fussing with her hair as we inched down the Long Island Expressway, a line of cars as far as the eye could see. "When will we start moving?" she asked Dad. "Or will we have to spend the summer in the car?"

"Do I look psychic?" Dad replied in a rare moment of irritability. "This is your home turf, not mine, Maxine."

We were all irritable. The heavy New York heat rolled over us like a carpet, so humid it constricted lungs and seemed to lick armpits. We'd been driving for days, and ever since the car's AC gave out somewhere near Pennsylvania, everyone had been losing it.

Dad had said that driving to New York would be an "adventure" and that we'd "need an extra car" at my cousins' house. But we all knew it was more about keeping costs down. Four airline tickets were nothing to sniff at for Dad, especially since his hardware business was struggling and his retirement savings had tanked in three months— along with everyone else's since the economy took a nosedive.

"This sucks," my sister, Eva, whined. She blew a giant Hubba Bubba bubble that exploded, leaving bits of stickiness across the back of my mother's headrest.

"Eva Marie, stop that!" Mom said. "And watch your mouth,

sweetheart. It's not pretty to speak that way, and you need to behave well in front of your cousins, please."

This was about the angriest my mother ever got with Eva, the family brat and apple of Mom's eye. Eva was nine, and she had the biggest, bluest eyes imaginable—so big and so blue they could take her "all the way to Hollywood," or so my mother never stopped telling her. Eva had been named after Eva Marie Saint, the actress from that old movie *On the Waterfront*.

I'm also named for an actress: I'm named after Mia Farrow, but unlike Eva, I look nothing like my whisper-thin, blond namesake. Luckily for Mom, she got what she had always wanted with her second kid: a beautiful replica of herself, who could live out the fantasy Mom had always dreamed of but never followed: to be a star. The last thing I would ever want to be.

"Mia, do you want me to put the radio on?" Dad asked. I caught Dad's eye in the rearview mirror and smiled because Dad was always tuned in to me. So on the favoritism front, you could say things even out.

"Not that station," I said quickly as the radio static turned to something recognizable. "I hate that song." "Forever" was actually one of my favorites. Until six weeks ago, when my boyfriend, Jake, had dumped me.

• • •

"I didn't plan this," Jake said.

We were standing outside school. I was trying not to look at Jake because I knew if I looked at him, I would cry. I stared at his shoes instead.

"It's just getting to be too serious too fast between us. I need space."

"So that's why you're hooking up with Gabi? To get space?" I spat back. "How does that work?" I lifted my gaze and stared him down, picturing Gabi Santiago draping her leggy body all over my boyfriend. "Correction," I snapped. "There *is* a lot of space when it comes to Gabi. Between her ears."

"You're going away for the summer. Gabi is here." Jake looked embarrassed. "It's just timing." He shifted awkwardly, rolling a skateboard back and forth under his foot like he couldn't wait to roll on out of there and away from me. "Mia, I'm sorry. I don't know what else to say."

But I thought I loved you! Even thinking the word "love" made me feel sick. This boy whom I had fallen for the minute I'd laid eyes on him. My first boyfriend. We'd only been together two months, but it had felt like forever. The way love should feel.

"How long has this been going on?" I asked, my voice low and hard. "What exactly *is* the timing of this relationship?"

"It's not a relationship, Mia, I—" Jake began lamely, but I was done.

"—Save it," I choked. I wheeled around and walked away, my eyes filling with tears. I didn't want to know any more. Jake was a cheat. I could see it in his eyes. I could hear it in his voice. Not that it mattered anymore. Because the relationship I'd thought was real had never existed. Jake could spin it any way he liked, but I obviously hadn't meant anything to him. I was just holding him back. If only I had held back from him! If only I could take back the three words I had said to him just last weekend, the words that had come tumbling out of my mouth.

But once you say something like that, you give something you can never get back.

• • •

"Who wants a snack?" Dad had pulled into a gas station that advertised homemade ice cream.

"Rhetorical question," I said, brightening. Who cared about Jake? He was far away now. And I'd promised myself I wouldn't think about him. I was on a vacation from heartbreak. I planned to treat myself to things that made me feel good instead. Like ice cream on a hot summer's day. But then Mom shot me one of her typical downers.

"Honey, snacking between meals is not the way to slim down."

"Thanks, Mom," I said dryly. "I forgot. You put me on a diet."

"Don't be sarcastic," Mom snapped. "I'm just trying to help you."

"Why do I keep forgetting that?" I shot back, but under my breath, because there was no point in making my words loud enough to hear. Mom would never get it: I was never going to be like her, thin as a toothpick. Graceful. Elegant. Small boned. Not unless I became anorexic. *Which is probably her big dream,* I thought angrily.

"Your new top looks very…tight," Mom had said to me one night as Jake and I were leaving for a party at my friend Kristin's. I'd bought a tank—something much more tight-fitting than what I usually wore, and Mom evidently thought I should go back to hiding my shape. "I just don't think clingy tank tops suit your build," Mom added. She thought she was speaking in a low voice, but Jake overheard her as he waited on the landing.

"You're wrong, Mrs. Gordon. Mia rocks everything she wears," Jake had said.

My mother was stunned and said something frosty in reply, something about young men not standing too close to girls' bedrooms while they got dressed. But Jake just smiled at me, his dark eyes warm and appreciative. He was there for me. *Was. But not anymore.* He had changed. Or maybe the real Jake was the lightweight who had stood with one foot on his skateboard ready to roll out of my life as fast as he had rolled into it, the new kid in town, the new boy in class, the first boy I'd ever cared about...

"Chocolate or vanilla?" Dad broke into my moody thoughts, leaning into my open window after parking at the gas station. "Or maybe you want to come in and see what else they have?" I shook my head. My mother. One sentence from her lips, and my appetite was instantly suppressed.

Once the car was on the road again, my spirits climbed with the speedometer. Every mile brought me closer to the ocean, and once I was in it, even my mother couldn't spoil it for me. I'm a good swimmer, and ocean swimming is my favorite kind. But we live in Athens, Georgia, and hadn't been up to my cousins' Hamptons beach house for several summers. Dad had expanded his hardware store when the construction business boomed, so he wanted to keep an eye on things year-round, especially during the summer when it got really busy.

There was the beach not too far away, but Mom would never think of staying there for even a weekend. She said it was "too blue collar," so that was that. Summers were spent at home, with chlorine substituting for salt, and, instead of soothing ocean sounds, the buzz of neighborhood lawn mowers accompanying each stifling suburban day.

But not this summer. "Business is so dead that we might as well enjoy the lull," Dad had announced to me and Mom. "We'll go up to New York this summer." And even though I knew Dad was worried about the store, I also knew he was glad to get away, that we all needed a break from home.

"Almost there," Dad said, as after what seemed like forever we finally took the turn-off and headed east along the south fork of the island. *Off Expressway. Yippee!* I texted my cousin Corinne.

"Thank God!" Mom smiled, and so did I as we exited the Long Island Expressway and cut along Sunset Road. Then we were on the Montauk Highway, inching closer toward the ocean. Still too far to see the water, but I could feel it getting closer. Just a little farther to my right were the barrier islands, tracing a long, skinny finger shape on the map, parallel to the mainland. Here the Hamptons beaches lie like a string of pearls, separated from the rest of Long Island by bays of blue water, connected only by long, thin bridges that lift you up and over toward paradise, leaving the rest of the world far behind.

Cool salt breezes swept through the stale heat of our car and I took a deep breath, inhaling like I hadn't breathed in years. Two months. Most of July and the whole of August. Eight weeks spent between the water and the beach, wearing the same pair of cutoffs every day and not caring. Best of all, it would be eight weeks of chilling out with my cousin Corinne.

Can't wait, cuz! I scrolled through old texts Corinne had sent me. *Another summer w/out u and I'll kill Beth!* If we weren't texting, we were emailing, and if we weren't emailing, we were calling, with Corinne gossiping about her annoying older sis, Beth, and me snarking on about Mom and Eva.

Corinne is only two months older than me, and every summer of our childhood we'd been inseparable. We hadn't seen each other for three years, since she lived in New York City and we hadn't come up in so long. But now we would be together again.

Except that Corinne had been unreachable lately. I stared at my phone, wondering why I hadn't received any messages from Corinne all month. The last I'd heard from her was after Jake broke up with me. I'd badly needed to talk to her. I knew she would have the right words to comfort me. She'd had serious boyfriends since she was thirteen. But after calling and emailing a two-page letter, all I got from her was a quick text: *Don't cry cuz. Always more fish in the sea!*

More fish in the sea. Was that really all she had to say? I shifted in my seat, the sweaty plastic unpeeling from the small of my back. It was kind of weird that Corinne had gone out of range like that, no words in weeks. But as the car slowed down, my mood kicked into a high-octane leap. Soon I wouldn't have to think about texts and phones. Soon I'd be seeing my cousin in the flesh, and when we were together, we'd be back in our old finish-each-other's-sentences groove.

"There they are!" Mom trilled, sticking her hand out the window as we drove through the open gates and up the gravel-chipped driveway to Wind Song, my Aunt Kathleen and Uncle Rufus Drexel's home in Southampton. "We're here!"

Before Dad had even stopped the car, I was out, sprinting across soft green grass. My aunt and uncle waved from the porch. Corinne and Beth were lying next to the pool.

I flew toward my cousins, shrinking time with each footstep, or that's what it felt like. All the lost years would be caught up in an instant. Corinne and I were two peas in a pod, both loving nothing more than to be barefoot and on the beach. We were also alter egos: skinny and solid, loud and silent, always together. It had always been that way, and this summer would be no different. We'd be best friends again in a nanosecond, and it would be like no time had ever passed between us.

Or so I thought. Corinne propped herself up on slim brown forearms. She shot me a lazy, sun-baked smile, held up a long-fingered hand, and gave a small wave. "Cuz! Come down here so I can kiss your cheek. I just poured lotion all over."

"Hey, Mia," Beth chimed in her soft, high, breathy voice. "We thought you'd only get here this evening."

"Didn't you get my text?" I said to Corinne.

"Bethy and I have ditched our cells this summer," Corinne replied. "The whole of New York calls us, like, every minute."

"We are so over being glued to the freaking phone," Beth added. "It's insane."

"So we made a pact," Corinne added. "We're detoxing our cellulars. We need a break from everyone."

"Oh," I said, the phone in my pocket feeling suddenly like the deadweight that it was. Now I knew why Corinne had been so silent. Her break from everyone had included me. "I uh, look really disgusting," I said, babbling to cover up the awkwardness I felt, having sent messages that no one wanted to receive. "It was boiling in the car. I'm dying for a shower."

"Hurry back." Corinne adjusted her iPod, looking anything but hurried herself.

"Okay." I tried to appear unfazed, but a wave of disappointment washed through me. It wasn't just the lukewarm greeting. It also had something to do with the fact that Corinne and Beth, who'd never got along, now appeared tighter than tight. Not that I wanted them to be enemies. But somehow their being best buddies didn't seem right.

Whenever we'd all been together in the past, Beth had always been the third wheel, too precious and prissy for Corinne and me—especially Corinne. When I'd last seen Beth at fifteen, she'd been the same as she had been as a kid—terrified of getting her hands dirty, constantly brushing her hair, and always sweetly smiling in a way that made her seem very pleased with herself, like she'd accomplished something amazing just by existing on the planet.

Corinne, on the other hand, was a spitfire. I'd always gotten off being near her wild, impulsive spirit. She'd made me feel like I was more alive just for being near her. Now I wasn't so sure. The two of them were mirror images—long legged, tanned, glowing and...I don't know...*poised*, or something.

As I turned away from my cousins, I knew that only one thing was for sure: if any of us was going to be a third wheel that summer, it would be me.

• • •

"You get your own room this time, Meemsy," Aunt Kathleen said to me, taking my arm and leading me along the second-floor hallway. I smiled as she used the nickname she'd given me when I was little. "Corinne has a friend coming," she added.

Own room... I had hoped for old times, long nights spent talking with Corinne in the dark. But I would be getting my own room now, whether I wanted it or not. Next door, Corinne would be sharing with her friend. A friend she'd neglected to mention to me.

"Wow!" I forgot my iffy feelings as I entered my bedroom. I'd always loved this room—a big, airy corner room right above the back deck, with windows framing postcard views of dunes, scruffy with beach grass, and the wide blue band of ocean beyond. Aunt Kathleen had put a bunch of wild roses in a vase on my night-stand, and the whole room smelled of a Long Island summer.

"I'm so thrilled to see you again, honey," Aunt Kathleen said warmly, taking my hand. "I've missed you so much."

"Ditto, Favorite Aunt." I squeezed her thin, elegant hand, and she laughed.

"I'm your only aunt," she said, fulfilling her part of the ritual we'd had going between us since I was a kid.

"But still my favorite."

Aunt Kathleen is my mother's older sister, and if Mom is beautiful, then Kathleen is exquisite. She has my mom's same china-blue eyes, cheekbones so high they seem dangerous, and skin so smooth it looks like it's been Photoshopped. And Aunt Kathleen has such killer natural style. Like now, barefoot and beautiful in a simple cotton summer dress, a silver charm bracelet tinkling on her left wrist. She looked so youthful standing there in my bedroom. It was hard to believe she was actually older than Mom.

"All set up here?" Mom peeked into the doorway. She had a smile on her face, but I knew her too well and saw something pinching at the corners of her eyes. After Mom and Aunt Kathleen had left to see about dinner, I sent out positive vibes in the hopes that Mom would unwind soon. Beach. Ocean. Light breezes. This had to be the cure for anyone's uptightness.

For as long as I can remember, Mom has been edgy. I cringe at restaurants when Mom uses the special snappy voice she reserves for waiters. *I asked for my dressing on the side!* Even shopping—her favorite occupation— is tinged with touchiness. *Is there anyone in this department store who understands the concept of customer service?* It has always embarrassed me to watch her frown and order around the sales staff at T.J. Maxx, like she's in an upscale boutique instead of a discount department store.

And ever since the word "recession" hit the airwaves, things had been going especially badly between my parents. Often, late at night, I could hear Mom's voice, sharp as cut glass, seeming to pierce through walls. "You should have sold when you had the chance, Chris! I told you, but God forbid you should listen to me!" In those moments, it was hard to remember that an angry voice is an invisible thing incapable of drawing blood.

Sometimes I think Mom still wishes she'd gone off to Hollywood and tried her luck, instead of marrying my gentle carpenter father right out of college. Mom met Dad when he made sets for a school production she'd starred in, but after they got married, they'd gone south so Dad could take over his family business.

I used to ask Mom about her acting ambitions. "Just pipe dreams," she'd tell me, but I'm not so sure that somehow, somewhere, they weren't still a real part of her she'd simply tucked away and tried to forget about, like a photograph of some lost love that it hurts to look at but you still can't throw out.

I have a photo like that. It's of Jake, his black hair flopping into his face, his slightly crooked teeth showing as he grins into the camera. I took the picture at a bowling alley. Jake is laughing at something I said. I no longer remember what he thought was so funny. I only remember how good it felt to have him look my way, and to capture the face of someone I loved and who loved me back. Or so I thought.

But the memory of that feeling still comes back to me when I think of that picture. When you know that feeling, it's hard to say good-bye to it, to tear it up and toss it away. Even though I don't look at it, that photo is in the drawer of my nightstand, hidden but still there. Maybe Mom's dreams are like that too, tucked away in a corner of her mind, never coming true but not forgotten either.

As for Aunt Kathleen, she achieved her dreams, and then some. Mom and Kathleen were brought up in a wealthy New York family, but the family had lost its money shortly after Mom came out as a debutante. They'd been forced to sell off all of their assets, but Kathleen was already on track. Before long, she'd become a successful food and wine critic and married Uncle Rufus, who was practically brought up on Wall Street itself in a big New York banking family.

First came the penthouse in Manhattan; then they'd bought back Wind Song, Kathleen and Mom's childhood vacation home in the Hamptons. It was supposed to be a triumph for everyone, but I knew that deep down, Mom resented it. She acted happy to be back for vacations, but I knew that secretly, in her heart, she was mad the house wasn't hers.

You can't really blame her. It's a beautiful house, the kind of house that could inspire a streak of possessiveness in anyone. Wind Song is a typical East Coast "summer cottage." It's built in the traditional style, with wood shingles, a gabled roof, and huge, old, paned-glass windows. The house is as much a natural part of the landscape as the dunes, the wetlands, and the beach spilling out wide and white like a giant's apron.

So much of the Hamptons has been destroyed by ugly mansions, but Wind Song is a pocket of heaven, an unpretentious rambling home with an ocean-facing back deck that stretches out across a piece of prime beach sheltered by dunes. The kind of place where summer lasts forever.

"You got the best room!" Corinne grinned from the doorway, and, looking at her, I felt stupid and childish for imagining some big void between us when I hadn't even given her a chance.

"I'm so happy to be here!" I sank back on my bed and kicked my legs up into the air. Suddenly I was full of energy. "I need a swim!"

"I need a drink," Corinne replied, turning moody. She crossed the floor, showing off her long-backed ballet posture, and leaned her long slim arms out of the window. "I'm just so damn *bored* here."

"Bored?" I blinked, confused. Corinne had always loved the beach. From childhood, she'd been like a seal in the water.

"My boyfriend, Alessandro, and his family go to the Italian coast every summer," she explained, doing a *plié* at the window, her long limbs sweeping out wide before she pushed up onto her toes and balanced. "I wanted to go, but Mom wouldn't let me. She wanted me to stay here in this wasteland."

"Wasteland?" I couldn't believe Corinne was talking like this about our favorite place in the world.

"Hello, hedge-fund scandal? Crashed economy? The whole of New York is flipping out. This place is a ghost town. There are even yachts abandoned in the reeds of the bay. Can you believe that? People are dumping their yachts because they can't afford to dock them. It's depressing." Corinne's beautiful face crumpled into a frown.

And then she recovered her smile and directed it at me. "But you're here. I'm really glad to see *you*." Corinne spun into a pirouette, twirled over to my bed, crossed her legs, and grinned, displaying her teeth, white as Tic Tacs. Corinne had gotten even prettier. She was still very thin, but then she was a ballet dancer, and it suited her long frame anyway.

"How's ballet?" I asked. Corinne's been a dancer all of her life and was training to be a professional at the prestigious New York City Ballet young dancers' program. Once, I'd gotten to see her dancing in *The Nutcracker* at the Lincoln Center. She'd beaten out hundreds of other little girls for the part of Clara, and it had been easy to see why: Corinne's jumps were high and silent, her pirouettes ferociously fast and perfect, and even when she wasn't dancing, she glowed from across the stage. You could feel that there was nowhere else she wanted to be.

"Don't say the b-word," Corinne said. "I was meant to join the Company this year, but I failed the audition." She shrugged. "Mom's practically suicidal over it, but whatever." Corinne tossed her hair, looking unperturbed. "I'm not even doing any training this summer. I'm just so over that scene right now."

"I'm sorry," I murmured, searching Corinne's face for signs of disappointment, but if she felt it, she hid it well.

Instead, she leapt up and leaned out the window again. "Want a cig?" she asked, whipping a box of Marlboros out of her pants pocket.

"Your mom could come back in here any minute!" I didn't add that I didn't smoke. Somehow I knew it was obvious to Corinne.

"Chillax," she replied, lighting up and exhaling a stream of smoke out the window. "They've gone to the fish market. Anyway, Mom knows, and she *so* does not care, trust me."

Aunt Kathleen not care? That didn't sound right. Aunt Kathleen was the world's most caring mother. I'd often secretly wished that she'd been my mom. She was always so funny and kind; she adored her husband and daughters and took such an interest in everything the girls did. Unlike my mom, who constantly ragged on my dad and was never much one for turning up to swimming meets or science fairs. Not that these were exactly Aunt Kathleen's scene either, but I knew if Kathleen was my mother, she'd put a spin on my admittedly less-than-glam talents. She'd be proud of me.

"When it comes to substance abuse, The Mother doesn't have a leg to stand on," Corinne said, staring with flat, unimpressed eyes at the view out of the window, her fingers playing with a slim, gold snake bangle in the crease of her elbow. "She's drinking like a fish."

"Really?" I was starting to not believe Corinne. She'd always been dramatic and loved telling stories. Maybe this was all just a performance for my benefit, to shock me or test me or something.

"Hey!" Corinne spun back toward me, her eyes lighting up. She looked so suddenly like the old sparkly Corinne that I was beginning to feel seasick from all the back-and-forth. "We're going to have a kick-ass party here this weekend after my bud Genevieve comes. She's staying for three weeks, maybe more. Her family has a house here too, but they just rebuilt and her mom is getting it all feng shui'd…"

"Wow," I said, trying to look enthusiastic as Corinne gabbed on about Genevieve, who attended the Professional Children's School in Manhattan with Corinne, where kids' school schedules were built around their lives as performers. Apparently Genevieve was pursuing an acting career, which was "pretty much in the bag" since her mother was a French model and her father was "Stanley Chu, the Internet bajillionaire."

"Gen's a riot," Corinne babbled. "She's a year ahead of me, and she's crazy. She set her own hair on fire as a Truth or Dare! Isn't that wild?"

"Wild," I repeated, while the other half of my brain tried to evaluate this new schizo Corinne.

"Gen's like a GPS for hot guys. *Turn left, hot guy.*" Corinne added, mimicking a computer voice. "She knows everyone out here."

"People from other schools?" I tried to follow along as I began to unpack my things, but I felt disoriented.

"No, Mimi!" Corinne opened her eyes really wide and then shook her head as if I'd said something endearingly backward and amusing. "College guys. And guys with their own software companies. But who aren't all dorked out," she added quickly, expelling smoke forcefully from her nostrils. "She also knows a lot of fashion people through her mom. She even knows Aram Amiri, Jr., do you freaking believe that?"

I always hate it when people pretend to know a word or a fact they've never heard of, so I just told Corinne the truth: "I don't know who that is."

"You've never heard of *Aram Amiri?*" Corinne looked like she might faint from disbelief.

I shook my head.

"The designer?"

"Maybe. I mean, I guess so," I lied, loathing myself for doing it but somehow unable to resist this time.

"He's only the most famous ready-to-wear name on the planet!" Corinne exclaimed. "This is one of his tops," she added, turning like a model to display the lemon-yellow, snug cotton T-shirt she was wearing. It had a slash just below the bustline and would have looked trashy on anyone with breasts, like me, but on Corinne it looked elegant, straight out of *Vogue.*

"Anyway," she continued, stubbing out her cigarette. "Aram Jr. is *ridiculously* gorgeous. He's going to be my project." Her eyes glinted as she ran a manicured hand through her thick, sun-tipped blond hair. "He dates Ivory. That girl who won *America's Next Top Model* last season. So I'm going to need my most hard-core strategies to get him." She widened her eyes in anticipation. "Fun."

"But what about Alessandro?" Maybe it was "dorked out" to bring up Corinne's boyfriend. But she'd begged the question, and I was having a very hard time keeping up with her.

"Alessandro." A faint smile crossed Corinne's lips as she turned to me, her eyes glassy and faraway. Either she missed him or she couldn't remember who he was. Then she seemed to snap back into the moment, flashing a wide grin. "He's not here, is he?" she said wickedly. "And even if he was," she added with a shrug, "he doesn't own me. He can't even get a hold of me unless he calls the landline!"

Weird. I couldn't tell if Corinne's "whatever," jaded attitude toward her boyfriend was for real or just an act to make her come off all sophisticated. And if it was for real...? What did it mean to go out with someone you weren't crazy about? As I unpacked a stack of T-shirts, I felt something I'd never imagined I'd feel: thrown off by Corinne. I couldn't put my finger on her. She seemed to be one thing one minute and another thing the next, a walking magic trick.

Whatever it was, it was happening too fast for me. Put it down to being from Athens, Georgia. Not exactly Manhattan.

And I got the unpleasant feeling that, for the first time in our lives, Corinne was trying to remind me of that fact.

• • •

That night we had a clambake on the beach. Corinne and Beth snuck off to smoke, but I was too busy enjoying the melt-in-your-mouth taste of shellfish baked in seaweed to feel left out. After dinner, Mom demanded that Eva perform like a seal, and being the kind of self-esteem-soaked kid she is, Eva enthusiastically broke the calm of Southampton with a song so loud and nauseating it could have caused a ship to wreck.

"My hand, your hand, four footprints in the sand," Eva warbled like she was auditioning for *American Idol*, which she and Mom both believe she will win someday. When she placed her palm across her chest like a pop diva, I took it as my cue and split the scene, heading down toward the water. But not before catching a glimpse of my mother, smiling indulgently, the way she'd looked at my sister since birth. Eva's surprise arrival seven years after me had given Mom a new lease on life. But even Eva couldn't compete with the ocean.

As I walked the tide line, the pounding of the surf drowned out my sister and lulled me into calm. I looked around for Corinne and Beth, but when I couldn't see them, it didn't bother me. I felt happy. Peaceful. Sure, I wanted to be close with Corinne again, but if I couldn't? I could amuse myself. Maybe it would even be better that way. After what happened with Jake, the last thing I needed was to be around my boy-crazy cousin and her scene.

The water shone, flecked with sunset-orange light. My feet were cool on the hard-soft sand at the tide line. I crouched down and picked up a small, pink spiral shell. It wouldn't be a lonely summer. I'd have the ocean for company. There would be long bright days, warm nights, and long walks looking for any kind of treasure the sea might throw up, from shells to souvenirs from old shipwrecks…

Okay, I hadn't found much real treasure before, but it never hurt to keep looking. That way if something was out there, I wouldn't miss it.

. . .

"Tanning's so boring, but swimming is worse," Corinne announced as we headed down a wooden walkway from the public-beach parking lot. I'd only had a quick dip after arriving the day before, but now I was about to have a real day at the beach, with Corinne.

Except that Corinne was less than thrilled about the idea of swimming. "The water is so polluted!" she said as we walked beyond the property line and continued up-shore, past dunes and houses, until we came to the public beach of Southampton. "Do you know that Long Island is one of the most cancer-ridden places in the world?" she added, lighting up a cigarette. "It's a toxic hazard, and *frankly*—" she blew a plume of smoke for emphasis—"I feel ill just being here."

I had to laugh.

Once we came to the public beach, we prowled around for the perfect spot, or at least that's what it looked like we were doing. Really, we were looking for Aram Hip Designer's son. I'd have preferred to stay on the slice of sand in front of Wind Song, but Corinne was convinced she could spy Aram Junior if we came to the main beach of Southampton. Apparently, he liked to "hang with the plebes"—this is what she actually said. We spread our towels on the sand. "I bet there are syringes in there," Corinne said, looking out to the surf.

"There are not. Come on! That water is perfect." I didn't believe for a second that the water was polluted; nor, it seemed, did anyone else. Mothers and babies were splashing around; boys with body boards were riding the small waves; and the deep, deep blue of the

Atlantic sparkled and shifted, changing color as small clouds skated across the sun.

"Appearances can be deceiving," Corinne replied, but I ignored her. No amount of pollution, no number of hoity-toity Manhattanites building large new houses out of pink cement and chrome and turning all the local restaurants into glitzy hot spots—none of that can ruin the Hamptons. Because nothing can spoil the color of the Atlantic Ocean right there on that shore: it goes from navy to slate, from green into blue. It's all of those colors, and then sometimes it's almost color-less, see-through. And for a whole summer, it was mine again.

"Okay, so I'm here then," a high-pitched, wounded-sounding voice piped up behind us as we arranged our lotions and books and snacks. "Nothing else to do."

"Bethy!" Corinne seemed excited even though, as far as I could tell in a day, Beth was still a wet blanket, not a shot in the arm. She seemed to look down her ski-jump nose at everything. Her voice had gotten higher and breathier over the years, and she appeared to have as much substance as a feather. From what I could see, she just went wherever the wind took her. Yet she always looked like she wanted to be somewhere else.

Or maybe that's just the curse of really beautiful people. Everything around them must look so ugly and second-rate.

"I should have gone to Budapest maybe," Beth said as she arranged her towel carefully, as if it were a napkin and she had to make sure it was neatly unfolded. "But I figured it would be dirty there," she continued. "And depressingly Eastern European, you know? Like black bread, et cetera."

She made a face, screwing up her tiny mouth into a little bud. And now I knew what her voice reminded me of: Hello Kitty. If Hello Kitty could talk, she'd sound like Beth. But these were the privileges of beauty—you could talk like Hello Kitty and come off sounding adorable instead of nauseating. "But now I wish I were there?" Beth whimpered, making sad questions out of her statements. "Instead of here?"

"Oh, Beth!" Corinne seemed to think this was hilarious. Beth was in her freshman year of college at Vassar and had opted out of a summer session abroad. I didn't see what was so funny, but they were both giggling now, and, though I felt downright fake doing it, I joined in.

I cringed, annoyed to hear my own laughter. I wondered why I was trying so hard, and not for the first time either. Waking up this morning, I seemed to have spaced on the lonely-happy scenario that I'd laid out for myself the night before. That "I'm Happy in My Own Company" trip was so out the window as Corinne passed me a basket of croissants and beamed at me over the breakfast table.

I felt blessed just being the object of her smile. Blessed and desperate, caught up in Corinne again. It didn't matter if she made a joke I couldn't get; I knew I'd be laughing like she was a star doing stand-up. Because the simple, embarrassing truth was that I wanted her to like me. I wanted her to think I was cool. I yearned to be in on the joke.

Ha ha ha.

As Beth and Corinne chattered on about people I didn't know and places I'd never been, they peeled denim sailor shorts down over muscular slender thighs with high knobs of hip bone and over endless legs, revealing miniature string bikinis that looked expensive even though they were about as big as postage stamps. I tried not to stare nor feel envious of their sun-kissed bodies, but when you see people like my cousins, no matter what your body type, you end up feeling squashy as a marshmallow and covered with hair, even if you've just gotten a bikini and leg wax.

Get over yourself, I coached myself as I removed my cutoffs and T-shirt. But I felt something in myself contract, like a hermit crab crawling back into its shell. It was bad enough having my mother criticizing my figure. Now I had to endure my cousins' quick information-gathering glances as I stripped down to my swimsuit.

Corinne sized me up, and I think I actually saw a touch of pity in her eyes. Or maybe I was imagining it, and her eyes were just a mirror reflecting my unconfident self back at me. I wondered why I hadn't ix-nayed a new summer bikini and bought myself a full-body wet suit instead, with matching goggles for disguise.

• • •

What about this one?" Mom held up a vertical-striped, one-piece swimsuit in Nordstrom "It's a retro look," she said, hopefully. But I wasn't buying it. All morning, while on our presummer shopping spree, Mom had encouraged me to try on "slimming" swimsuits with "flattering thigh frills," suits that made me look like I was heading off to Gilligan's Island instead of Long Island.

"This one's comfortable," I said to her after settling on a navy bikini with low-rider briefs and an athletic cross-back top. Since I have a decent stomach I've worked my abs off for, I thought I'd earned the right to tan it. But by the time we'd bought the suit, I wasn't so sure. Mom's pointed comments had done their bit to drag me down. As always.

This exercise in mutual mother-daughter disappointment was nothing new. Mom was Miss New York State when she was eighteen, a fact that still makes her proud even though, in her words, the beauty pageant world has become "very lower class." What doesn't make her proud is having a daughter who doesn't take after her at all—not in body type, not in interests. If my mother had her way, we'd be shopping every day and talking like sorority sisters. Except that I hate shopping, especially with Mom. And I would never join a sorority—much less be accepted into one.

• • •

"I'm going in," I said to my cousins, my voice extra loud and confident to make up for feeling the opposite. But a swim would help. It always did, wiping out my worries. And in the water, everyone is weightless.

I exercise a lot: I've always been on the swim team, and I work out often. But no matter what, it just isn't in my genes to be delicate boned and sea-sprite-ish in a bikini. I think I would have been okay with that, if it weren't for the fact that my mother always made a big deal about "slimming." But though I ignored my mother and the fashion mags as best I could, there are only so many things you can do to make yourself feel good in your own skin. Lying on the beach with two bronzed girls as dainty as sea horses is not one of them.

"Enjoy," Corinne said, picking up a thick *Vanity Fair*. "And try to drown," she added with a grin. "The lifeguard is sex on a stick!"

I laughed, and this time it was genuine. Corinne still had those flashes of lightheartedness that appeared every so often, that sparkled like the bits of sea glass we used to collect as kids. I hoped she'd hang onto them and throw me a few more this summer.

I plunged into the sea, swimming a fast freestyle out through the breakers, dipping my head under a breaking wave, and coming up to strike the glassy water between the swells.

Home.

That's what the ocean has always felt like to me. A wave smacked my muscles, smoothing out all my knots, leaving no space for unhappy thoughts. Then, flat calm, the sun burning a lazy stillness into my skin. I floated, drifting, the life on shore far from my thoughts.

But when I finally crawled out of the ocean, dreamy and tired from a long swim, awkwardness stung me again. It was as if the world and everyone in it were waiting to drag me down once my feet touched dry sand. Only suspended in the water could I truly let go.

chapter two

orinne's friend Genevieve drove up from Westchester on a Wednesday, screeching into the driveway in a midnight-blue Audi sports car. After that, there was a lot more screeching as Corinne came rushing out to greet her.

"Aunt Maxine, Mia, this is Genevieve Chu, the craziest girl I know," Corinne introduced her friend, her long, tanned arms around Genevieve's neck. "Gen, my aunt and cuz."

"Very nice to meet you, Maxine." Gen certainly knew how to charm everyone, especially my mother, who loved nothing more than a Euro-style double kiss on each cheek. To me, Gen just said, "Hi, cuz." Then she flashed me a dazzling, thousand-watt smile, but it disappeared as fast as it had appeared, replaced by an aloof sizing-up nod. Gen was also stunning. Apparently setting her hair on fire hadn't ruined it: she had a pixie cut perfectly suited to her glossy, straight black hair. She also had those pillowy lips that belong to the daughters of rock stars, and her almond-shaped, bottle-green eyes glinted with a "been there, done that" look.

Within minutes of her arrival, Gen sucked the whole house into a tornado of excitement. But underneath her bright laughter and easy charisma there was a hint of hardness, and I got the distinct feeling that when you got boring, she would switch you out for someone new.

I knew people like that. My own former boyfriend. And even my own formerly favorite cousin. I had enough fickle people in my life. I didn't need to befriend another one.

• • •

"Bo-ring," Gen flipped through the pay-per-view menu and rolled her eyes at the DVDs spilled on the floor in front of the flat-screen TV. We were in Corinne's room, and even though it was a beautiful afternoon, Gen and Corinne just wanted to stay inside and watch movies.

"Oh, I love this one!" Corinne waved the remote at a cable channel as a trailer for an upcoming movie played. "Oldie but goodie. *The Virgin Suicides*. Didn't you dig it, Gen?"

"Ish," Gen replied with a sniff.

"I thought it was so sad," Corinne said wistfully.

"Sad?" Gen scoffed.

"All those girls dying," Corinne replied. "It was sad and creepy."

"The only sad part was that they died virgins," Gen weighed in while I watched the trailer, a group of blond girls smiling flirtatiously at the camera. I hadn't seen the movie. "No one should die a virgin."

"I just thought it was *completely* unrealistic," Beth chimed in. I was surprised. Beth never seemed to have opinions. "A house full of teenaged virgins. What girl of fifteen is a virgin? *Puh-leez!*"

"It was a period piece," Gen commented. "They had to set it in the early eighties because there aren't any virgins of our age left."

As they all laughed in agreement, I heard myself laughing too. A horribly fake laugh, but it would sound real to anyone who didn't know me. "*So* true," I added, my voice sounding like it came from somewhere else. Someone else. *So true?*

I chuckled along with the gang like we were all on the same page, dimly trying to remember what it felt like to be there, oh so long ago. And even as I snickered with the others, I could feel Corinne's eyes on me, curious, suspicious, alert to the fact that I was so obviously the very thing I was laughing at: a virgin. Apparently I wasn't fooling her. So why couldn't I just give up and be me? It's not like I was thirty years old or had joined one of those teen Waiting for Marriage clubs—so what was the biggie about just admitting it?

Plus, though I've never been the most verbal girl on the block, I've never been afraid to pipe up when I have a different take on something. But as I sat there on the floor of Corinne's bedroom, I surprised myself. I'd become like a trail-ride pony, dumbly following those in front of me, unable to pick my own path and go at my own pace.

Yeah, I'd definitely gone on vacation—and forgotten to pack my brain.

I stood up. "See you later. I'm going to the beach." A swim would clear my head and remind me that even if I felt socially inferior around these sophisticated girls who spoke about sex I hadn't had, music I didn't know, and places I'd never been, I wasn't spending my summer here to impress them. They didn't own the beach. They didn't own me.

• • •

"Isolating yourself won't help you fit in, hon," Mom lectured me the next day as I sat on the porch in an Adirondack chair, watching the sunset and writing in my journal.

"Mom!" I rolled my eyes. "I'm not isolating myself. I'm just *being* myself. I need time on my own."

In fact I had tried to talk to my cousins and Gen the previous evening. But it was just more of the same: nobody ever asked me what my life was like in Georgia, or anything else about me. Apart from a brief talk with Corinne about Jake, I hadn't spoken about myself at all since arriving in the Hamptons. It was all me asking questions and trying to follow in-jokes.

It gets to be embarrassing when you nod and smile and pretend to follow a conversation that no one ever breaks open to help you follow. They hardly ever stopped mid-chatter to explain to me who, exactly, they were talking about, or why what he'd said was so funny, crazy, brilliant, or whatever. So after a while—when I felt that smiling one more time at nothing might make my face crack—I'd just removed myself from the room. I still had a shred of pride left.

"Trust me, they don't miss me," I added as Mom pressed me about rejoining the flock. Instantly I regretted the bitterness in my tone. It was just the kind of thing Mom would pounce on.

"Mia," she said firmly, "I think you're being oversensitive." Her voice softened. "And I understand why. You've had a rough time. You're still hurting."

"I don't want to talk about it," I snapped. *Especially with you.* Ever since the breakup, Mom had tried to get me to talk about

Jake with her, but I always cut her off. I didn't want to talk about him. And even if I had, Mom wouldn't get how I really felt. She'd never understood me before. Besides, she hadn't even liked Jake to begin with, so sharing my pain over the cheating loser I'd had the bad taste to fall in love with was the last thing I wanted to do.

Mom perched carefully on the arm of my Adirondack chair. "If you give them a chance, I just know the girls can help you have a fun summer," she said gently. "Sometimes it takes time to reconnect," she said patting my knee. "You and Corinne will hit your stride soon. And Gen seems lovely!"

I bit my lip. Gen was exactly the kind of girl Mom would have wanted me to be: popular, naturally skinny, and magnetic in every possible way. She was also a professional actress and, as far as I could see, she was very talented, easily able to impress parents and make them think she was great. But underneath the act…was there any substance to her at all? I doubted it. Or maybe in some stupid, shallow way I was just jealous.

You could buy the shirt, the lipstick, the shoes, but you couldn't buy the pitch-perfect coolness of someone like Gen. She was born lucky, and not just because her dad was "Stanley Chu, the Internet bajillionaire." Gen had the ability to make even boredom seem interesting. *It's like she even owns the air around her*, I had written in my journal. How could I not be jealous?

"I have nothing in common with Genevieve," I told my mother. It was true. Gen is one of those girls who does everything long before a girl like me has even thought of it. She knows how babies are made when everyone else still believes in the stork. She's disabling the parental controls on her laptop when you're still printing coloring pages off PBS Kids. And when you're still afraid of the dark, Gen is the girl climbing out the window to go clubbing.

But…she was definitely not the girl who would ever get dumped by her boyfriend. That was one—the only—way in which I was more experienced than Genevieve.

"I still think you should try to be more outgoing, honey," Mom finished. "Nothing comes from nothing."

A flare of anger burned in my chest. What she was really saying was that if you weren't a social butterfly, you were worthless. In one way or another, my mom had been telling me this my whole life. She only saw what I wasn't, what I didn't have. What I did have a reasonable amount of—brains—didn't please her.

Mom had always thought I was way smarter than I really am: a brainiac mutation instead of an intelligent but normal girl. But her hyper-inflated opinion of me wasn't parental boasting. I worried her. If my mother could have traded me in for a beautiful block-head who talked constantly even though she had nothing to say, I had a feeling she'd have done it, pronto.

"Is that Maxine? My Maxine?" a deep voice rang out, just as I was about to tell Mom to leave me alone. We turned to see a man step out onto the porch.

"Shep!" Mom shrieked in delight. And then she flew into the arms of one of the handsomest men I had ever seen. For an old guy.

"Shep Gardner! As I live and breathe!" Mom sounded so preten-tious. *As I live and breathe?* Then again, what kind of man had a name like Shep? This could only be someone from Mom's past. Someone from a powerful family like Mom's had once been.

"I used to know your mother when she was Miss New York State," Shep said, confirming my guess after we shook hands. He had silver-flecked black hair, and his amber eyes gazed intently into Mom's. He wore an expensive-looking salmon-colored dress shirt, and a gold pinkie ring shone on his deeply tanned left hand. "Maxine and I used to be beach buddies," he added.

Mom giggled like a girl. *Beach buddies?* I didn't even want to know what that meant. Nor did I want to know what Shep was getting at with "my" Maxine. Thankfully Mom was already maneuvering him off the porch and into the house, where cocktails were flowing, as usual.

Since we'd arrived, I noticed Mom—and even Dad—had started much earlier on the drinks, maybe to keep up with Aunt Kathleen and Uncle Rufus, who definitely kept their glasses well-watered. I'm not saying the adults walked around blind drunk, like Corinne had implied, but the gin and tonics started before sundown and were constantly refreshed by Uncle Rufus.

I guess the drinking just made it easier for everyone. Mom and Dad had their problems, which must have been uncomfortable for my aunt and uncle to be around. And then there was the economy. Uncle Rufus had a permanent smile on his face, but I knew he was dealing with crises at his investment bank. He often paced the lawn talking into his cell phone, and I caught snatches of conversation between him and Dad. "We're just the feeder funds, Chris," he'd said once. "But everyone's scapegoating us. It's a witch hunt, a blame game."

But at cocktail hour—like right now—everyone seemed happy. Mom and Dad acted like everything was great between them; Uncle Rufus looked as though he didn't have a care in the world; and Mom and Kathleen reminisced about when they were young. Sometimes they even demonstrated dances they'd learned when they were debutantes.

"Christopher! More ice!" Mom called out from inside the house, her voice ringing out like a bell clear across the back deck. Mr. Handsome Beach Buddy must have been important because Mom was being theatrical and affected. She never called Dad "Christopher" unless she was playing to an audience she wanted to impress.

I frowned and pulled my cardigan around my shoulders, picturing Dad with a forced smile on his face, socializing with aristocrats. It wasn't his scene. It wasn't mine. But Mom was in her element with people like Shep Gardner.

The sea turned choppy and gray as the wind picked up. From out behind the dunes, I heard a tinkling wind-chime laugh—Beth, no doubt sneaking vodka shots from her and Corinne's secret stash. From the front porch, I heard a roar of laughter—my uncle.

And there was me: alone, no drink in hand, the only one not trying to give cold reality a warmer glow. Since Jake had dumped me, I'd sworn off alcohol. I'd never been a big drinker anyway, and Jake would get wasted at parties and rely on me to sober him up. That was one thing I wouldn't miss about him. It wasn't the good part of him. That would be his laugh. The smell of his T-shirts. The way his hands felt around my waist.

I closed my eyes, tears pricking the back of my throat. I could use a little buzz right now, something to make me forget the memories that washed over me when I least expected them, like a freak wave. But I didn't move.

I was being strong. Even though I felt weak.

• • •

The next morning I overheard a conversation. Corinne and my aunt were in the kitchen, talking in tense voices, unable to hear me coming in off the porch from an early walk on the beach. "Your first priority is Mia," my aunt said. I froze midstep. "You should be including her in everything you do."

"Shut up, Mom!" Corinne snapped.

I waited for my aunt to reprimand her. If I ever told my mother to shut up, I'd get my head bitten off. But Aunt Kathleen didn't say anything. "She's different from me," Corinne continued. "She's, I don't know, *awkward*."

"Maybe she's feeling awkward because you're not paying attention to her."

"Lay off, Mom," Corinne grumbled. "Mia is fine without me hanging all over her. She can take care of herself."

Don't worry—from now on, I will. Tears sprang to my eyes as I heard the hardness in Corinne's voice.

"What is the matter with you?" Aunt Kathleen demanded icily. I paused, forgetting my hurt pride for a moment. I'd never heard my aunt speak to her daughters with such coldness—bordering on disgust. "You're incredibly selfish. You know that?"

"Get over it, Mom," Corinne replied, her words dropping like bricks into the still morning air. "I'm just like you, and you know it. You're not exactly Mother Teresa, and we both know what I mean."

And right then, they sensed me. Or saw my shadow. Something. Because suddenly, there was quick whispering. Busted, I walked into the kitchen, trying to seem like I'd heard nothing even though my heart was slamming into my rib cage and my face was tingling in a telltale blush. *Great!* Not only did Corinne think I was a loser, but now she'd think I was sneaky too, pulling a Nancy Drew behind the pillar. This event would go a long way toward our cousinly bonding.

"Meemsy!" Aunt Kathleen shot me a brilliant, warm smile and held up her coffee mug. "Cup of coffee? Your uncle will be up any minute now to make his famous raspberry pancakes."

"Sure, I'll have coffee," I somehow managed to say. Corinne smiled and poured me a cup, and Aunt Kathleen hummed as she took eggs out of the fridge. And I just stood there smiling back, suddenly as big an actress as both of them. Even though my aunt had challenged Corinne—out of love for me and decency—I felt humiliated that she'd done it. And cut by Corinne's response. I was also confused by the cold space that had seemed to exist between Aunt Kathleen and the daughter I'd thought she was so close to.

You're not exactly Mother Teresa, and we both know what I mean. What *did* Corinne mean?

Standing in the kitchen sipping coffee, I felt cheated out of the perfect summer I'd longed for. Even before I'd seen Corinne, I had suspected things might not be the way I'd anticipated, but I'd also hoped I would be wrong. And now I knew I wasn't wrong: those suspicions were more than confirmed.

And I had a feeling things were only going to get worse, that I might find out more things I'd rather never know.

• • •

"Tomorrow night's going to be a blast," Corinne announced. I was in my favorite turquoise satin Chinese pajamas, reading in my room. My book was about the ocean and global warming, and I didn't really hear Corinne, in that way you can sometimes hear things but also not hear them. I was too lost in a chapter on the earth's melting ice caps and their effects on rising sea levels.

Or maybe I was ignoring her.

But as Corinne came and sat on the edge of my bed, I pulled my eyes from the page. Corinne chattered excitedly about the big party she and Gen were organizing for the young high society who happened to find themselves on—what had she called it the day I got here?—*the wasteland* of Long Island this summer. I watched her over the top of my book. "Mimi?" Corinne looked suddenly unsure of herself. "Mia, I…"

"What?" My voice was flat as a sheet of polar ice.

"I just want to say that I know I'm not always the best host, you know?" Corinne twisted her hands in her lap.

"I don't need a host," I said, still frosty. I didn't need Corinne to kiss up to me. The last thing I wanted was her pity, especially if, as I suspected, she was only doing it because she knew I had overheard her being snitty about me.

"I'm a bitch," she said after a while. "I guess you must hate me."

"I don't hate you," I said robotically, but inside I was wishing her away with every fiber of my being. I wasn't here to make her feel better about herself.

"Hey, Mia?" Corinne said.

"What?" I said, determined to push her out of my room with monosyllables.

"Remember when you were last here?" Corinne said suddenly, a mischievous smile playing at the corner of her mouth. "Remember Mr. Hollis and his Just Fabulous son…what was his name…Marky?"

"Marty," I said. "Marty Hollis."

In spite of myself, I began to smile at the three-year-old memory of an annoying family that had rented the house next door to Wind Song. The house was big and new and showy, and seemed to suit the family that had rented it. Mr. Hollis was fat as a puffer fish and had a voice like a chain saw. He used the word "just" in front of everything: "just amazing," "just awful," et cetera. And he had an incredibly serious son, Marty, who was at Harvard, where supposedly he was Just Fabulous at everything, especially gymnastics.

But we found Marty to be just terrible. He wore high-waisted, pleated khaki pants every day, with a golf shirt like an old man. His pants practically skinned his armpits, but Marty thought he was quite the stud and often worked out on the beach with weights, pretending not to be trying to impress Beth.

"Remember the demo?" Corinne asked, and right then I cracked up. We had been invited to a seafood barbecue at the Hollises— and while giant Mr. Hollis zipped around on surprisingly small, delicate feet, refilling glasses and talking your ear off, Marty Hollis did stretches on the lawn, as if he were preparing for an event. Which, as it turned out, he was.

"Marty, get on the trampoline and show them your stuff," Mr. Hollis said. "He's just fabulous."

Marty spent three seconds pretending to have his arm twisted, but then he was springing up and down on a portable trampoline. He wore a very intense look on his face and a pair of teeny silky shorts, and before long he began to spring higher and higher, gearing up for a big trick. And it was. Marty sailed up through the air and seemed suspended for a moment—arms straight up next to his ears and legs stretched into splits—his features scrunched up with concentration. And then somehow, from too much enthusiasm, Marty whizzed sideways, way clear of the trampoline, and fell into a crumpled ball on the grass, his silky shorts half off and revealing a chunk of hairy, saggy butt.

"You said to him later, 'That was just fabulous,' remember?" Corinne reminded me.

I nodded, recalling the way Marty had gotten up, pulled up his shorts, put on his Ray Bans, and carried on like he was the coolest guy on the planet. Later, we all laughed about it and Aunt Kathleen said, "It's not nice to laugh, but dear God, that was a most *unfortunate* display."

"I wonder who's in the house this year," I remarked and Corinne rolled her eyes.

"Awful people. Rich, of course, but they're super-tacky. From the Midwest or something." She wrinkled her lightly freckled nose.

"All the dregs come here. I don't know why, because we don't want them."

"Now you're being a bitch," I said, and Corinne laughed.

"That was a fun vacation," she said, sounding wistful.

"It was perfect." It had been. We'd spent weeks exploring the beaches, getting up early to go clamming with our dads in Shinnecock Bay, and riding our bikes through the streets, stopping to explore forests and ponds.

"Please hang out in my room for a bit." Corinne reached out and grabbed my hand. "It would be *just fabulous*, don't you think?"

I smiled tentatively. Maybe it was time to meet Corinne halfway. Maybe she was self-absorbed, always talking about her world. But maybe she filled the air with words because I was tight-lipped. Awkward.

As I closed my book and set it back on my nightstand, I vowed to be less hypersensitive. Corinne and I weren't peas in a pod anymore, but that didn't mean we couldn't have fun together. And the fact that she remembered minor, silly things we'd shared, like the sight of Marty Hollis's hairy butt, made me think that perhaps Corinne had missed me too.

Just then my phone rang. I picked it up off the pillow and looked at the screen. *Jake.*

"Oh, my God," Corinne said as she read the name. "What the hell does he want?"

As the phone cawed like a bird (I had a seagull ringtone), my body tingled. Jake. I didn't want to answer the phone.

I did.

I didn't.

I grabbed it, unable to resist.

"Hello," I said, tonelessly.

"Mia," Jake said. "You answered."

As he started talking, babbling about how much he missed me, I wished I'd turned my phone off completely when I got here, like Corinne and Beth had. I could tell he'd had a few beers. And even though he said all the things I had, deep down, wanted to hear in the weeks since our breakup—that he was sorry, that Gabi meant nothing, that he had broken up with her because he missed me so much—it made no difference. It was too late.

"Jake, can you hold on a minute?"

I took a deep breath, snapped the phone shut, and threw it out the window.

It clattered off the roof, and Corinne let out a whoop. "Mimi! That was amazing!"

I was amazed too. *Whoa!* I didn't do things like throw cell phones out the window. But letting go of my usual self felt as right as letting go of Jake. As Corinne and I stood laughing hysterically, she grabbed both my hands in hers, and I felt light. As though I were made of air.

• • •

"I don't know about this dress," Beth whined to Corinne.

"Ish," Corinne remarked, waggling her hand in a *so-so* gesture at what I thought was a stunning gray asymmetrical dress that clung to Beth's angular body in all the right places. "I'm just over that one-shoulder look," Corinne added, folding her arms and eyeing her sister critically. "It's so last summer. Like Roman gladiator sandals." She shivered. "Ick."

Thank God I didn't bring mine. I flushed. I had a pair of Roman sandals, and, where I was from, it was still okay to wear them.

"Yeah, lose the frock, Beth," Gen called over from the other side of the room. She was dressed only in bikini briefs and a black lace bra, and had draped herself in the window bay. "Mia, pass me those cancer sticks, would you?"

I picked up the box of cigarettes on Corinne's bed and tossed it to Gen. "Catch." Eva was sitting on Gen's bed. *Good,* I thought, as my little sister wrinkled her nose. It would be good for nine-year-old Eva—who'd already decided to be Gen's devoted slave—to see her hero puffing out the window.

But Eva had other demands on her attention. "Evie, keep your head still!" Beth had lost interest in her dress and was busy applying makeup to Eva's face, putting glitter on her eyelashes. I was amazed at the transformation. Eva looked like a teenager. A beautiful one.

"She could be your sister, Corinne," Gen commented, as Beth applied ruby gloss to Eva's perfectly bowed lips. "She's your spitting image."

"I've always wanted a little sister," Corinne yelped, crushing Eva into a tight hug. "And Evie and I totally look alike."

Even Eva, at all of nine years old, fit in with these girls better than I did, like a model with her lipsticked pout and sulky eyes. I looked away, eager for a distraction.

Corinne's room was strewn with clothes, her tall closets wide open, revealing rainbow-colored stacks of pale rich-people clothes on the shelves: cotton shirts and cashmere sweaters in pastel Jordan Almond colors that suited only those with light hair and just the right lightly sun-burnished skin. Corinne possessed a lot of other hipster clothes, but she also had the preppy basics of her tribe. I had an urge to go to her closet and run my fingers through those piles of luxury I could never afford.

"Mimi!" Eva commanded me back. "Look at me."

"You can be the party mascot," Corinne said as Beth applied gel to Eva's hair.

"Mom won't let you be at the party," I said, almost without thinking, to Eva.

Eva leveled her gaze at me, and I saw a coolness and superiority that surprised me. "Mommy won't care. Anyways, I can make Mommy agree with me."

"No you can't, Eva." I stared her down. Suddenly she was no longer just my annoying little sister, but now one of The Group, with their long legs, skinny jeans, and tiny T-shirts. She looked like a miniature version of them, right down to the way she smiled, full of a grown-up kind of self-confidence that took my breath away.

"You have a bedtime," I said to Eva, knowing I'd blown it with the others just by that comment alone. Once again, Mia was proving herself to be a spoilsport and a square supreme. "Though Mom and Dad are way too wasted these days to notice," I added without thinking. Instantly I felt embarrassed for exaggerating about my parents like that. And for talking about them like that in front of Eva. But it was the right thing to say to get me in with the others. Gen laughed and then the others joined in.

"The parentals are definitely tucking into the old Jack D.," Gen agreed.

"When in Rome," Beth added, and stepped into a pair of heels I knew I could never walk in, even if my life depended on it.

• • •

Later, lying in my bed, I tossed and turned, my body coiled tighter than a spring. I climbed out of the window and sat on the flat roof that stretched over the back deck. The only light outside came from lamps along the wooden walkway connecting Wind Song to the beach. Everything else was in darkness.

"You have awesome cheekbones," Corinne had said to me earlier, stepping back to admire the makeover I'd finally agreed to.

"Thanks." There was still some distance in my voice. But as she smiled at me in the mirror and brushed sparkles onto my okay cheekbones, my iciness melted and I smiled back.

"*Much* better," Gen said, evaluating my reflection in the mirror.

Who asked you? But to my surprise and irritation, I was pleased as Gen nodded approvingly.

"Those are your colors," Corinne announced. Together we gazed at my eyes in the mirror, rimmed with electric-green liquid liner and smoky shadow. "It's *you*, Mia."

Was it me? I blinked. I looked so different. "I love it," I said. And I did. At least, part of me did.

It was exciting to let go a little. Wearing electric-green eyeliner. Tossing Jake out the window. These were not things the Mia I know would ever have done. Which made them that much more thrilling…

But in the darkness, alone, I was less sure I could move on—be a new, confident me, go to a party, actually have fun again. I wanted to step out of myself and be a part of the world. But I also wanted to crawl deep inside myself and be alone. That way nothing and no one could hurt me.

I rested my chin on my knees, my thoughts like the waves I could hear shifting somewhere in the darkness. I turned to the other problem on my mind: Corinne. It wasn't just a matter of me slotting in with her universe. I had also seen how fast she went from smiles to sulks, from kindness to coldness. She was like beach weather, changing without warning. Could I keep up? And did I really want to?

I stretched an arm out into the black nothingness. It was so dark I couldn't even see my own hand in front of my face, nor anything else in front of me, for that matter.

chapter three

eemsy! You're gorgeous!" Aunt Kathleen said as she popped her head around my bedroom door.

"Thanks, Aunt Kath," I murmured, unconvinced.

In Athens, my summer party outfits involved a T-shirt or peasant blouse with jeans or khakis. At a push, I might wear Candies sandals instead of Converse sneakers. But I was worlds away from that tonight. There was the dramatic eyeliner (I'd let Corinne apply it), and I had a dress on: it was simple, white, and strapless, made of shimmery silk. I'd let my mom talk me into getting it in Georgia for the summer, "in case there's an occasion."

I stared anxiously into the mirror. I'd decided to get ready in my room, alone, because I still wasn't sure that I didn't look like a white elephant—in more ways than one—in my dress, and I didn't want the others to see me in it before I was ready to be seen. Corinne had said it would be a real "chi-chi bash" so I figured I'd better make an effort.

Going strapless was a big deal for me. Luckily the dress was well-cut, as Mom had pointed out, and it had a built-in bra…although the top was edged with little beads, which at first I'd thought was cool. Now I worried that they emphasized my bustline too much, especially with my dark curls loose on my shoulders instead of scrunched back.

"The boys will all be fighting over you tonight," Kathleen said, kissing me on the cheek. "Brains and beauty, Mia. That's what you are." *Hardly.* I gazed uncertainly into the mirror, but my aunt squeezed my hand and I felt grateful she was there.

"Sweetheart, you look fabulous," my mother said in an unusually generous tone of voice, coming in just after Aunt Kathleen left. "Isn't this exciting?"

Her eyes sparkled, a little too brightly, I thought…and was I imagining things or were her lids rimmed in red? "Mom, are you okay?"

"Spectacular!" Mom said in an overloud voice.

I frowned. Since Mom had arrived at Wind Song, everything was "spectacular" and "fabulous," but somehow the more she cranked up the vocab, the less I believed she was truly having a good time.

"Are you and Dad fighting again?" I asked her, point-blank, even though I knew she wouldn't answer me straight.

"Dad and I are just fine," she said.

"Then why are your eyes red?" I persisted, but she cut me off with an impatient wave of her hand.

"Stop analyzing me, Mia," she muttered crossly. "I'm not upset about anything. Especially not your father."

Her tone flashed with irritation at the words "your father," and I turned away from her, rolling my eyes. I really didn't need more details. I could fill them in myself. I'd seen Mom and Dad's fights a million times before, and they were always the same: Mom railroading Dad for not paying more attention to her or for disappointing her in a gazillion tiny ways. Dad hardly ever argued back, which riled Mom up even more. Unfortunately, Mom always seemed to dwell on what she didn't have, even though she had the best husband ever.

Dad has all of those qualities that never play a starring role, but take them away and everything falls apart. Chris Gordon is as simple and easy to read as his name: stable, loyal, no complicated motivations, happiest having dinner on our back deck at the table he made himself from old barn-wood, but ready to go with the flow if Mom forces him out to some stiff cocktail party. Because he loves her.

But Mom always seemed to want more than Dad could give. And maybe being back here, with Kathleen and Rufus and their flawless marriage and among all of their sophisticated friends, Mom was starting to feel the fault lines between her and Dad even more.

Or maybe it was something else. Someone else.

Shep Gardner. The image of Mom's polished, aristocratically good-looking *beach buddy* alarmed me. What if Mom was having some kind of midlife crisis? What if Shep was? He was all over Mom when I met him, and she'd been dropping his name ever since. I hadn't heard a single thing about his wife, or even if he had one.

I felt a bit wobbly as I slid into my beaded sandals. Who was to say Mom wouldn't give her beach buddy a second chance after a life spent in a town she'd never loved, with a husband who never seemed to measure up to her dreams?

I must have looked shocked and scared because Mom switched gears. "Really, everything's okay, honey," she said, in a tender voice she usually reserved for Eva. "I just want you to have fun tonight."

She came over, tucked a corkscrew of hair behind my ear, and smiled. "And Mia?" she added.

"Yes?" I smiled. Me and Mom have had so few really good mother-daughter moments, and I was enjoying that simple gesture of her tucking a piece of my hair behind my ear. Her soft voice.

"Don't forget to suck in your tummy."

• • •

"This is incredible!" I said to my aunt as I walked into the living room. There were giant plates of crudités and crab dip, a tray of oysters on the half shell, and salads with roasted pine nuts and goat cheese. I'd never seen such a spread for a teen party. Outside, a guy seared tuna steaks. "Is that one of Beth's friends?" I asked Aunt Kathleen.

"He's from the catering company," my aunt explained.

"Catering company?" Since my aunt is a gourmet cook, I'd figured she would mix some barbecue sauce herself, and we girls would make salads and slice bread rolls.

"We're on our way out," Aunt Kathleen explained, snapping shut a black patent-leather purse and running a hand through her hair, her diamond rings winking in the low light. "We don't like to hang around and be a bore at the kids' parties," she said. "And believe it or not, we fossils still like to kick up our heels. So we're going to the club!"

My parents appeared with Uncle Rufus. "You're going too?" I said to Mom and Dad, my jaw dropping as Mom nodded and removed her pashmina shawl from a coat hook. My parents leaving me at an unchaperoned party? This was a first.

But though Dad looked a little concerned, Mom beamed at me. "Dad and I trust Bethy and Genevieve will make sure you and Corinne behave like young ladies."

Gen and Bethy setting examples? *Smart thinking, Mom!* But then I realized Mom had her own agenda for the evening too. The fact that my uncle and aunt were members of the Southampton Club was a big deal to my mother. Mom lived for places like that—where you got voted in by a panel of highbrow socialite types. Going out for such an exclusive evening was right up Mom's alley.

Especially if Shep Gardner would be there. Was that why she was so keen to leave?

Dad nodded as Mom finished her speech about "trusting" me at sixteen, but I could tell he was less sure. Not about trusting me, but about the others. Dad keeps to himself, but he notices a lot. And I could tell he'd noticed enough about my cousins and their friends to be concerned. But no doubt he'd opted out of rocking the boat this evening, and maybe that was the smart thing to do.

"When the girls are at home, I know they're safe," Aunt Kathleen said to Dad. "It's when you don't give them any freedom to have some fun that everything goes wrong."

"Plus we have our little eyes and ears over here," Mom said, looking up as Eva appeared in the stairwell wearing one of Corinne's—or maybe Aunt Kathleen's—dresses, a long red piece of chiffon that dragged behind her on the floor. "Is she a vision or what?" Mom cooed as Eva shot us a coquettish smile.

She *was* a vision, in a creepy child beauty pageant sort of way. Her hair was curled; her lips practically dripped with red gloss; and she had a feather boa around her neck. The other adults looked disturbed too, but, as always, Mom was blind as a bat when it came to Eva. Funny, because Mom is also the first person to point out tackiness and "vulgar behavior" in everyone else.

"Romeo-Romeo-wherefore-art-thou-Romeo." Eva rushed the words, breathless with excitement as she leaned over the stairwell.

Mom clapped her hands together. "Shakespeare!" she breathed reverently.

Give me a break. I resisted the temptation to make gagging motions. Personally, Shakespeare has always gotten on my nerves. All those people poisoning each other. All that "forsooth and verily" stuff. Having to read it at school was bad enough. But now my very own personal Juliet was sliding down the banister.

"It's acting! Gen taught me!" Eva exclaimed as she reached the bottom of the landing. "She taught me how to die too. Watch!" Eva clutched her throat and fell to the floor, rolling her eyes back in her head.

"You're a natural," Mom declared proudly, as Eva's eyes fluttered open to receive her applause. "Make sure she's in bed by nine thirty," Mom added, turning to me. "I don't mind her staying up to see everyone arriving, but I want her in bed at a reasonable hour."

I nodded, but I knew there would be nothing I could to enforce Mom's rules with Eva, not while my cousins and Gen were running the show. One look at Eva's angelic smile and I knew she knew it too. There was not a chance in hell that devil in a red dress would go to bed when I said so.

"Have a good time," Dad said to me, giving me a hug. "You look beautiful."

"Thanks, Dad."

"Keep your wits about you around this crowd," he added in a whisper. "And your clothes on."

"I'll try," I replied, laughing as we broke apart from the hug. If there's one person who trusts me implicitly in this world, it's Dad. But as I waved good-bye to my parents, I doubted myself. Everything was weirdly off-kilter. It's not like I was planning to do anything crazy, but I didn't feel centered either. And watching my parents disappear into the darkness gave me a strange chill.

Randomly I thought of my house in Athens, the green front door framed by a bower of wisteria. I'd been so glad to get away, get out of town, and leave the misery of my breakup behind me. But now I felt homesick.

"Whoo-hoo! They're gone!" Corinne yelped as she, Beth, and Gen came slinking down the staircase. They were dressed like they were about to hit an underground, rock-star-owned club with a dress code involving next-to-nothing tops, black leather pants, and spiky heels no thicker than car radio antennas and almost as long.

And there I stood: the Ultimate Virgin in my white party dress, surrounded by sirens. Cue the laugh track.

"You look…fresh," Gen said as she took in my dress. I no longer felt elegant. Now I felt like a special guest who had traveled all the way from the Victorian period to be here tonight. *What were you thinking?* I glanced down at the offending garment. I'd thought it was a safe bet: simple and well-cut and a little bit funky with its beaded detail. But now I realized it was all wrong for New York. Miserably I stared at the beaded fringe hanging off my hemline. I looked like one of the lampshades in the corner of the room.

"I thought we were…doing the dress thing." Why did the floor never open up and swallow you in real life, when it really counted? "I should change, I guess." Not that I had anything to change into. Nothing even remotely sexy like the others were wearing, and even if I had, I couldn't carry it off.

"Don't change. You look sweet," Corinne chirped, tossing her golden hair. It matched the color of her pale suede top and contrasted with the black leather of her pants. She looked both sophisticated and natural at the same time. And I, apparently, looked "sweet." I looked down at my sandals and then across to Corinne's stilettos. It's a long way from Payless to Prada.

• • •

"Oh, my God! Aram is here," Corinne whispered into my ear, as a guy with waves of long hair stood in the hallway, locked in a bear hug with Gen. And then a beautiful black girl stepped through the doorway.

"Ivory?" Corinne hissed under her breath. "I thought she was modeling all summer," she muttered, seething. Quickly recovering herself, Corinne marched over to the door. "Hey," she casually greeted Aram. "I'm Corinne Drexel. And you are…?"

Aram Famous Designer's Son was as beautiful as his girlfriend. According to Gen, his father was from Iran "or Turkey or something." Aram wore surfing shorts and a T-shirt with a hole in it. His long, messy hair was sun-bleached to orange highlights, and he had huge, smoldering, cat-shaped eyes and a lean, muscled body. Just the fact that he wasn't dressed up made him somehow even cooler. I knew it, and so did everyone else. Including him.

As for everyone else, only the cream of young Hamptons society had been invited to the party. It wasn't a big bash; it was too exclusive to be big. The guests were children of fashionistas and media moguls, of CEOs and art dealers, and of the lawyers to media moguls, CEOs, and art dealers...and me.

I've never seen people in real life who looked as glamorous. Some wore punky-chic outfits like Corinne and Beth and Gen; some looked more conventionally cool in leggings and kimono shirts or painted-on jeans and tight tanks, hoop earrings glinting against their skin and sun-streaked hair.

But all of them looked like they'd been fed only the best food ever (entirely fat-free, I might add), worn only the finest fabrics ever made, and had their hair carefully cut into the latest homage-to-the-eighties styles by hairdressers to the stars. They looked young and old at the same time. Older than me, for sure.

"This is my cousin, Mia," Corinne said, making an effort to introduce me to her friends, no doubt on the heels of a pep talk from my aunt. "Mia, this is Thea/Clarissa/Chloë/Tanya."

Were rich people born with longer necks than the rest of us? Or did your neck grow an inch when you looked down on the world from up there? I wondered. All of Corinne's friends had vacation homes in the Hamptons, or in Amagansett or Montauk, and almost all of them were in college.

They smiled at me when Corinne introduced us. Some were polite and asked me where I was from and if I was having a fun summer, but I noticed their gazes flicker sideways during the answers. Except for one girl, Stacy, a beauty with a shiny strawberry-blond mane and a scattering of freckles on her nose so perfectly placed, it was like a stylist had painted them on.

"Athens, Georgia?" she said. "I always laugh when I hear that name. It's so funny how in the South you have all these podunk places named after famous European cities." She sniffed, raising a plucked eyebrow. "Paris, Texas. Yeah, *right*. Paris in *Texas?* I'm so sure!"

"And where are you from again, Stace?" Corinne cut in suddenly.

Stacy wrinkled her tiny nose. "Cambridge?" she said, uncertainly.

"Cambridge, England?" I asked, my mouth twitching with a smile as I caught on to Corinne's train of thought.

"Cambridge, Mass." Stacy's pretty face fell into a scowl, and Corinne winked at me before she disappeared into the crowd. I didn't know whether to be happy that Corinne had come to my rescue or bummed that I'd needed it.

Once the party got into full swing, everyone started dancing. The music was sexy and loud, hip-hop and electronic stuff. The girl DJ was supposedly one of Gen's best friends. I watched as Corinne worked the floor, dazzling all of us, and then finally—expertly—managed to get herself into a suggestive dance with Aram, his girl-friend Ivory pouting in the shadows before slinking off.

It was like watching a National Geographic special about being top of the food chain. Corinne and Aram were like lions at head of the pack. Gen was the vulture, circling the room in her black clothes, looking ready to sink her stylish claws into whatever poor unsuspecting conformist preppie might make the mistake of smiling her way.

And the frumpy relative remains on the sidelines, I chided myself, after I realized that for the last hour, I'd been as silent and still as one of Aunt Kathleen's potted ferns beside the bookcase. Feeling conspicuously inconspicuous, I took a deep breath, marched over to Gen, and asked her for a shot of whatever she had.

Gen grinned, her arms around a tanned guy who was drinking straight from a bottle of vodka. "This is Justin," she informed me, running a fingertip along his cheek. "I think I'm falling in love with him."

"I'm Eric," the guy corrected her. "That's Justin." He pointed at a nearby guy who raised his cocktail in the air.

"Whatever, Justin!" Gen slurred cheerily. "Just pour!"

Gen's eyes were sly and amused as she handed me a shot glass. "Chin chin."

I swallowed the vodka under Gen's gaze and what felt like everyone else's too. I felt like I was on stage with everyone watching me, which, unlike Corinne, was the last place on earth I'd ever want to be.

Paranoid! I opened my eyes to see that, in fact, Gen was not watching me at all. She had disappeared into the forest of elbows and tanned shoulders and hips moving to the music. I was alone, a bad dancer in a stupid dress.

Except suddenly I no longer cared. The vodka spread and burned, a warmth moving through my blood, the room's hard edges softening. Around me, the bright colors muted and separated and blurred together until everything seemed like a collage: hoop earrings, a flash of black leather, Eva's feather boa (she was out on the dance floor with Beth), and, booming through my chest, the thud, thud, thud of the music.

I knew I was dancing like a hick from Dipstick, Nowhere, compared with the others who were clearly used to clubbing and professional performing-arts programs and did all sorts of complicated hip-rolling maneuvers all over the room. But it didn't matter. I felt light-headed, lighthearted, and loosened up, and now they were having a retro Motown moment, playing music I actually knew and even liked. That Dusty Springfield song about the son of a preacher man...

Just before ten, I somehow remembered Eva and looked around for her to try and coax her into her pajamas. But as I grabbed her hand, a guy scooped her up and put her on his shoulders. Eva spun around the dance floor, already the star of her own show, while the DJ spun classic Michael Jackson. "PYT! Pretty young thing!" Corinne and Gen sang, clapping for Eva.

Then they moved off the dance floor, heading outside with Aram and some of the others like Zoe and Tanya, or was that Chloe and Thea? Their names combined in the haze of my mind, their faces fuzzy smears, all alike.

"Where are you going?" I asked, grabbing Corinne's arm and linking my arm through hers.

"To the beach." Up close, Corinne's eyes were bright and strange. "To smoke pot. I'm sure you don't want to come."

Aram slid his hand around Corinne's waist. He also looked weirdly baked, his light eyes glassy as beads, his girlfriend nowhere to be seen. Hadn't they already smoked enough?

I took a deep breath. "I'll come," I said. "I'll just put Evie to bed. Then I'll join you guys," I said.

Corinne broke away from Aram and said into my ear: "You don't want to come, maybe." Her voice had kindness in it. She wasn't making fun of me; she was simply pointing out what we both knew to be true.

But here I was, insisting I wanted to go, maybe hoping that with a little vodka in me, I'd relax. "I'm coming."

"Okay. We'll wait for you," Corinne replied, leaning into Aram.

After I'd managed to convince Evie that Mom and Dad would have her head on a stake if she didn't get up to her room, I returned to the front porch. They weren't there.

Okay. I tried not to take it personally as I scanned the garden and then followed the wraparound deck to the back of the house. They'd obviously gone to the beach. Slipping off my shoes, I crossed the deck. I still felt warm and loose from the vodka, and I was determined not to be judgmental about myself or anyone else.

This could be a crazy summer night that Corinne and I would laugh about later, one of those shared experiences we so badly needed...and hey, maybe I'd even smoke a little pot myself. Just one hit. You're supposed to try it once, right? I stepped onto the wooden walkway, looking out toward the dunes, moving quickly before my inner Good Girl caught up with me.

No one.

Then I was on the beach, my eyes adjusting to the night, looking out for shapes on the sand, listening out for voices. Nothing, except dark sea, waves slapping the shore.

After ten minutes of looking, walking up and down, and calling names, I went back up to the house. Inside, the music throbbed like a headache, and there was laughter, a sound of glass breaking, and someone shouting, "Oh shit!" followed by giggling.

Deflated, I leaned against the balcony of the back deck, looking out at the sea. I no longer felt buzzed. Now I just felt idiotic. My dress was all wrong. And what was that about me smoking pot? *Please*. I couldn't even fake being cool. I so obviously wasn't.

I was just a "nice" girl. A boring nice girl that nobody who was anybody wanted to hang out with. Worst of all, I couldn't really blame them, because right now even I didn't want to hang out with myself. I was beginning to see why Jake's eyes had wandered.

Looking out to sea, I caught the lights of a boat passing nearby and pictured what the view from there might be. Maybe the people in the boat could see me, could see the twinkling lights and hear the music floating in the air and mixing with the sound of the wind and the water. Maybe, to the people in the boat, the scene at Wind Song looked magical, romantic. But from where I was standing, it felt anything but.

"Thinking deep thoughts?"

A tall guy leaned against the wall behind me, his face silhouetted in the light falling from an old-fashioned gas lamp hanging from one of the eaves.

"Not really," I replied, wishing that whoever he was, he'd just go away. I didn't feel like company. I'd tried it, and it hadn't worked. Maybe I should say company didn't feel like me. That much was clear, since I'd been ditched—and no doubt this guy would ditch me too, just as soon as a better bet came along.

"That Charleston can really take the breath out of you," the boy said, still in his position by the wall. "I am *beat*."

"Charleston?"

"I thought you of all people would know what I'm talking about," he replied. "You look like a flapper from the twenties in that dress, my dear."

"Twenties?" I didn't really know what he was talking about. Was he making fun of me?

"Use your imagination," the stranger persisted. "The setting is perfect. We're out in the Hamptons, playground of the rich. We're standing on the deck of an old summer cottage, an uninterrupted view of the ocean before us. You're in a beaded dress, and I'm lookin' sharp—a touch more mod than the twenties, but it'll work. I admit the music is a little off," he continued as a loud hip-hop beat pummeled the air like an invisible fist. "But everything else…?" He opened his arms wide and walked toward me. "It's positively Gatsby-esque!"

"Do you always talk this way?" I asked, as the stranger came closer. He wore a vintage-style suit jacket that hung off his lanky frame. And he had on shiny, lace-up two-tone shoes.

"I can not talk if you'd prefer that."

He was nice looking, I noticed; skinny, but it suited him. Not a face you stare at across a room, but a face you like to look at up close. Slightly crooked nose. A good smile with some kind of electricity flickering beneath it, as though he was trying to suppress a joke. And he had an unusual voice, very deep and sort of rasping, like he'd been chewing on gravel. "Would you prefer it if I didn't talk? Because I can be the strong, silent type, you know. I can *not* talk if you—"

"Can you?" I said pointedly.

That shut him up. For a moment anyway. We stood looking out to sea. I'd read *The Great Gatsby* in school, in eighth grade: a sad story about unhappy people in fancy houses trying to impress each other.

"I'm Simon Ross," he said after a while. "I don't know if you noticed me noticing you earlier. Noticing your dress. There's not a lot of elegance around here."

"I didn't notice—you noticing me, I mean," I fumbled. I didn't want to send the wrong message. I didn't want to send any message. I still couldn't tell if he was making fun of me in my dress, and, even if he wasn't, I didn't need some stranger hitting on me. Or pretending to. Or whatever it was he was playing at.

"*The Great Gatsby* is my favorite book," Simon continued, unde-terred by my not-very-encouraging signals. "It's a story of impos-sible love. Jay Gatsby and the ravishing Daisy Buchanan." He stopped, cocked his head, and looked me up and down. "She broke his heart."

"A classic American love story, I guess," I added unhappily.

"You make an excellent Daisy in that dress. The question is…are you going to break my heart?"

"I don't break hearts," I muttered, darkly. *But I know what it's like to have one broken.* I pictured Jake at a party chatting up some new girl. Jake was an easy-talker type, like this guy. Whereas witty, flirty conversation was not my thing.

"I gotta go," I said, turning, but Simon grabbed my arm lightly.

"Stay," he said. "I'm sorry. I was just kidding around. I didn't mean to offend you."

"Who are you anyway?" I asked suspiciously. I hadn't seen him at the party, and he didn't seem like someone my cousins would hang out with. He was on the gawky side, and Corinne, Beth, and Gen surrounded themselves with surf-toned studs whose shoulders were so broad you could practically run a marathon on them.

"I'm an infiltrator. An uninvited guest," Simon admitted. "We're renting the house next door. I've been watching the parties over here for weeks now. You can see the lights all the way down the beach." He paused and lit a cigarette, and I waved the smoke away from my face. Did everyone smoke here except me?

"You're renting the house next door," I repeated, remembering Corinne's words. *Awful people…all the dregs come here…we don't want them.*

"Yup. Unfortunately, my parents like tacky houses, so I have the dubious honor of staying in the ugliest house in Southampton. And that's saying a lot because there are some butt-ugly pads out here."

We watched as two drunk, giggling girls passed by, casting shadows onto the deck as they wandered down to the beach. We were silent as our eyes followed the girls' silhouettes weaving down toward the beach, their laughter tinkling through the still night air.

When Simon next spoke, he surprised me. I'd almost forgotten he was there. He began to quote from *The Great Gatsby*, his voice throaty and deep as he delivered the narrator's description of his neighbor's summer parties, with music wafting across the garden and people flitting like moths in the evening light.

The words hung in the salt-perfumed air. "*The Great Gatsby*," I said, stating the obvious because I wasn't sure what else to say. Back in eighth grade, I'd speed-read the book. Its long sentences had gotten on my nerves. I've always preferred books with hard facts, the real world over stories. But the words caught me now, so perfectly tuned to where we were.

"Fitzgerald." Simon shook his head and gave out a low whistle. "That guy kicked serious ass," he added, straightening up. He was a least a head taller than me, I noted, with knee-jerk pleasure. I'm pretty tall, and most guys make me feel like a hulk of a girl.

"I remember the movie more than the book," I blurted out, then cringed, wondering if Simon would think I was shallow for saying so. But it was true: I had seen the movie at least twice. My mom had it on video. It was one of her favorites.

"The movie's pretty good," Simon replied. "Robert Redford. Mia Farrow as Daisy—that's your part," he added.

"Hardly. I'm not much of an actress. And I'm certainly no Mia Farrow." I laughed. Simon couldn't know the secret meaning behind my laugh. Because he didn't even know my name yet, much less that I was named for Mia Farrow. Mom had all Mia Farrow's movies, just as she had a library of films starring other blond beauties like Grace Kelly, Jean Harlow, and Eva Marie Saint, my sister's namesake. Unlike Eva, however, I was sadly miscast in my role: the movie Mia is a blond slip of a thing with a babyish Hello Kitty voice, like Beth's.

"Fitzgerald set the story here on Long Island, but he changed names around: West Egg—that was supposedly Great Neck. And that's where all the unfashionable people lived in the twenties. And East Egg—that would be Sandy Point, where all the swanky people owned houses. People like you guys."

"I'm not swanky," I said back. "Anyway, you live next door." I added defensively. "Not exactly slumming it."

"True, true." Simon thought about this for a bit. "But it's not all money, is it? Being accepted, I mean."

"No, it's not," I agreed. Even if I had pots of money, I still wouldn't fit any better with my cousins and their friends.

"Me, I prefer staying out of the cool set these days."

"If you're not into the scene, then why are you crashing this party?" I shot back.

"To meet you," he said smoothly. "I saw you arrive last week. And I thought, that's someone I'd like to meet!"

"That's a crock," I replied, turning away. I still couldn't figure him out. Was he mocking me? How would I know? I had no talent for interpreting these people out here. They were full of sudden smiles and clever comments…it was disorienting. That's when I decided it had been a long enough evening.

"I have to go." I pushed past Simon and headed back across the porch, looking for my shoes, which I'd abandoned somewhere when I'd realized Corinne and her friends had abandoned me.

"Hey!" he called after me as I opened one of the glass sliding doors.

"What?"

"I didn't catch your name."

If I told him the truth, he wouldn't believe me. "Daisy," I said, smiling. And then I went in.

• • •

After I'd heard Corinne and Gen giggling and sneaking upstairs, I heard my aunt and uncle and my parents come in. I couldn't believe they'd been out so late, that they'd outlasted us all. *Lucky for us.* Their lateness had bought me time to pile paper plates into garbage bags, stash booze bottles in the garage, and sweep cigarette butts off the porch.

"Don't sweat," Beth had said breezily from the couch, where she'd been lying in the lap of some guy. "The maid's coming tomorrow."

Maid or no maid, I didn't want to leave the place looking like a sty. For one thing, we'd surely get in trouble…though on second thought I wasn't so sure. Aunt Kathleen and Uncle Rufus had already surprised me. They gave their daughters so much freedom and never seemed to get on their case for anything like cleaning up or meeting curfews or any of that. If I didn't know them better, I'd think they were the kind of parents who just didn't care.

But I did know them better. They'd always been doting parents. And they obviously gave Beth and Corinne a long leash precisely because they were loving enough to be cool so that their daughters would be happy and have a fun summer. Beth and Corinne were so lucky! But they didn't appreciate it. It was like they wanted to get caught getting drunk or smoking or whatever. They didn't do much to hide it, which seemed dumb to me.

Whatever. That was them, not me, and I didn't want my uncle and aunt to think I was a slob who didn't care that their house had been trashed. So I cleaned away the worst of the mess, which took a good forty-five minutes. Still no parents.

After I finally got up to my room, I wrote in my journal, reviewing the party and Simon. I didn't know what to think of him, so I wrote his name and put a string of question marks after it. Who was he? And would I see him again? Not that I wanted to start hanging out with some guy. I didn't trust instant friendship, especially not from a boy. And especially not a boy who could quote from great American novels. Either he was interesting or else he was just pretentious.

Only time would tell.

I put my pen down, climbed out the window, and sat on the roof. Simon's house was up-shore and to my left. But I couldn't see it from where I was sitting, no lights even. You couldn't see much by day either. The property was adjacent to Wind Song's, but it was still fairly far down the beach, and trees and bushes obscured the front and sides of the house—"mercifully," as my aunt had put it to my mother, describing the new renovations that had been done by the latest owners.

"There's so much glass and metal on the outside of the house that it acted like a magnifying glass. It actually burned the first lot of trees they planted..." my aunt had told my mother.

I tried to imagine Simon in his vintage suit reading old classics in that house. And I'd thought *I* was out of place? The image made me smile. But my smile disappeared when I thought of the flirty lines that had tumbled so easily from Simon's lips. *I saw you arrive...and I thought, that's someone I'd like to meet!* He was a charmer all right.

Or maybe he had just been teasing me. Either way, I wasn't in the market for some guy's games.

I got up and went back to bed, glad that Simon only knew me as a fictional character. I liked the distance. It suited me fine.

I was just drifting off when I heard my mom crack open my door. "Mia, are you awake?" she asked softly, but I didn't answer. Mostly I just didn't want to talk about the party. I didn't want to hear my mother's anxious questions. Had I met any interesting people? Had everyone liked my dress?

She had dreams for me, in spite of the fact that she knew I was not the girl she wanted me to be. And somehow, telling her I had spent time talking to a boy, and, yes, he had liked my dress…well, I had a feeling Mom might not be so impressed by Simon. Because if he wasn't in the "in" set, then he wasn't somebody. That's the way she thought.

chapter four

I woke up before the rest of the house, at seven. Though I was tired, I couldn't go back to sleep, so I decided to go for a swim and wash the smell of smoke from my hair.

The beach was empty, as if it existed only for me. I took a long walk up the shore. The tide was low. Bits of mussel and clam shell gleamed in the morning light, and small waves collapsed over my feet.

I passed old wooden houses and beach shacks. Behind and beyond them, newer houses rose up, towering over the old: dome-shaped time-shares and giant concrete vacation homes with huge pillars and so much glass it hurt to look at them. I thought again of my aunt's description of Simon's house magnifying the sun.

As I wandered along the beachfront, I realized that there weren't many people out here who really liked ordinary things. Their vacation homes looked like city homes to me. I'd thought the whole point of vacations was to leave everything behind.

Out in the water, I faced out, away from the beach and toward the horizon line. I imagined there was nothing behind me: no houses, no parties, no Corinne, only me floating like a piece of seaweed, insignificant, just a tiny spot drifting in the sea.

I swam until my muscles burned and waded back to the shore, pleasantly tired. If only the beach could always be so empty. That way I wouldn't care what I looked like and I wouldn't be comparing myself to anyone else.

As I sat drying my hair with my beach towel, I watched as two distant figures made their way down the shore. Even from afar you could tell they were a man and a woman. At one point their hands linked, and I felt jealous, a lonely onlooker. I felt something else too: déjà vu. For a moment, I couldn't place why this scene seemed so familiar and so important. The couple receded farther, little more than two dark smudges on the pale tide line—almost still, like a painting. And then I remembered...

• • •

"This one is called *Green Sea*," Miss Elliot motioned for the group to gather round. We were at the High Museum of Art in Atlanta. Our class was on a field trip, and we were almost at the end of our tour. It had been a long day, starting with an early school bus departure. I stifled a yawn as I followed the sound of Miss Elliot's voice. I wasn't much of an art buff, so I'd let Jake pull me behind columns and into stairwells, while Miss Elliot guided us through rooms of European masters and contemporary sculpture, all of it no doubt important but none of it feeling nearly as important to me as Jake's lips grazing mine, his hands in my hair. We'd been together for a month, and all I wanted was to be with him.

"*Green Sea* was painted in 1958 by American artist Milton Avery," Miss Elliot announced as I leaned through the sea of heads in front of me to catch a glimpse of the painting.

"*Green Sea* was painted by a moron," Jake muttered jokingly, his hand snaking around my waist. "Come on," he whispered in my ear. "Let's skip this masterpiece."

But the painting pulled me in. It was a simple landscape, a diagonal line dividing it in two, pale sand on the left, dark-green white-capped sea on the right, and a band of sky above. In the center, two smudged figures moved down the beach.

The colors of sand and sea stopped me like a memory, as though I had been in the painting myself. I knew those exact shades. I smiled, thinking of the summer just ahead. The ocean in front of my aunt and uncle's house looked just like that on a windy day. The figures on the canvas were little more than a squiggle of brushstroke, but, as they walked toward me, I pictured them as me and Jake walking on the beach in front of Wind Song, the white-capped sea one side of us, a shimmering blanket of bright, pale sand on the other. Two figures close together on an otherwise empty beach.

I squeezed Jake's hand, an idea forming in the back of my mind: maybe, just maybe, Jake could come and see us that summer at Wind Song. Maybe our parents would let him come out for the tail end of our trip or something, giving me and Corinne time to ourselves but also allowing me to introduce my new boyfriend to my extended family...

"What do you think?" Miss Elliot asked the group.

"I think my dog could do better," Jake quipped. Everyone laughed. "Seriously," Jake added, "the guy couldn't even paint a face on those people. But now his painting's all famous? What a scam, man."

"Anyone care to answer Jake?" Miss Elliot looked around the group. "What's the effect of leaving the figures so undefined? Or do you think Avery just didn't know how to paint properly?"

Before I even realized it, I was speaking. "I like that you can't tell who the people are," I countered, sliding out of Jake's embrace. "This way you can use your own imagination, maybe even put yourself in the picture. The people could be anyone, and the beach could be any beach you want it to be."

"That's a very thoughtful interpretation, Mia." Miss Elliot nodded at me. "One of the interesting things about Milton Avery is the tension between the abstract and the literal in his work," she continued. "We recognize the forms, but then they break away from realism. He wasn't trying to paint a photograph. He was trying for something else, something new."

"That's just what my dog says," Jake shot back, and the room erupted in laughter again. I smiled weakly, but though Jake's goofy side had always charmed me, this time it grated on me. I wasn't even really sure why.

While Miss Elliot continued talking about Milton Avery and his groundbreaking use of simple shapes and flat color, how peaceful ocean scenes of summer had captivated him, and how his work was celebrated by later Abstract painters, I felt a twinge of sadness. Hard to define. Like the feeling you get when summer is over. Somehow I just knew—deep down, without even realizing it—that Jake and I would not be walking on the beach together near Wind Song. That image truly had been an abstract fantasy. It would never be real.

But on that day in the museum, I didn't know that Jake and I weren't going to last. I shrugged off my feelings, told myself that I was just being oversensitive, making something out of nothing.

"Don't be touchy," Jake murmured, sliding his hand into mine. "I forgive you for liking bad painting," he teased.

"Last stop, the African Art permanent collection," Miss Elliot announced. I looked back at *Green Sea* as the group moved toward the elevators. This time, the two figures on the beach looked different to me: they weren't walking toward me, but away.

• • •

Back at the house after my swim, Mom was moody and barked at me for coming to the breakfast table without combing my hair. Aunt Kathleen looked tired. She smiled as she scooped a poached egg onto my plate, but there were dark circles under her eyes, and I noticed the way she stiffened when my mother started talking. Had they had a fight? I stared at my mother angrily. No doubt she'd found a way to pick at my aunt—who, frankly, was the nicest person I knew.

But nice finishes last, I reminded myself darkly, thinking of how Corinne and the others had ditched me the night before. Maybe if I'd acted less keen to hang out with them, they'd have wanted me to? Reverse logic? Was that the way to navigate through my vacation and have a good time?

Whatever. I left the table as soon as I could, packed a banana and a bottle of sparkling water into my backpack, and took a bicycle out of the garage.

I cycled west, all along Dune Road, its length and flatness making it perfect for coasting, past the beaches of Southampton all the way to where the finger of land I was on petered out, the Shinnecock Inlet dividing our spit of sandy beach from the next. I stood with my bike, looking out across the narrow blue strip of water that prevented me going any farther. I was cut off, but I could see over to where Dune Road and land began again and would continue all the way down the coast, from Hampton Bays to Tiana Beach and over to Westhampton.

To my right, the inlet widened into Shinnecock Bay. The marshland glowed green and gray, and, in the distance, I could make out the shapes of men lifting clams from the shallow, sandy floor, the Ponquogue Bridge arching high up over them and touching down in the town of Hampton Bays. The scene was calm and still and dreamy. Like a painting.

Back on my bike, I rode in the opposite direction until I hit the town of Southampton. From there, I took streets at random, riding past small cottages, trying to peek at mansions hidden by manicured privet hedges, and stopping to admire old houses like Wind Song, with shingled roofs, deep porches, and hanging baskets of geraniums.

I kept going, along causeways and down to dead ends, looking over inlets and ponds, grand old homes, and shiny new ones, sloping down to the water. I got pleasantly lost and then doubled back until I found streets I knew. It was a great feeling, flying through the landscape with no destination. And briefly, instead of lonely, I just felt free.

• • •

By the time I got back, the girls lay on deck chairs in robes and dark glasses, drinking tomato juice. Corinne's so-called friend Stacy, the one who'd tried to insult me the night before, had stayed over. But she looked meek now and dipped her head toward her tomato juice when she saw me, obviously embarrassed to remember how she'd tried to slur my hometown for being "podunk" but just ended up sounding ignorant herself.

Mom and Aunt Kathleen had gone to the library, and the dads were heading out to go fishing. "Want to come, anyone?" Dad asked, and I knew he meant me. I love fishing and didn't often get the chance.

But I didn't want to seem antisocial, so I shook my head. "No, thanks." And then I smiled at the other girls. It was a new day, and, after cycling away my bleak vibes, I felt fresh and forgiving. So I'd gotten left behind last night. So what? The summer had barely begun. "Anyone want to swim?"

"Ouch!" Gen put a hand to her head. "Could you keep the decibels down, Mia? Some of us are delicate."

"Sorry," I mumbled, trying not to giggle. The girls looked funny, like they were dressing for a scene in an old movie. They wore silk head scarves and huge Jackie O. sunglasses, and held cold glasses to their foreheads, extravagantly hung over.

Gen lit a cigarette the minute the fathers left, and Eva appeared in a Hannah Montana swimsuit and one of Mom's big straw sun hats. "Genny, will you swim with me?" she asked, ignoring me altogether, as I ignored her.

"God!" Gen moaned, clutching her head in distress. "Give us a break with those vocal cords, would you, Evie-pie? Run along now. Go find some kids, would you?"

Eva blinked. "Are you sick?" she said uncertainly, looking from Gen to Corinne to Beth to Stacy.

"They're not sick," I murmured to Eva. "They're just tired, Evie. I'll swim with you if you like."

"But I want Gen to," Evie pouted. "Gen said she would."

"Eva!" I snapped, irritated. "You have to learn to take no for an answer."

Eva flounced off inside, and Gen shot me a grateful look. "She's very demanding, isn't she?"

"It's my mother's fault," I replied with a sigh. "She's obsessed."

"Thank God, my parents never reproduced again," Gen said, making a face. "All this early-morning Nickelodeon activity. It's not good for my pores." She refilled her glass and adjusted her sunglasses. "Definitely a soft-focus day for me."

Do people really talk like that? I wondered, not for the first time. Gen put on such an act that it was absurd and—I had to admit— kind of entertaining. But later, when everyone had finally dragged themselves to the beach and lay limp as rag dolls, her mood darkened and she seemed even more irritated by Eva.

"Get that thing out of my grill!" she barked when Eva came up to show her a small crab. "Eva, you're like a mental wedgie right *here*—" Gen squeezed her temples. "Just go make a *sand castle* or something, can't you?"

"She's only nine," I remarked as Eva's face twisted and she stalked off, embarrassed.

"Do you have to be so nicey-nice all the time, Mia?" Gen replied coldly. "It gets a little old."

"Lay off, Gen," Corinne said from underneath her hat. "You're just hung over."

"Sorry," Gen said tonelessly, shooting me a not-very-convincing apology smile and lighting up another cigarette. "But Mia doesn't care, does she?" she added lightly. "Mia isn't fragile." Her eyes traveled the length of me. "She's a big girl."

A big girl. Did she intend a double meaning? Was she making a veiled reference to my weight? Even if she wasn't, her comment made me bristle. *Mia isn't fragile.* Gen didn't sound sincere. If anything, I got the feeling she meant the opposite of that statement. And maybe I *wasn't* as tough as her, and maybe I wasn't as sophisticated. But replying would only make it worse, especially since I'd felt my face fire up like a lamp and I knew in a million years I couldn't say anything quick enough to put her in her place. So I pretended I hadn't heard her, which was all I could do. Anything else would make me seem "fragile."

"I hate tan lines," Gen said, thankfully changing the subject. She whipped off her bikini top to reveal her perfect small breasts.

"Me too," Corinne agreed and followed suit.

"Ditto," Stacy said, whipping her top off. Beth, who hadn't uttered a word all morning, also reached up as she lay on her stomach and undid the bow on the back of her string bikini.

Gen turned to look at me, her green eyes flashing with amusement. "Shocked?"

"I'm not shocked," I replied. "It's natural." But it was obvious I wasn't about to strip down.

"They do this in Europe all the time. It's no biggie," Corinne explained. I was annoyed that she felt she had to explain to the almighty prude what they were up to. Like I even cared that they were topless. We were on a virtually private beach, hidden by a sand dune.

But I was uncomfortable with all eyes now on me. They were waiting for me to join in. *Yeah, right! Don't mind me, I'll strip down in a minute—I'm just looking for the support of a spare crane to keep my breasts perky!*

I spotted the question mark in Gen's eyes. *Trust Gen to think this up.* This was a test. She wanted to see if I really wanted to be a part of the group or if I just wanted to sit on the sidelines. "Don't suppose they do this in Georgia," she added with a little fake-Southern twang, drawing out the sound of Georgia so that it came out more like *Gaw-giaah.* "But you can't disapprove of Mother Nature," she added with a virtuous smile, replacing her sunglasses.

Something inside me exploded, a hot firework of irritation. What did she know anyway? She was just another rich kid who didn't know anything about anywhere except her own backyard. Someone who acted like anywhere but here was nowhere at all.

"Are you kidding?" I shot back. "They go full-frontal down there. Total nudity. Don't you know we Southern folks are looser than y'all? It's all those mint juleps we drink."

"Seriously?" Gen replied, her mouth parting in shock.

"Touché, Mimi!" Corinne laughed. "Score!"

But though I smiled, enjoying cool-as-a-cucumber Gen being caught out for once, I was tense as a tightrope walker as I lay back down on my towel. They were waiting for me to flash it to the world. A part of me would have loved nothing more than to be as free with my body out there as the rest of the girls, but I knew I didn't have the kind of body that would look right without a considerable amount of Lycra keeping everything in place.

It's easy for other people to say they "wish" they had big breasts. I know people get implants all the time. But when by the time you're twelve everyone is staring at your chest, you start making wishes of your own, and they tend to be prayers for bee-sting boobs like Corinne's.

"Don't let us turn you into an exhibitionist, Mia," Corinne said with a kind smile. "Indecent exposure is not a compulsory part of our beach activities."

I swallowed hard, sucking down the embarrassment. I knew Corinne was trying to be nice, but that somehow made it worse. I just wished they'd all forget about me and get back to their tanning already.

"I'll pass," I said, with a self-deprecating laugh that I hoped would put a lid on the subject once and for all. Gen rolled her eyes but said nothing. And after a few minutes she got up and walked, slinky as a cat, down to the water, her long bronzed back disappearing into the waves.

"Don't mind Gen," Corinne said to me, pushing her sunglasses up onto her head as she watched Gen sashaying into the water. "She just got naked for a part in this art-house movie, and she thinks she's quite the badass."

"No big deal," I said breezily, and Corinne smiled and lay back down, closing her eyes.

I tried to read my book about global warming and the ocean, but I couldn't concentrate with Stacy splayed out next to me, smoking a cigarette and checking me out with a sidelong sweep of her long lashes, up and down, up and down, her tiny nose tipped up to the sun. I turned a page. Stacy was near enough to inflict some damage upon. She was so thin I could probably deck her on the side of the head with a pack of Marlboro Lights and she'd hemorrhage internally. That would teach her to keep her eyes to herself.

But of course I did nothing, said nothing. I just stared at the same sentence over and over again while the others fell into a sun-worshipping silence, motionless, as thin and brown as pretzel sticks. When I caught Stacy checking me out a second time, I stared back at her. Quickly she asked me about my book to make it seem as though that was what she was looking at.

"It's about global warming," I replied coolly. "Do you know jelly-fish are taking over the ocean?"

"Tell me about it," Stacy giggled, looking in the direction of an overweight woman walking into the water. "Right before our eyes."

As the others laughed, I decided for once not to be a pseudo-version of myself just to fit in with everyone. "Hilarious," I said dryly to Stacy and snapped my book closed. I got up and fetched Eva, who was sulking on a nearby dune. "Come on," I said, taking her hand. "Let's take a walk, see if we can find anything cool."

We moseyed along the beach, and I kept my eyes open for Simon as we passed near his house. I looked up at the big, white deck and across to the sloping lawns. A gazebo had been built at the bottom and stood empty on the green grass like a giant bird-cage. But there were no signs of life, and, for a strange second, I wondered whether I'd imagined the whole thing: maybe Simon was like an imaginary friend I'd dreamed up for myself at a party where I'd found myself alone...

. . .

Up at the house, in Corinne's room, I casually asked my cousin if she ever saw the neighbors.

"I see the annoying son around," she replied. "Simon. They rented that house last year too, and he attached himself to us like a barnacle."

"Really?" I said, trying to sound offhand, but somehow I was disappointed by this news.

"He had a huge crush on Stacy. But she wouldn't touch him with a ten-foot barge pole."

"Why?" I asked, fiddling with a bottle of Corinne's Chanel Barely There nail polish even though I knew the answer already. A snob like Stacy would never pay attention to anyone from anywhere that wasn't her own backyard. Someone as off the New England map as Simon would never pass muster.

Corinne shrugged. "He's a dweeb," she said. "Tried too hard to impress us with all of his big talk about Kentucky Derby horses and artwork his father supposedly owns. Like we *care!*"

I'd hoped Simon would not be the guy Corinne described. The only thing I did know about him was his easy way with words. *All of his big talk.*

"Plus he dresses so *offbeat* all the time," Corinne added. "Thinks he's some kind of artist dude."

Beth came in during the conversation, padding silently into the room like a cat. "His father is supposedly some mega mortgage broker," she added, curling up her tiny rosebud mouth as though she'd just tasted something foul. "I bet he lost major money in those toxic loan things." She arranged her lanky frame on Corinne's bed, her sunlit hair fanning out on the white coverlet. "A Hamptons summer rental must be a big ouch for that family," Beth continued. "Doubt they'll be back next season."

"Like gladiator sandals," Corinne quipped, and Beth tittered at the joke.

"Not that having money matters *at all*," Corinne added quickly, seeing my stone-faced expression. "It's just…" she groped, looking for words. "Simon's just…LC," she said at last. "Lower class," she explained, stabbing an emery board in the air for emphasis. "No matter how he tries to act like he's stylish. I mean, that *house*. Sure, they're just renters, but…"

Simon's just LC. Lower class. Corinne sounded like my mother. Though we aren't exactly high society, words like "lower class" drop from my mom's lips all the time. She often reminds me that even though we aren't rich, we're "well-bred" and "good stock is good stock." For Mom, it's all in the details: God forbid we string Christmas lights *outside* the house during the holidays. Like having your family portrait taken at Sears, it's just "not done." And even Eva gets corrected when she sounds too Southern for Mom's liking.

I've never gotten how Mom could reconcile Dad's owning a hardware store with anything swanky, but she'd always found ways to set our family apart from being ordinary. In Mom's world, little meaningless things marked you as in or out, as the "right" kind to mix with, or not.

I hate that kind of talk. Upper class, lower class. Old money, new money. *Nouveau riche.* That was another of Mom's favorite phrases. The only way she forgave the newly wealthy for existing was if they had the sophisticated airs and graces Mom believed in. Like Genevieve: her dad might be an Internet bajillionaire rather than an heir to an old fortune, but Genevieve knew how to double air kiss on each cheek.

All this class BS apparently meant something to my cousin too. I felt sorry for Simon as Corinne turned up her nose at him. But at the same time, maybe he wasn't worth feeling sorry for. If he was so busy gate-crashing my cousins' parties and trying to kiss up to Corinne's friends by bragging about his wealthy family, then he obviously wasn't worth getting to know. Which was too bad. I'd thought he was different. He'd seemed so much like his own person.

Look who's talking, I thought dismally. I stopped in the middle of painting my thumbnail. Every day since I'd arrived, I'd tried in some way or another to fit in with Corinne's scene, even though I'd felt conflicted all the way. Hell, last night I was ready to go smoke pot with everyone, not because I wanted to but because they did! And today, when Gen had made fun of me, laughing about *Gaw-giaah,* I'd joked my way out of it, instead of telling her what I thought of her on the spot.

I looked over to where Gen lay passed out on her bed, still topless, dead to the world, probably dreaming the empty, happy dreams that people like her surely dreamt: dreams that mimicked their lives, where everyone followed them like stray dogs...

*Gaw-giaah...*I swallowed. What was wrong with me? Since when had I ever wanted to hang out with snotty types?

Then again, beggars couldn't be choosers. Maybe snotty types were the only people I'd have contact with this summer. A black cloud settled over me, and, despite how gorgeous and sunny it was outside, I couldn't shake the feeling.

• • •

That night, I slipped off to my room while the others went to watch movies in Beth's room. I spent an hour writing in my journal and then climbed out of my bedroom window onto the roof. Taking care not to make a noise, I stole past Beth's bedroom and slipped down the rose trellis that ran up against the side of the house. It was easy to get down, and I jumped the last part.

I trudged moodily up the shore. A light rain was falling, tickling my cheeks, but I kept walking, thinking back to the girls lying out on the beach with their flawless bodies, bodies they were proud to flaunt, whether out on the dance floor or in the water. Everyone here wanted to be around them, even people like Simon. Even people like me. For whatever reason, they seemed to suck me in against my will. I couldn't help wishing I was more like them. Or at least that I *looked* like them.

Near Simon's house, the beach was lit up tonight by floodlights sweeping down over a section of sand. As I passed by, I looked up from the bright white sand to the walkway. But beyond were only dark lawn and the ghostly silhouette of the garden gazebo. I could see no lights in Simon's house, no signs of life at all.

In spite of what Corinne had told me about Simon, a little part of me was still curious about him. But I ordered myself not to be curious about him anymore. I wasn't on vacation to befriend a smooth-talking boy. I was there to escape from one.

• • •

The days that followed passed in a blur of prickly moments—barbed comments from Gen, tactless words from Mom, or overheard snippets of tense conversation between Mom and Dad. But everything dissolved in the darkness. I climbed onto the roof and slipped to the ground via the trellis, and then I walked, absorbing the wordless night sounds. At night, I finally felt as though I was on vacation.

I looked up at the stars on clear nights and pieced together the sky, testing my knowledge. My dad had bought me a telescope for my fifteenth birthday. I'd gotten to know the major constellations and had learned about trippy things like black holes. The black holes stuck in my mind: vacuums of Nothing that were also Something; invisible dark vortexes that pull everything into them and make things disappear, even light. They were deadly; they were out there; and you couldn't see them at all. They fascinated me, and I still couldn't get my head around them, no matter how many books I read on the universe.

How could Something be Nothing?

People think science is dull, but there are things I've learned in science that blow my mind and make it hard to relate the same way to the world, once you know there's more to it than meets the eye. Like when I learned that color is just a reflection of light, and matter isn't really solid but made up of a gazillion moving atoms that skate around each other and never stand still.

Matter is not solid.

Color is only a reflection.

Nothing is Something.

I'd look around me—at the dark sea, at the night air, at the stars—and wonder what was real in the world and what "real" even meant.

• • •

"Daisy!"

"Huh!" I yelped, jumping back from the hoarse, gravelly voice booming out through the stillness of the beach , while I was out on a night walk. "You scared me," I said, stating the obvious, as Simon grinned ghoulishly at me, a flashlight underneath his chin. "That doesn't scare me though," I added.

"You shouldn't walk alone at one o'clock in the morning," he said.

"Why not?"

"There are people like me out here, that's why." He fell into step next to me. "Strange people wandering about like lost ghosts in the night."

"Maybe I'm one of them too." I paused to remove a piece of shell that had gotten stuck between my toes. "What are *you* doing out here?" I asked. "And where have you been all week?" I added, but then regretted it. I didn't want to act like I'd been checking up on him, watching his house for signs of activity.

"I come down here at night. To have a smoke. And a swim." Simon clicked his cigarette lighter—one of those mini-blowtorch things—and I caught a glimpse of his strong, bony face and big, square hands in the burst of orange light. "We went into the city for the rest of the week. My father had business. He thought I was checking out Columbia University, but I played hooky and went to art galleries instead."

"Why?" I asked. "I mean, whatever. None of my business," I mumbled.

"It's okay," Simon said cheerily. He sucked on his cigarette, the tip glowing brighter in the darkness. "My father's plan is for me to go to Wharton when I graduate next year. Famous business school in Pennsylvania," he added, in response to my blank look. "Business school!" Simon snorted. "Me!"

It did seem a weird choice for Simon. His retro style and flamboyant way of talking didn't make him seem a match with business school.

"My mom finally convinced my dad to let me check out Columbia's economics program," Simon continued. "As a compromise to transfer into if I don't like Wharton once I'm there. Not that I have any interest in Compromise Columbia."

"Why not?" I asked. "It's Ivy League." *Ivy League.* I smiled thinly to myself. Those were my mother's two favorite words when it came to discussing colleges. Most important to Mom, Ivy League schools were not "lower class." They were prestigious, the "right" schools to go to. And if "lower class" kids got in, they were the exception, not the rule. This is how Mom's mind worked.

"Columbia's a great school," I amended, embarrassed at my Ivy League reference.

Simon laughed. "Sure, it's a great school. But I don't want to go to college." He paused, tapping his cigarette to ash it. "And if I ever do go, I definitely won't be studying economics," he added. "Even so, my father's obsessed. Wharton means everything. Most people who go there do an MBA, but Dad wants me to get a head start, enroll as an undergrad. It's absurd."

Simon took another drag of his cigarette. "Even if my grades aren't good enough, he's already taken care of that. He donates money to the school. He's tight with the admissions people," he added, a sliver of bitterness beneath the amusement in his voice. "He'll do whatever it takes."

"Oh," I said, suddenly uncomfortable with the urgency in Simon's voice. He seemed to emit intensity like radio waves, and it wasn't just his voice. It was his whole body—the way he jerked his head and paced in long strides, only to turn around and walk backward. Everything about Simon seemed wired, like he was ready to spontaneously combust.

"It's a little tough for my old man," Simon said. "All I really want to do is backpack around Europe. My father's not exactly the type to go for that." He snorted. "He's been grooming me for college since I was born. Then he wonders why I don't want to go."

"Ever?" I tried to picture what my parents would think if I decided I wanted to backpack around Europe after school. But I couldn't picture their reaction. For the last year, I'd been dead set on getting all As, so I would get into a good school when I was done. I would only be a junior next year, but I already felt the pressure.

"Maybe one day. But on my own terms. Not to sit around studying business with a bunch of bankers' sons. Forget that. Swim?" Simon said suddenly, tugging off his shirt.

"Now?" I stopped walking.

"Sure, why not? It's a perfect night."

It *was* a perfect night. There wasn't a breeze in the air, and though the moon wasn't full, it gave just light enough for us to make out the breaking waves. We were at the best part of the beach too, a small cove near Simon's house.

"I call this Indigo Beach." Simon pulled off his watch and threw it onto his shirt, the metal clinking as it landed. "Even in daylight the water is so dark here, almost purple-blue."

"I don't have my suit," I said. But that wasn't the only thing holding me back from the swim. I wasn't yet sure I wanted to hang out with Simon. I couldn't read him. He seemed to want to talk to me, but maybe that was just because I was the only person who would talk to him. After all, Stacy wouldn't touch him—what had Corinne said—*with a ten-foot barge pole?*

Simon was probably just latching onto me because Something was better than Nothing…but I didn't want to be anyone's fallback plan. Especially not some random guy I'd never even talked to in daylight.

"We could go skinny dipping," Simon suggested.

"Highly likely!" I said sarcastically.

"Come on, Daisy! I can't exactly see you."

"Still."

"Have you ever been skinny dipping?" Simon asked me, removing his khakis to reveal—thankfully—a pair of baggy swimming shorts. "It's the best."

"I'll take it from you," I said.

He shrugged and took off, crashing into the water and yelping.

I thought about disappearing back to the house while he was still out there. It was late—very late I noticed, looking at the glowing hands of Simon's watch on his pile of clothes. But it was a beautiful night. So calm and quiet…

"I feel completely re-energized!" Simon half-panted, half-shouted as he came out of the sea a moment later.

"I didn't notice you'd run out," I said.

He laughed and shook his hair, sending droplets in every direction, and then patted his face dry with his T-shirt. "You should try night swimming sometime. It washes away all of your sins."

"I don't have any sins," I joked, but as soon as I said it, I felt like an ass. It hit a little too close to home to say it, even to my ears. *Do you have to be so nicey-nice?* Gen's words came back to me and I winced. Nobody would ever accuse me of being wild and crazy.

"Come swimming with me tomorrow night," Simon suggested, as we headed down the beach. "Hey! That could be your first sin!"

"I don't think so," I replied, laughing. I may not have known what I wanted yet, but swimming with this virtual stranger in the dark wasn't it.

"You'll be sorry," he said as we neared the walkway to his house and I slowed to a stop. "Why are we stopping here anyway? I'm walking you home, young lady."

"I don't need a chaperone, old man," I said as Simon jiggled from one foot to the other to dry off in his damp clothes.

"Who said anything about being a chaperone?" Simon reached for my arm. I tried to snake out of the way, but he held on, gently.

"Daisy," he murmured with a half-smile. "Give a guy a chance, would you? You're so arm's length!"

"You should be used to it," I returned smoothly. "Didn't Stacy say 'No thanks' too?"

The minute I said it, I wondered why I had. It was harsh. But I guess I was testing Simon the same way he was testing me by clinging to my arm. I wanted to know whether it was true that he'd made a fool of himself over Corinne's snotty friend. If that was Simon's idea of worthwhile, then I wasn't sure he and I had much in common as friends after all.

"Ah. Stacy," Simon said, letting go of me.

Idiot, I chided myself. Who Simon had tried to hook up with last summer wasn't my business at all. He and I were barely even acquaintances. I should have kept my mouth shut.

"I was a dick last year. I'll cop to it," Simon said with a shrug. "Tried to hang with the cool crowd, you know? Tried to show them I had the right stuff." He sniffed, shook his head. "Naïve. Weak."

"You don't have to explain yourself to me," I said.

"Stacy ignored me in front of her friends. Even though she let me—"

"I don't want to know. Really, this is none of my business," I broke in, holding up a hand. For some reason, I was blushing in the dark. I felt foolish listening to Simon's confessions. "I'm not friends with Stacy. I can't help you hook up with a lost love or anything."

All I wanted was to get into my room and ditch Simon. I guess I'd been hoping all along he would deny what Corinne had told me about him being into Stacy. But the fact that he didn't made him seem less interesting to me now. No longer someone to be curious about. Just another rich kid trying to get on the inside track.

"Look." Simon suddenly seemed sheepish. "I didn't—I—um." It was weird watching him grope for words. He was so verbal, such a natural with conversation. "I just want to talk to you. Get to know you a little better."

"Why?" I blurted out coldly. "Because I'm not who you think I am, trust me. This isn't my house. I'm not friends with Stacy. Seriously, we don't have anything—"

"I know who you are," Simon said softly. "I mean, I know who you're not. I watched you at the party. You're different."

Different. I flinched at the word. It felt like the way people say "special" or "challenged" when they mean handicapped. "Define different," I said, folding my arms.

"Hard to define," Simon shot back swiftly. "That's what's different about you."

"It's late," I said. "I have to get back in."

"Tell you what." Simon grinned. "You tell me your name, and I will promise to earn your respect and trust and friendship the old-fashioned way."

"I have to go to bed," I said. This was way too late for me. Or perhaps just way too much talk for me.

"Why?" Simon challenged. "Need to be somewhere in the morning?"

"I don't want to be tired tomorrow."

"Never mind tomorrow. If you sleep, you'll miss out on tonight. Why do people always choose day over night?" He shook his head. "Beats me."

"Yeah, well. I'm a morning person," I replied feebly and slipped away.

"Good night," Simon called out into the darkness. "Whoever you are."

After scrambling back up to the roof and climbing through my open bedroom window, I looked back behind me. Simon was walking back in a long, dawdling zigzag, the white of his shirt shining in the night as he wandered down to the shoreline.

I watched him until he disappeared, a pale dot sinking into the darkness. I watched him, and I tried to define exactly what I thought of him. I couldn't, so I went to sleep instead.

chapter five

echnically, I'm not interested.

I repeated these words to myself as I climbed out of the window the next night and wandered across the beach, keeping my eyes open for Simon.

And I *wasn't.* Not romantically. The way I saw it, to fall for someone meant you had to have that instant connection, the one that makes you feel as if you've been wired to an electrical socket. It had been that way with Jake. From the first moment I saw him, I just knew he was the one I had been waiting for. It felt like destiny. Like it was written in the cards. And actually, it was.

"The new boy even does magic tricks?" flirty Gabi Santiago had said, sliding into a seat next to Jake. We were in the cafeteria. I was in my usual place, eating with my friends Kristin and Lacey, when Jake had come over, a pack of cards in his hand.

"Man of Mystery," Gabi purred as Jake smiled and cut the deck.

"I need someone to do this with," Jake replied, flicking his long black bangs from his dark eyes.

"Oh, yes, pretty please!" Gabi squeaked.

But it was me Jake smiled at. "Mia, would you pick a card?"

My heart clanged like a gong against my chest. Kristin's elbow dug into my ribs. She knew how I felt about Jake. She knew that even though I'd never give him a flirty Gabi Santiago glance, he was the boy I'd been dreaming about. And she knew that for me, this was big.

"Take the card, Mia," Kristin said, shooting me an intense look.

I took it. Queen of hearts.

I'd always held back from boys. I didn't fall for them the way my friends did. While Kristin and Lacey hooked up with different guys and had crushes that were returned or rejected or fizzled, I just waited. Sometimes I wondered if the boy I was waiting for even existed. Until Jake came to our school. Then I knew. Except I never thought he'd even look at me. He was far too cool and far too cute to notice a shy, ordinary girl in a sea of admirers. And yet here he was, my queen of hearts in his hand.

All through Jake's magic trick I said nothing. My face burned, but he just smiled his lopsided grin at me. The trick was complicated, expertly pulled off. He wrote my name with a Sharpie on the queen of hearts. Then he wrote his name on a card he chose: king of hearts. After much shuffling, he somehow found both cards and pressed the two of them together in his palm. When he let go, there was only one card: on one side it was the queen of hearts, with my name on it. On the other, the king of hearts, with his name on it.

"Oh. My. God!" Gabi crowed, amazed. "He's like David Blaine."

I wasn't so gullible as to believe Jake had really pulled off some impossible magic. I couldn't work out all the details, but my analytical mind told me it was just a sleight of hand. And planning: Jake had come to the table with a trick card in his pocket, a card with two sides, one with my name already on it, one with his.

But it was still a kind of magic. A different kind: Jake had come to this lunch table with my name in his pocket. He'd come to this table for me.

. . .

Jake's and my relationship had begun with a brilliant illusion. But it had all felt so real. When we hooked up a week later, it felt unbelievable and inevitable at the same time. After dreaming about being in love for so long, I finally got what it meant to actually be in it.

Or so I thought. When those three words tumbled out of my mouth to Jake in the second month of being together, we were in his car. I hadn't intended to say what I felt. I was still nervous around Jake, and I still hung back. But this night I just felt the words fall from my lips.

"I love you," I whispered to him. We had been kissing for what felt like hours. Jake kept pushing for more, sliding my unbuttoned shirt off my shoulders, but I stopped him, grabbed his hands, and held them in mine. I wasn't ready for him to see me. Even in the darkness I felt shy. Still, I wanted him to know that I felt what he felt, that I knew he was the one for me, and that everything else was just a matter of time.

I should have known something was off when Jake just smiled, pulled his hands away from mine, and ran his fingers through his hair. I should have known something was off when he just leaned over and kissed me, but quickly, his lips light and dry.

"I should let you go," he said. And I promised myself there was nothing in his voice, that he was just scared, not ready to tell me his real feelings. I promised myself that when it came to Jake telling me he loved me, he would when he was ready.

He broke up with me a week later.

• • •

A chilly beach breeze made goose bumps rise on my skin. I folded my arms, hugging them tight to my chest. If only there were a scientific way of measuring love, of knowing when it was real, of knowing what it meant to feel right with someone who turned out to be so wrong.

But I didn't have anything else to compare my relationship with. I'd only kissed one other boy apart from Jake—just some stranger I met at a Dave Matthews Band concert. And to be honest, part of the reason I allowed myself to kiss him was because I knew I'd never see him again, and I didn't want my first kiss with the boy I loved to be awkward. I wanted to know what it was like so I'd be ready when it really counted. So I wouldn't screw it up.

So much for first love, I thought bitterly, trudging along the shore. Luckily, with Simon, there had been no heart-stopping craziness the moment we met. But I did find myself thinking about him. Maybe because I couldn't figure him out. Either he was just another lightweight or he was actually someone worth being friends with. I hoped so. Because I could use a friend—and from my experience, friendship lasted a lot longer than love.

As I passed the gazebo below Simon's house, I pretended not to be looking for him and pretended not to be disappointed when I didn't see him. I walked on, wind blowing tendrils of hair into my mouth.

But Simon was out after all.

"Over here!" Simon called out as I passed by the cove he'd called Indigo Beach. He was sitting on the sand, smoking. I got closer and shone my flashlight on him. His hair was dripping, and he squinted at me in the harsh light.

"Ouch. Serious beam."

"It's Cold War technology," I replied, shifting the beam so that it cast a long light into the darkness. "It works for up to fifty feet, depending on moisture particles in the air. Like mist. Or fog. The Russians made it."

"Impressive."

I clicked off the beam. *Moisture particles? The Russians made it?* I tended to get a little stupid and unnecessary when I was nervous. And I had tended to be nervous ever since I'd arrived in the Hamptons, watching my words around my cousins' scene, trying not to say the wrong thing so that I didn't sound like a fool. I bit my lip. I didn't want to sound like a fool in front of Simon either.

"Swim?" His voice came through the darkness.

I looked out toward the dark blur of sea ahead. "No thanks."

"Okay." He stood up, and we started walking, drifting along the sand together. Now even if I wanted to be alone, I'd have to think up something interesting to say, something to kick-start conversation. I swallowed hard. This wasn't my strength.

"Did you know that sea horses are the only animal where the males go through the pregnancy?" My face grew hot. *Stupid. Unnecessary.* I closed my eyes. Where had that come from?

"So if the males are the pregnant ones, how do you know they're males?" Simon asked.

"They fertilize the females. And then the females pass over the eggs to be carried by the males…"

My awkwardness didn't faze Simon. He was happy to chat about the sex life of sea horses for several more minutes, as though he'd brought up the subject himself. He also fired questions at me—about my hometown, my friends, school. He wanted to know everything. And I told him everything—except for Jake, that is. I didn't want to talk about him.

"…So you like it out here?" he asked after I'd satisfied his curiosity about Athens, Georgia, and my entire family tree. "The beach. The people?"

"Yeah. I mean, some of it," I answered evasively. "I mean the beach. Obviously."

"Not obvious," Simon countered. "I, for example, do not like the beach. Not out here. It's ruined. Full of awful houses, like the one I'm living in. Nighttime is the only time I can stand this place. That way you can't see how it's all gone to shit."

We'd found ourselves right in front of a monster-big shadow of a house, a house that said in stone what Simon had been saying with words. It was less a house than a faux castle, complete with Gothic towers. Spotlights and glaring fluorescent floods lit up the sand in front of it. A few lights were on in windows, but I knew no one was home.

This was Dragon's Lair, the house everyone had been talking about for years. My aunt was on the local board of residents that had fought to prevent the owner from building it, but he'd managed to go ahead anyway, defying the building codes only to go bankrupt in the process, partly from local lawsuits, partly from his own wild spending.

And now no one wanted it. There it stood, a skeleton of scaffolding still creeping up an unfinished turret. The owner had lived in it for only a few months before leaving. With even nice houses standing empty in the recession, it didn't stand a chance as a summer rental.

"Dragon's Lair." Simon mused. He looked up at the house with its dark turrets pointing spookily up into the sky. "Proves my point."

"Did you know there's a shark tank inside with live sharks?" I asked. "I haven't seen it, but that's what my aunt said."

"I heard there's a waterfall. And an indoor barrier reef." Simon shook his head as we stared up at the house. I couldn't tell if he was kidding or not, but I laughed anyway.

"I take back what I said the other night. About living in the ugliest house in Southampton," he said. "This one wins the prize."

"What kind of person would build something so offensive?" I asked.

It was a rhetorical question, but Simon answered. "Someone like my father."

"No way." I figured Simon was exaggerating.

"He's maybe like *this* close to the Dragon's Lair type." Simon held up an index finger and thumb in the air. "If he could afford it, who knows? Maybe he'd put in an offer. Or finance some other bonehead to buy it." We turned, starting back toward Indigo Beach. "My father wouldn't know taste if it flew down and smacked him in the face."

"Taste isn't everything," I commented. I wondered whether Simon was a snob at the same time as I wondered whether I, myself, was one too. I also laughed at the kind of people who built vacation houses better suited to Disneyland than the beach. But so what if they did? It was a free country.

"It's not everything," Simon agreed. "But I won't pretend I don't care about beauty. Beautiful things. Beautiful places..."

And beautiful people, I finished silently, an image coming to mind of physically perfect Stacy. She was so pretty it was nauseating.

"I have to get going," I said, pausing as we rounded the shoulder of a dune. My bedroom light shone out at me from the other end of the beach.

Simon nodded. "You need your beauty sleep."

"Do I?" I said coolly.

"I didn't mean," Simon stuttered. "I meant...you're a girl and all."

"Thanks for telling me," I said frostily, even as a part of me felt bad for making Simon stammer along. It was the second time I'd seen him at a loss for words. I knew he hadn't meant anything insulting, so why was I making him squirm?

"I'll see ya," I said in a neutral tone. I wasn't sure whether to be annoyed by Simon or by myself, or by both of us. "I can walk home," I added as Simon trudged alongside me to the walkway leading up to Wind Song.

"I can see that. You're very talented at it."

I rolled my eyes. "You know what I meant."

But Simon was several footsteps ahead of me now, walking backward, holding his arms out wide. "Can you imagine this place way back when…?" He shook his head, still lost in his beauty kick, imagining the unspoiled paradise of what Southampton must have been once upon a time.

"Hard to picture." Not true. I'd often imagined the shoreline free of houses.

"Try harder," Simon replied cheerfully.

"I'm a realist," I replied stubbornly, "not a romantic. Romantics are always disappointed."

"Maybe they're disappointed because they're always surrounded by realists." Simon countered.

I shook my head, smiling in the darkness at Simon, at myself. At the nonsense coming out of my mouth. A realist? I'd spent years dreaming of the perfect guy and the perfect relationship. And, okay, I know it's cringe-worthy, but I'd spent time in front of the mirror, moving my head in slow motion and looking over my shoulder, imagining I was in a music video or a movie, the subject of my incredible boyfriend's fascination and love. I'd thought I had found that love with Jake. But I was so wrapped up in my fantasy of me and Jake that it had blinded me to the reality.

And, let's not forget, ever since I'd arrived here I'd obsessed over the beauty of Corinne and Gen and Beth, as if hoping that by being near them, some of what they had might rub off on me. Then again, deep down, I'd always known I could never be a bright light like Corinne.

Ever since we were little, I'd always been her sidekick. And I didn't truly believe that what girls like Corinne had was something you could pass on, especially not to me. As for being a music video muse? I wasn't *that* out of it. So maybe I was a realist after all. Could you be both at the same time, realist and romantic? A dreamer who didn't believe in dreams?

"Sure you don't want to take a quick dip?" Simon badgered me as we neared Wind Song. "It's safe, you know."

"No, it's not," I corrected him. "There's a low-pressure system coming in, and it's peak high tide."

Simon cocked his head. "Do you work for the Weather Channel?"

I reddened. "There are big waves out there."

"Safety First. That's your motto, huh, Daisy?"

I turned up the walkway. "My name is Mia," I said over my shoulder, into the darkness. I could almost hear Simon's thoughts as he puzzled over whether I was just kidding him with my Gatsby movie-actress reference.

"For real?" Simon's voice came back at me.

I smiled. Yes, I was real. But there was no harm in keeping him guessing a little longer.

• • •

Simon was wading out of the water when I passed him a few nights later. I'd spent the past couple of nights walking the opposite direction, wanting to be alone after busy days trying to keep up with the social scene out here—with my cousins and Gen, that is. But tonight I found myself back at Indigo Beach, looking for Simon.

"It's really warm," he said, as he came up toward me, water dripping from his shaggy hair. Thick hair, I noticed, half not noticing that I'd noticed.

"Define 'warm,'" I replied.

"See for yourself."

I looked out toward the sea. The sky was pale and the ocean an inviting milky-gray. It was a still night, thick with mosquitoes, and the idea of water on my skin was tantalizing. Which was why I had my suit on underneath my clothes. I'd finally decided to try a night swim. But now that I was about to go in, I was having second thoughts.

"Don't be frightened. We won't go out far."

I hesitated, but a mosquito nibbling on my shoulder made the decision for me. "I'm in," I said, slipping off my cargo pants.

"Daisy takes the plunge," Simon teased, splashing in beside me. He grabbed my hand, and I let him. But I broke away when the water reached my waist. The surf wasn't big, but it was dark enough to make the rising black shapes out there seem a little scary—and that scariness made it thrilling too. My heart pounded as I heard Simon shouting above a breaking wave somewhere ahead.

"Hey!" I shouted. "Are you okay?"

Simon answered with a whoop.

"Come on out here, Safety First!" he chuckled during a lull.

"Don't make fun of me," I retorted as Simon swam up near me. But I was smiling. Being out there, just the two of us in the water, was a rush in the way that day swimming with all the crowds never could be. Darkness added to the excitement.

"See what fun it is to do what Simon Says?" Simon teased, drawing closer toward me.

"Maybe," I replied, circling my arms wide underwater, pulling myself backward toward the shore. "But don't let it go to Simon's head."

● ● ●

"I want to be a great painter," Simon said. "But I'll settle for being a good one."

We'd been sitting on the sand after our swim. The ocean had unspooled my muscles and my mind. For the first time since I'd met Simon, talking felt easy. He told me he lived in Minneapolis and had two older brothers—one at Wharton, the other in the navy—neither of whom he could stand. I commiserated on the sibling front, sharing un-cute stories of un-cute Eva. I told him I was on the swim team and that I might study oceanography when I got to college. He told me he had a thing about old jazz and dreamed of being an artist.

"I try not to get too serious. But painting really makes me happy. Maybe I'll show you some of my stuff sometime," he said. Then he shook his head. "That sounded pretentious."

"I think it's pretentious to pretend you're not pretentious," I teased. "Admit it—you show your paintings to all the girls. To impress them."

Simon shook his head slowly back and forth. "You're a tough lady, aren't you?" He smiled. "Why are you so hard on me, Daisy? And here I thought things were all cozy and we were getting to be good friends."

"Sorry. But my grandmother told me never to trust a man who offered to show you his paintings. Or could quote from books. Or wore white socks," I added with a laugh.

Simon nodded, faking a serious expression. "Pretty profound…
Hey, have you ever noticed how little old people actually know?
You're supposed to get wiser the more life experience you have, but
I think it works backward. Like after a lifetime on earth, you have
to reduce it all down to things like white socks…which, I might
just take this opportunity to inform you, I have *never* owned."

"Really? I could have sworn…" I kidded.

"*My* grandmother," Simon interrupted me, wagging a finger, "*she*
knew what was really important in life. The woman was an inspira-
tion. A passionate believer."

"Yeah?" I folded my arms in a challenge. "In what?"

"The lottery."

"Did she ever win?"

"No." Simon laughed. "But she always believed she would."

As we joked around, it occurred to me that Simon was lonely. He
was a natural talker. But I got the impression he didn't have a lot of
listeners. At least not out here, and maybe not back home either.

"It's late." I said finally, getting to my feet and brushing sand
from my lap.

"Not yet a night person, are you? Still conforming to the sleep
patterns of the world?"

"It's already day," I replied, smiling as we started walking.

"Thanks for the swim. You are a majestic swimmer," Simon said
as we neared the walkway to Wind Song.

"You talk a lot of crap, you know that?"

"I thank you for appreciating my verbal stylings," Simon replied,
with a formal bow.

"You're welcome." We were in front of Wind Song. Suddenly neither of us seemed to know what to say. So we just stood there. I looked up at the moon. It was heading toward full moon and bulged out, bright against the dark backdrop of sky, as white as an eyeball. "Waxing gibbous," I said, more to myself than to Simon.

"No need for bad language," Simon joked.

"The moon," I explained, laughing. "That's what it's called when it's more than halfway toward full moon."

"I never did understand that waxing-waning business," Simon commented as we gazed at the moon. "How can you tell by looking if it's waxing?"

"It's the direction…" I began. Mid-explanation, I could tell he was no longer listening; he was just staring at me. "What?" I asked. "Is this boring?"

"I was just thinking that it's cool you know about these things." Embarrassed, I shifted my weight from one foot to the other. "Don't worry, I'm not going to stop being your friend because you understand moon phases," Simon teased. "Hey," he said, after a pause. "Let's meet every night."

"Every night?" The idea of a regular nightly meeting made me nervous.

Simon thought a moment. "Here's an idea. Text me when you're out here if you want company."

"I can't."

"Why?" Simon sounded disappointed.

"I threw my cell phone out the window." I blushed in the darkness, thinking of how impulsively I'd acted, and that half the reason

I'd done it was to impress Corinne and Gen. "It's complicated. Basically I'm phone-free for the summer."

"That's silly. And charming."

I thought of Corinne, whose idea it was to go phone-free. But I didn't feel like explaining further, so I just smiled as if a phone-free summer was my own silly, charming idea.

"You take your flashlight out on your walks, right?" Simon asked.

"Depends on the moonlight."

"From now on, take it with you every night. When you're out walking this way, you'll pass the gazebo, where, chances are, I will be smoking."

"Then what?"

"You can signal—say, three times if you want to take a walk with me. Twice if you want to walk alone. That way I'll just let you walk on. It'll be like a military code. No one gets hurt."

I laughed. "That's silly and charming."

"I try. I can signal back with my cigarette lighter too," Simon said, holding up the lighter and firing off three short bursts of flame. "So, like, if I see you first and *I* happen to not wish to talk to *you*, I can fire off two bursts and block you in your tracks."

"Sounds fair," I agreed.

"Now go away." Simon flicked his lighter twice. "It's your bedtime."

• • •

The day after our second swim, I saw Simon on Dune Road.

Gen had asked me to go with her to pick up cigarettes. Corinne was off with Aram somewhere, and I rode shotgun with Gen in her sports car, annoyed to find myself pleased she'd asked me along.

As we turned out onto Dune Road, an old-fashioned yellow convertible puttered slowly in the road, nearing the driveway of Simon's house.

"Look. It's a blast from the past," Gen said, her lip curling in a mocking smile as we approached the car and the driver. It was Simon in a checkered cap.

"Hey!" Simon held up a hand and waved as we whizzed by, and I managed the briefest of smiles and the smallest of waves before Gen's fast driving flashed us past him altogether.

"Do you know him?" Gen shot me a curious glance.

I kept my eyes ahead. The social cachet of knowing Simon was clearly nil—and at worst, a liability.

I opened my mouth to answer but hesitated, checking myself, my eyes flicking over to the rearview mirror, where Simon grew smaller and smaller. I had a hard time with the question, maybe because in the light of day the question seemed as out of context as Simon himself. "Are you guys friends or something?" Gen pressed.

Friends. I could think of only one answer, and, in that moment, it seemed to be true. "Ish," I said.

I checked the rearview mirror again. Simon was gone.

INDIGO BEACH

chapter six

"Why don't I see you on the beach during the day? Are you a vampire or something?"

Simon laughed. We were lying in the shallows at Indigo Beach. There were almost no waves that night. It was low tide. A warm breeze blew at the backs of our necks and shoulders. "And *don't* tell me it's because you can't stand to see all of the ugly houses around you," I added, flipping onto my back.

"I'm probably the only person out here who doesn't like the sun," he replied.

"You don't like the *sun?*" That seemed impossible. Like being allergic to water.

"I'm a freckle-head," Simon explained. "Red hair. Burn easily. Never tan."

"Really?" I smiled, because it struck me as weird that I didn't know such a basic thing about him. But I hadn't seen Simon in daylight, with the exception of that one time in the car. Even then I'd barely seen him, just a smudge of face and his checkered cap. And though we'd been swimming three times already, it had always been at night. I'd thought of Simon as having blondish-brown hair.

"See?" Simon held a flashlight up to his hair as we got out of the water and dried off. "Carrot top."

I studied Simon's dripping hair in the white of the flashlight. "I can't tell."

Simon held the beam of the light up to his forearm, and I could make out a sprinkling of tiny freckles. "My mother's family is Scottish. I shouldn't even be in this climate. I should be out on the moors in the rain, with my brethren," he added. "In a kilt. With bagpipes."

"So what do you do if you don't go to the beach in the day?" I asked.

"Listen to music. Paint. I mess around with oils. I like the light, but I like to see it from a shady place. Under a tree. Or sitting in my window bay." A look of longing came into Simon's eyes. "I can really see myself next year just drifting, in search of soft light. Going to Italy, sitting in cafés and painting. Siena. Venice. I want to go to Venice before it's all underwater. This college crap… everyone is so programmed."

Simon stopped abruptly and laughed. "There I go, giving you the long answer. Always too many words. That's been my father's criticism of me my whole life."

I smiled. That was the exact opposite of my mother's criticism of me. "So now I know what you do all day."

"Occasionally my father forces me to go fishing. And yeah, sometimes I go to the beach. I've seen your cousins out here. Tanning topless."

"They do that." I wrapped my towel around my upper body.

"They're very pretty-pretty, your cousins. Not my type."

"Not your type?" I said wryly. "They're everyone's type. They're like the blueprint. Or something," I added the "or something" in a lame attempt to cover up the wistfulness in my tone. I regretted feeling wistful at all on this subject, and I especially regretted revealing it to Simon.

But I couldn't help it. Corinne, Beth, and Gen seemed to get even lovelier as the days wore on. The sun agreed with them, making their skin and hair glow no matter how many boxes of cigarettes or bottles of vodka they went through.

"Nobody is everybody's type," Simon countered, as we sat down on the sand. "And it's funny, you can think someone's your type and then they turn out not to be. Or the other way around. Know what I mean?"

"Like Stacy?" I asked.

"Like Stacy." Simon nodded, his profile outlined in the low light, his hands playing with a pebble, turning it over and over. I liked Simon's hands. He had long, slender fingers, hands that seemed to belong to an artist. My own hands aren't elegant like that. They're big and chunky, good for palming water in a breaststroke. Not hands an artist would admire.

"Last year I acted pretty stupid," Simon admitted, his gaze fixed straight ahead, as he rolled the stone in his hand. "I guess I thought I'd fit in better with Stacy if I could charm her crowd somehow. Renting a summer house here doesn't exactly mean you fit in with the people who've owned houses here for years." He shrugged. "I couldn't have cared less about that kind of stuff...until I met Stacy. Then suddenly being in that scene mattered because it meant I could get near her.

"I had to go the extra mile, prove myself. So I told stupid stories. Half of them weren't even true. But I figured if I was going to win Stacy over, I needed to impress more than just her. So I was larger than life. A real 'colorful character.' Know what I mean?"

"I guess," I rested my chin on my knees. But I wasn't sure that I did. I myself had never been a colorful character.

"In the beginning, her friends were okay. I was crazy about Stacy. I thought she was the most beautiful girl I'd ever seen."

"Uh-huh." I swallowed, trying to be a good listener. But no girl likes to hear stories about beautiful girls. No matter who you are or how "nicey-nice." "I got invited over to all of the parties. My brother, Hunter, the business school bozo, was here, so he came too. At first I thought Stacy liked me a lot. We'd started having a thing. I thought I was in love. I'd never met girls like her before, who seemed so much older. Who seemed to know everything."

I thought of Gen and Corinne. I could easily see how any guy would be hypnotized by them and their friends, especially a guy who hadn't seen girls like them before. A guy who came from some place else, some place less sophisticated than New York City—which as far as I could tell, was everywhere else on the American map, if not the whole world.

"As it turned out, Stacy wasn't interested in me." Simon tossed the stone he'd been holding. From somewhere in the darkness came a soft thump as it hit the sand. "It didn't take long for her to figure out that I wasn't quite the hotshot I'd made myself out to be. I can't compete with these people. I'm not from the right family or whatever. My dad has money. But he's a mortgage broker. From Minnesota. Doesn't cut it with this crowd.

"Being with the 'right' sort of guy—that really mattered to Stacy," Simon continued. "She strung me along for a while, meeting me in private after she worked out I wasn't good enough to be seen with in public. She seemed like she was torn. But she treated me totally differently in front of her friends, like she didn't know me. And one night, at a party at your cousins' place, I found her with my brother, Hunter, in one of the bedrooms. In one of the beds."

"God." I hugged my knees to my chest, picturing the scene, how humiliating it must have been.

"She acted like it was no big deal. She said we weren't a couple or anything, so what was the problem? She denied everything about us, to my face. I went completely nuts. Hit my brother. Screamed at Stacy. Caused a real scene. Because I knew what she was doing. She wanted to send me a message…" Simon paused, took a long drag on his cigarette, and exhaled, forming a perfect smoke ring that floated up and then broke apart, dissolving into nothing. "After that, she totally froze me out. Told her friends I was an idiot, a wacko, a confused head case who'd imagined something between us that didn't even exist. And maybe she was right."

He was silent for a while. Then he shook his head and gave a little laugh. "I thought the world had come to an end. I really thought I loved her. I spent the rest of the vacation moping around in my own private Greek tragedy. Pretty stupid, huh?"

"I don't know." I didn't. Love was a mystery to me. I'd once thought I knew what it was, but in the end, I'd only known what it was not.

"Served me right," Simon said with a bitter laugh. "I spent so many days staring over at those girls and their guy friends, watching them hang out in their little clique and wishing I fitted in so that Stacy would go out with me."

He shook his head. I waited for him to continue.

"I put on this big act just to get into her orbit, and, when I did, I felt like I'd arrived. But she wasn't worth the price of admission, that's for sure…Still, it took me months to get over it and see it all for what it really was."

"That's why you don't hang out at the beach," I thought out loud. "Because you don't want to see them. Especially Stacy."

"Nighttime is my time." I could hear a smile in Simon's voice. "No people. No brightness to blind your eyes and burn you."

I thought of the way I felt out on the beach during the day. "I know what you mean."

"Your cousin Corinne is all right," Simon continued. "I mean, she doesn't invite me to her parties or anything this year. She's loyal to her friend, and Stacy acted like I'd humiliated her in front of the world, instead of the other way around."

I remembered the nasty way she had described Simon. *LC. Lower class.* "If Corinne ignores you, then why do you think she's okay?"

"I'm not saying she's not a snob of the highest order in the elite forces," Simon replied. "But underneath, she's not as bad as the rest. Not as bad as her sister. That Beth girl doesn't say a whole lot and has the sweetest smile in the world when she turns it on, but she's hard as nails. I can just tell. Sorry for saying so."

I thought of Beth's permanently wounded smile and soft voice. But she was anything but vulnerable. Beth looked down at the world from the top. That made her untouchable. Maybe hard too.

"But you think Corinne is okay?" I was still confused.

Simon shrugged and shot me a rueful smile in the low light.

"She's as decent as she can be. They're all pretty weak characters. Like I was. Desperate to be a part of the group. Going by the rules of their own game. So yeah, your cousin sticks to the plot. Ignores me if she's in company. But if she's out here alone, and I'm on the beach, we'll talk. Maybe even take a walk."

I guessed Corinne must have showed her soft side to Simon. I'd seen flashes of it too. But I hadn't thought of her as weak. She was a born leader.

Could you be a leader and a follower too? Maybe Corinne did what was expected of her when her friends were around and only got real in private.

"Maybe we're all weak," I suggested, thinking of myself, how I'd pretended that I wanted to get high with my cousins and their friends. I felt a stab of guilt too, as I remembered the half-assed way I'd waved at Simon from Gen's car. *Ish*.

But I was weak because, like Simon, I was the odd person out. The uncool one. I figured if you were popular, a queen bee like Corinne, you didn't have to suffer through the hard stuff of compromising yourself to fit in.

Or maybe I was wrong.

"I'm not such a sucker anymore," Simon stated, buttoning his shirt. "I feel like I know what I *don't* want, which is pretty much like knowing what you do want." He smiled confidently. But his smile was tight. Was he still hurt?

"So why were you at the party then?"

His face fell, and I could tell that he wished I hadn't asked. "I figured I needed to see Stacy. Now that a whole year has gone by. Show her I'm over her. Pretty pathetic, I guess. But I suppose everyone wants that kind of an ending, don't they?"

I tried to picture Simon brokenhearted over Stacy. He was so intense, so I could see him falling in love, even though Snotty Stacy wasn't the girl I'd thought he would fall for. But apparently Simon had been different last year. Wanting different things, trying to impress people by pretending to be someone he wasn't. That didn't seem like the person here now.

"Thing is, I worked myself up to it…but by the time I made it to the party, I decided I didn't want to see her after all. I didn't need to." Simon flicked his lighter on, cupped the flame toward himself, and lit a cigarette. "She wasn't worth it." He exhaled in a long, contented sigh. "That's when you found me outside."

"When I first met you," I began slowly, "you said you'd crashed the party because you'd seen me and wanted to meet me. So you lied." My voice was steelier than I'd meant it to be. But I remembered Simon's flirty talk. I'd caught him out now, and I wanted him to know he couldn't fool with me.

Simon lay back on his hands and stared up at the sky. "I had seen you. I was curious about you. And I tried to disarm you by flattering you. That's what I do when I'm intimidated."

"Intimidated?" I gave a little snort. I couldn't imagine any guy being intimidated by me.

"You looked so pretty in your white dress. Untouchable. And you were so guarded. Being a guy can be nerve-wracking, you know, Mia."

I pulled on my sweatshirt. I'd dried off enough to get dressed, and it felt good to have the warmth of dry cotton on my skin. I weighed options in my mind. Simon had been open with me. How open should I be with him?

Lying back on my towel, I turned to face him. "I've never been in love," I confessed in a quiet voice. My voice surprised me. I hadn't known those words would come out. I'd planned to tell Simon about Jake, about how much he'd hurt me. But right then, the story of Jake didn't matter. All that mattered was what I had learned from being with him. "I thought I was once, but I wasn't," I added.

"Me neither." Simon looked over at me, his face very serious. "I was in love with love, but that's not the same thing. The first time I saw Stacy, everything went slow-mo. It was like the world was about to stop spinning. Do you know what I mean?"

"Yes."

"You can convince yourself of anything when you have that 'love at first sight' epiphany."

"Epiphany," I repeated. "Just because you go to a private school doesn't mean you have to hold it over me."

"You know. The proverbial chorus of angels." Simon laughed quietly. "It's like you have your own internal orchestra. It's when for a moment everything in the whole world makes perfect sense. But love at first sight…it's just an illusion." Simon sighed. "Once I finally got to know Stacy, she was nothing like I'd dreamed she would be at all."

Simon's words made me think of Jake, writing my name on the queen of hearts card and his name on the king of hearts. I'd wanted so much to believe we really were meant for each other. But in the end, it was all just a nice idea, a good card trick. What remained between us wasn't strong enough to last.

I listened to the slight crackle of tobacco burning as Simon inhaled from his cigarette. "Stacy…" he murmured into the darkness. "What did I see in her? I can't even remember."

His question drifted off on the night air, and I found myself wondering more generally about what it means to be drawn to people—what was it about certain people that made certain other people gravitate toward them? I'm not someone who's impressed by shallow things, like money, or how cool or great-looking a person was. And I didn't think Simon was impressed by these things either.

But beautiful, popular people like Stacy and Corinne and Gen have their small, subtle ways of drawing you toward them in spite of yourself. The fact is that they're everything you are not, and their nearness creates some kind of illusion where you feel maybe, by being near, you might become like them—even though the nearer you are to them, the less you feel you have to offer by comparison.

I saw myself then, lying on the beach with the girls topless around me. Close up, they were even more perfect than they seemed from afar, and, sitting near them, I'd felt much less confident than I would have if they hadn't been there at all.

But Simon had had a different experience with the same people. He'd found that as an outsider, the insiders seemed even better, brighter, and more hypnotic than they really were. Once he'd gotten close, he'd seen that Stacy wasn't nearly the golden girl he'd thought she was. He'd thought he was in love with her, but he was only infatuated with an image.

I stared up the stars and thought about light, how bright and powerful it had to be to travel so far, all the way across the galaxies to our eyes…

Or maybe it was our eyes that were powerful. I'd never thought of it that way before.

• • •

It was two in the morning when Simon walked me home. When we reached the walkway to Wind Song, I told Simon the girls were planning another party. "I'm inviting you," I said. "If you want to go."

"Do you want to go?" he asked me.

"No. But if you come, it will be bearable."

"Just bearable? Not the night to end all nights? Not the dream summer date you've been waiting for?"

"Don't push it." I smiled. "But please come. I know it's not your dream date either, but the food will be good."

Simon did something then that surprised me. He leaned over and kissed me suddenly on the cheek. "You're a sweet girl," he said quietly.

There are better compliments than being called "sweet." And even if I wasn't the edgiest, most dramatic person in the world, I could sometimes imagine myself being another, sharper, more powerful version of myself…But I guessed I could handle being called sweet. Sweet was a start.

At least he hadn't called me "nice."

chapter seven

Simon came down to the beach a couple of times in the days that followed, while I was lying out with the girls. The first time I saw him, I waved. I could see him from a distance and knew he was probably scanning first for Stacy. Then, as he came over, I found myself squirming in discomfort.

Nighttime with Simon felt so easy. We were becoming really good friends. I also felt that our friendship had something to do with being out there in the dark while the rest of the world was asleep. Just the two of us talking and laughing about whatever random thing happened to catch our attention. Like how much we loved the Indian place names on Long Island, the rough but also beautiful and sometimes funny way they sounded when you said them out loud. *Speonk. Yaphank. Montauk. Quogue.*

Nighttime was another place. It was almost like we'd broken off from the world for those hours and were looking back at it from the outside—from some other part of time and space where nobody else existed except for us.

In daylight, everything seemed different. Simon looked different. He was handsomer than I'd thought he would be, his hair the color of dark copper, his eyes an intense gray-blue with chips of light in them, like marbles. It was weird to really look at each other, be able to properly see each other. It occurred to me how strange it was that because we'd always met in darkness, I hadn't even known what color Simon's eyes were. And now that I had the chance to look into them, I looked away.

As for me, I knew there was no way I'd look better by day. It shouldn't matter since we were just friends, but as I saw Simon make his way up the beach that first day, I tensed up.

Never mind that we'd talked about how people like Stacy and Corinne were no longer Simon's "type." Never mind that he'd told me he wasn't interested in the same superficial things and people he'd been interested in before. And it didn't matter that I knew deep down I was perfectly okay and had a normal body. I still couldn't be open and confident while I lay on that beach in my navy bikini next to those thin, magazine-worthy, silky-haired specimens. Especially not with Simon around to see the difference.

• • •

"Hey," Simon said casually, wandering up to me, my cousins, and Gen one afternoon on the beach.

"Whoa!" Gen muttered, giving Simon a cool once-over from behind her sunglasses. "Is that a seersucker cap? That's so dorkus, man. You remind me of my Latin tutor."

"Latin?" Simon wrinkled his nose in mock horror.

"Gen aces Latin," Corinne said, giggling. "AP Latin, no less. We don't even have Latin at school. But Gen has her own special tutor."

"Shut up," Gen said.

"Speaking of dorkus!" Simon retorted. "I guess I'd better keep moving! Don't want to be seen sitting with crowdus dorkus maximus!"

Even Gen had to laugh at that one. And with jokes like that, Simon melted the frosty exteriors of Corinne and Gen. They respected you if you were funny, even if you were trying to make fun of them.

But as the conversation floated up around me, I found myself thinking about my night conversations with Simon. *Patchogue. Rockaway. Shinnecock.* And I wished I was there in the darkness, instead of here with all these thin girls around me, and only two little pieces of Lycra between me and the world.

I also felt two-faced sitting with Simon and my cousins when my day and night worlds collided. I'd started to share some of my doubts about Corinne and Co. with Simon. I'd told him that I didn't feel part of the scene. Yet there I was, still trying. Because in a way I didn't feel I had a choice. Was Simon doing that too? Or was he just dealing with the others as a means to hang with me?

You do *have a choice*, my inner voice snapped back at me. No one was holding a gun to my head, and since when had I ever admired people just because they were beautiful?

But my cross-examinations couldn't cure me. I was caught up in my cousins and their universe, unable to push myself away. It probably went all the way back to childhood, when I'd see glamorous Aunt Kathleen with her handsome, blond husband, Uncle Rufus, and their angelic daughters. They always looked so happy, so glowing and perfect.

One time, shortly after they'd bought Wind Song, my aunt had sent us a picture of the family at the Southampton marina. The girls and my aunt and uncle all had matching navy-and-white striped T-shirts on, and they were laughing into the camera as my uncle cracked a bottle of champagne against the hull of their brand-new yacht.

I'd stared hard at the picture when it came inside a letter from my aunt. I wasn't envious of the family as I looked into their beautiful faces. I admired them too much to be envious, and besides, their beauty seemed more than skin deep. It was like a promise of happiness and goodness, a physical proof that perfect worlds existed. That I could hold this in my hands and look at it felt like a privilege. I had a blood connection to the ideal family. And I loved them all unconditionally.

I still loved them all.

Even self-absorbed Corinne and even—*even*—chilly, smug Beth. Even though they could be mean. And yes, they were sweet to Simon's face and seemed to enjoy all of the funny things he said, but they changed their tune the minute we were alone.

"That guy is such a case," Corinne muttered as Simon left us that afternoon. "He's cracked."

"What do you mean?" I swiveled my head to look Corinne in the eye. "Cracked how?"

"He made a real fool of himself last year with Stacy," Beth said. "Told her he loved her even though she had just been having it off with his brother. I mean, talk about no shame! It's sad."

"No shame." I repeated the words quietly, sending daggers with my eyes into Beth's eyes. What about Stacy herself, knowingly cheating on a guy with his brother, even if she didn't like him?

But Beth just reflected my gaze right back at me, her eyes like two shields. Simon was right in his assessment of her. She *was* hard as nails.

Corinne shrugged and lit a cigarette. I remembered what Simon had said about her being nice to him when she wasn't going to be judged for it. "Thing is, Mimi, he pretended to be someone he wasn't. He pretended he was this highflyer society guy when he's just some mortgage broker's son in Iowa."

"Minnesota," I corrected her.

"Which is *totally fine*," Corinne continued. "But he tried to be more than he was."

"And then he made this big, ugly *emo* scene," Beth chimed in. "He freaked out, big time. He was so deluded. Him and Stacy? It's just *sad* to see that…" Her voice got breathier and higher as she filled Gen in on the details of last year's scandal. "…You just end up feeling sorry for a guy like that?" she said, finishing with her trademark question-mark delivery. But there was nothing timid about the words she left dangling in the air.

*Pretended to be someone he wasn't…Tried to be more than he was…*A hot, hard kernel of anger tightened somewhere deep inside my chest. Here these girls had just pretended to like Simon, yet they didn't approve of the fact that he'd pretended just the same as they had. So that they would like him. It was all so stupid. So hypocritical.

And the wild thing was, just a few minutes before, I'd actually thought they *did* like him. And I'd actually thought maybe he liked them too. Maybe even more than he liked me.

Right then, I wasn't sure what was real, or who was. They all seemed like a bunch of poseurs to me. Maybe even Simon. Maybe even me. After all, I was still sitting there with them, wasn't I?

I swallowed. I could feel Gen's eyes on me, curious, waiting to see how I would respond. "I like Simon," I said, looking mostly at Beth, who returned my steely gaze with a skilled smile that managed to look caring even though I knew it was condescending. "I think he's smart, and I think he's funny. And I've invited him to our party."

"That's *completely fine*," Corinne said hastily as I stood up. "We just wanted you to know he's a loose cannon is all."

"Thanks for filling me in," I replied, my voice hard as stone. "But I can take care of myself."

And with that I walked down to the sea—and threw myself into it.

• • •

I signaled back. Twice.

A low full moon beamed a long light across the water as I took my late-night walk. Simon's lighter had flashed three times the moment my feet hit the sand. I felt in my pocket for my flashlight. I paused before clicking on the beam and nixing our hanging out.

That was the first time I'd done it. Sent the message telling Simon I wanted to be alone. For a second, no signal came back. I guessed Simon was startled. But I needed to think things through. Was it possible Simon was all talk about hating pretentiousness and cliques, and that he really only wanted to get back in with the crowd after all?

And if that was the case, should I hold it against him? Couldn't I be his friend and let him try to fit in with the people I myself couldn't help envying, even though I disliked them for the same reasons I admired them?

I wasn't sure of anything. Except that iffiness did not need company. So I kept going. Past Simon's house, past Indigo Beach. I walked way up-shore, way past my usual places, past the dark silhouettes of houses, the sea sweeping back and forth on my right, hissing and seething in time to my tangled, restless thoughts.

Right then, even though I had longed to get away from home and the memory of Jake, all I wanted was to be back in Georgia where I didn't think so hard about fitting in and measuring up. I had people I'd grown up with who didn't need me to prove myself all of the time. But out here I felt like I floated with the tides, unable to choose a direction of my own, and, even if I put up resistance, sooner or later I seemed to give in to more powerful forces.

I had become as much a mystery to myself as the people around me were. A black hole in a galaxy of bright stars.

Eventually I turned around and made for Wind Song. I stopped halfway and sat on the sand, remembering all of the times I'd been out here when I was little. Corinne had always been with me, the two of us joined at the hip. Even then she'd had a special kind of brilliance about her, but I'd never felt like it took anything away from me or asked me to be anything in return...other than my usual self, the quiet observer, happy to be in the shadows if it meant I could be near the light.

But that was then.

As I passed Indigo Beach, I saw the flicker of Simon's light. Three times. A question. He was still out there, wanting to talk. I flashed back. Three times. Silence hadn't helped.

Simon stepped into the beam of my light. "I found something for you," he said. "Treasure." Simon knew I liked to look for anything the sea would give up, but I just shrugged. Right now I couldn't get excited over a piece of sea foam or a shell. "Check it out." Simon held up two objects. "One asthma inhaler. And what seems to be an old tuna can."

"Score." I shot him a weak smile, and for a moment we were silent.

"What's up?"

I shrugged and we sat down on the sand. Even if I could explain all of my misgivings to Simon, I wasn't sure he'd be receptive to them. I didn't want to tell him I had my doubts about why he wanted to be friends with me. Or that I had doubts about who "me" even was anymore.

"Look. Aren't they romantic?" Simon said, pointing out two fireflies dancing together, their glowing lights making spirals in the dark.

"Not necessarily," I replied. "There are firefly species where the females trick the males into thinking they want to mate, but they eat them instead."

"Oh, yeah, I think I know a few of them." Simon laughed but I didn't join in. My mood was too black to even smile in the dark.

"You know a lot of things, Daisy," Simon commented.

"Yeah, well. Sometimes the more you know, the less you understand…" I trailed off. We watched the fireflies until they disappeared into the night.

I kept thinking Simon would give up and leave, but he was unfazed by my moodiness. I could feel his eyes on me.

"What are you thinking?" he probed after a long silence.

"I was just thinking how I hate it when people ask me what I'm thinking," I answered drily.

"Are you looking forward to the party?" Simon asked.

I sighed. "No, I'm not." I couldn't lie. Not with him watching me so closely.

"Me either."

"You're worried about seeing Stacy."

"It's not that."

"You still think about her a lot." There was a hardness to my voice. I didn't think Stacy deserved to be thought about. Especially by Simon. But I knew what it meant to care against your will.

"I don't care about Stacy anymore," Simon said softly. He sighed and rolled onto his elbow. "I just hate pretending like I like them, you know? Like everything is cool."

I waited for him to elaborate. He'd certainly acted like he liked talking to everyone on the beach. If he hated pretending, then why was he so good at it?

"I guess I'm a natural at acting," Simon admitted, as if he could hear my question. "I've always been good at making people laugh and making it seem like I feel great even if I don't."

"You're lucky," I replied sullenly. "That's a skill I don't have." As my mother kept reminding me. Social graces, she called it. The art of not wearing your heart on your sleeve. Apparently I'd never had a lot of talent for it, though I was certainly trying hard lately.

Simon laughed. "Lucky! It's not about luck, Mia. It's about what matters. You're not like the rest of us. We all put on a performance, even your cousin Corinne. We act like we're having fun when we're not. We act like we're comfortable with people when we'd rather be alone. You're different. You know yourself."

"Know myself!" I laughed and shook my head, amazed Simon could see me that way. "I don't know myself any better than anyone else does. I act the same as everyone. Pretending things."

"But you're not very good at it, as you just pointed out." Simon grabbed my wrist and forced me to roll over and face him. "You did the two-flash tonight and stalked past me into the night. That's not pretending."

"Yeah, well." I smiled. "Can we talk about something else? This is hurting my head."

"How about we not talk at all? How about we take a swim?"

I looked out at the ocean. It was a lovely night. Moonlight reflected off the dark water, like glitter on a sheet of black velvet.

Hard to resist.

· · ·

In the water, I relaxed the most I had all day. It was unusually warm, almost soupy, and the tide was medium, so I had to concentrate on staying in the shallows and trying unsuccessfully to stop Simon from going too deep. Every one of our three swims so far, he'd always wanted to go farther than he should.

I smiled as Simon ducked under a wave and then swam furiously out into the blackness, splashing loudly. I lay in the shallows grabbing fistfuls of sand, the watery moon tracing a shimmery trail from the horizon to the beach.

Several silent minutes passed. I started to worry. "Simon!" I yelled. "Come back here."

Nothing.

I felt two strong hands clenching my ankles, pulling me forward and under.

I gave him the finger as I came up to the surface, half-choking on a mouthful of seawater, half-laughing. Simon swam up behind me, grabbed my shoulders, and pulled me toward him.

"Hey, we're friends, aren't we?" he said into my ear, his arm heavy around my waist. "So why don't we go skinny dipping?"

I untwisted myself from his grip. I could see Simon grinning at me in the bright moonlight, and I shook my head. "No."

"Why not? It's night. It's not like we can see each other."

"It's a full moon, Simon."

"But have you ever tried it?"

"It's not my thing," I shot back weakly. "Don't you know me by now? I Just Say No."

"Don't knock what you don't know!" Simon retorted, grabbing both my arms, playfully. "C'mon! It will melt all your troubles away!"

"Maybe so," I replied. "But I'm not exactly the skinny dipping type."

I pulled away from Simon's grasp and tipped my head back, smoothing my hair in the water.

"Seriously, Mia, I'm not trying anything. But being naked in the water—I did it all the time out here until you came and spoiled the fun."

"Well, don't mind me then. Go for it."

Simon chuckled and slid down into the water. "If you take it off, I won't look. Promise."

"Forget it."

Simon held up his swimming shorts, dripping with water. He squeezed them out, aimed, and tossed them onto the beach where they landed somewhere on the sand with a plop. "No turning back now," he said. "See ya." I caught a flash of his pale back and then he was in a wave.

I could hear Simon whooping as I walked back to my towel. The noise made me smile. He was putting on a big show for my benefit. How great could a naked swim really be? Although I had to admit, the idea was appealing. No sand trapped in Lycra. Nothing between you and the water…But I wasn't like him. Or the girls. And I especially couldn't let loose and flop around out there with a guy in the water.

So I didn't swim with Simon, and I didn't look at him either when he bounded up to the towel, butt-naked. "Here," I said, keeping my eyes averted as I held up his towel.

"You missed something."

"Yeah, well, I'm trying not to look, so cover it up."

"Chicken."

• • •

After that, Simon swam naked every night. By the third skinny-dipping session, I secretly peeled off my bikini top while I was in the water. It was safe. Simon was splashing somewhere ahead of me. He couldn't see.

It was an amazing feeling. I felt free. Or at least half of me did. And right then that seemed to fit with the person I felt I was on Long Island: half-cautious, half-spontaneous, surprising myself with my random behavior, my sudden moves away from who I thought I was.

"So how was it, your half skinny dip?" Simon asked as I was drying off.

"You were watching me?" I blushed, horrified.

"Just a hunch," he replied. "Feels good though, right?"

I hit him with the towel.

chapter eight

"Anybody want to go sailing?" Uncle Rufus asked cheerfully, striding into the living room on the day of the party. "It's clearing up."

It was drizzling and the mood of the house matched the gray weather. Corinne pouted on the couch, annoyed because Aram had said he would come over, but he still hadn't showed by noon. So she'd tried to call Alessandro, her supposed boyfriend in Italy, but he'd told her he would call right back. And he hadn't.

"You know I hate sailing, Daddy," she snapped, in answer to Uncle Rufus's invitation. "It's tedious." Her eyes were flat and bored. "All that water and wind and nothing. All that nothing everywhere."

"It's called fresh air, sweetheart. You should get some. It might help," my uncle teased. Corinne rolled her eyes and stalked up to her room.

"Gen? Mia? Feel like hitting the sea?" Uncle Rufus pressed. "It could get a little rough, but it will be fun. Mia, your dad's coming."

"Pass," Gen replied, paging through *Rolling Stone* from her perch on a daybed. "Yachting is so not my vibe."

"I'll go," I said, and went upstairs to change.

On my way to the bathroom, I passed Corinne's bedroom, and I heard her hissing at her mom through the half-closed door. My aunt said something about Corinne "cleaning up her act." Maybe Aunt Kathleen was just referring to her daughter's sulky attitude. Or maybe my aunt had finally caught on to the fact that Corinne and Gen had been raiding the liquor cabinet after hours. I couldn't tell.

I wanted to eavesdrop, but I was nervous they'd catch me again— so I only caught what had floated past: that comment of Aunt Kathleen's followed by Corinne calling her mother a hypocrite.

Again I wondered what was really going on between them, and I was reminded of the last time I'd overheard them arguing. *You're not exactly Mother Teresa, and we both know what I mean.* Had Corinne been referring to Aunt Kathleen drinking maybe more than usual?

So what? I wondered why Corinne was so mean. After all, her mom was an adult, and she was also the nicest mother anyone could ever ask for. She constantly praised her daughters and told everyone how proud she was of them. My mom never said things like that—not about me anyway.

But I guessed Corinne just didn't know what she had, so she couldn't appreciate it. Which seemed to be true for a lot of things in Corinne's life. Her favorite bad-mood word, I'd noticed lately, was "tedious." Everything was tedious. I guessed she was so spoiled she didn't know what else to call anything. And I'd had enough. Was it really so "tedious" at the top of the social order? How bad could it be?

"…Mom, you're the actress around here, not me!" I heard Corinne snap as I came out of the bathroom and walked down the

passage to my room. I wasn't sure what that meant either, but...
whatever. If Corinne wanted to be awful to her mother, then that
was Aunt Kathleen's problem and had nothing to do with me. Still,
I was glad to be bailing out of that house. I'd never thought Wind
Song was the last place I'd ever want to be, but suddenly I couldn't
wait to get far away from it.

• • •

"William! Meet my brother-in-law, Chris, and my niece Mia.
Maxine's family."

My uncle docked his yacht at the marina belonging to the
Southampton Club on Shinnecock Bay. The clubhouse is a beautiful
stone mansion with rolling links—one of the most exclusive golf
courses in the world. As we walked across green, manicured lawns
and onto the gleaming decks of jetties at the water's edge, people
like this William padded around, looking privileged and well-kept.
They all looked the same: tanned, slightly weather-beaten, and in
casual, understated clothes, the kind of clothes that didn't draw
attention to themselves but cost the earth just the same.

And as my uncle introduced me to his upper-crust friend, I
remembered Simon laughingly telling me how his father had tried
to "buy" his way onto the club golf course the previous summer.
Like they would ever accept him! Simon had made fun of his father's
aspirations to high society and told me how his father wore all
of these "conservative, Waspy English country-gentleman" clothes
over the summer, because he thought that was the correct uniform
for the Hamptons. *But he never managed to get it right...he stuck out
like a sore thumb anyway...*

For a moment I felt sorry for Simon's father. He didn't sound like the greatest guy, but his wanting to fit in was something I could relate to. And though Simon dissed his dad every chance he got, I knew that somewhere underneath, he had some sympathy for his dad too, because Simon knew the truth firsthand: in the end, it didn't matter if you had good taste or no taste at all; there were some clubs you couldn't join unless you were born into them.

Maybe that was why this William person seemed strangely unfriendly to all of us. He'd mumbled only the curtest greeting and had been frosty even to Uncle Rufus. Was it because my uncle had brought his poor relations to the club? Was it my imagination, or were other people staring at my uncle, at us? Had we done something terrible?

Like worn the wrong brand of boat shoe?

But as the yacht drifted away from the marina, everything receded like the view of the clubhouse. Insider, outsider, it didn't matter what you were out on the water, and I was more than glad as my uncle shouted directions. I wasn't a pro sailor, but my uncle taught me something new every time. I was beginning to feel like I knew the ropes—some of them at least.

And with the wide gray skies and the metallic water all around me, I felt myself disappearing into the immediate present, into the wind and the bay, the flapping of the sails, and the voices of my uncle and my father. It was exactly what I needed. And I knew I had to make the most of it, breathe deeply, and unwind like the sails unfurling from the masthead. Because soon enough I'd be back at Wind Song and facing something that would require much more complex navigational skills than I had—another party.

• • •

By early evening, Corinne was in a better mood and the weather had lifted too. Once again, the parents were going out, to a barbecue "at Shep's new house in Amagansett," Mom gushed, her eyes shiny and excited. A tremor of alarm rippled through me. Mom looked away from my searching gaze. Whatever Shep meant to her, she wasn't about to tell me.

Once again, we had a huge catered spread for the party, laid out by my uncle and aunt. Yet another reason why Corinne ought to appreciate them better instead of acting like a brat. And maybe she thought so too, because she gave her dad a really big hug before the parents took off, and I noticed she clung to him longer than I'd seen since she was little. Mostly Corinne seemed to ignore her father these days. Beth did too. They obviously thought their parents were a drag, same as any other kid. Which would have been understandable if they were any other parents.

But I tried to put it all out of my mind as I got dressed. This time, I dressed like I would for any other barbecue. A peasant blouse, jeans, a baggy cardigan, and my hair in two braids. The only glam effort I made was a shimmery copper lipstick.

"Very fresh, very Peace Corps," Gen chirped as I wandered into the living room.

"Huh?"

Gen surveyed me from the couch. "You look very, I don't know… *real.* I can't pull off that look. Whenever I put a cardigan on, I feel like I'm about to go and volunteer, or apply to med school or something." She looked me up and down, and nodded again, serious for a moment. "I guess that just isn't my look."

"Not to worry, Buffy," I shot back, taking in Gen's long black boots and the scrap of leather masquerading as a dress. "You help out in other ways."

Gen laughed—the good-natured, genuine kind. "Point to you, girl. One point."

Gen never seemed to appreciate anyone unless they mocked her or at least tried to. She just didn't seem interested in a person who wasn't sparring with her. Which certainly made for some sparks in conversation. I mean, no one could call her "tedious." But no one could call her nice either, and I guessed that was the way she wanted it. I'd seen that in her since the moment I met her: being nice just wasn't something she cared about. Maybe she thought it was out of fashion.

Maybe it *was* out of fashion.

"Let's murder some drinks, shall we?" Corinne declared, traipsing down the stairs. "Thank God, the Geritols have gone out. They are *so* tedious."

"Absolut!" Gen agreed, nodding as she whipped out a brand-new bottle of vodka she'd hidden in her Diesel backpack.

They hit the vodka, and I drifted out onto the deck and chatted with the guy at the grill. He worked for the catering company. I felt a little embarrassed around him at first, since he was cooking our food and would be serving a bunch of teenagers all night. But he seemed not to care about the setup. It turned out he was studying marine biology, and this was just a summer job to pay for school. So I asked him a whole lot of questions, and, by the time I checked back inside, the party had filled out.

Aram was there with some of his friends, all of them tanned and sleepy-eyed, giving off waves of superior breeding.

Where was Simon? I scanned the room anxiously as sun-kissed girls in spendy clothes shrieked and hugged each other as though they hadn't seen each other in years. If Simon was there, maybe I'd even have some fun. But he hadn't showed.

I could feel myself retreating back into my shell even though I really wanted to be open and friendly, because it was a party after all...and parties were sink or swim, smile and be chatty, or stay silent and be lonely in the corner. *Make an effort. Nothing comes from nothing.* I could hear my mother's voice inside my head. In situations like this, though it bugged the hell out of me, she had a point.

"Mia, did you meet Guy?" Corinne slipped her slender arm into mine and led me across the floor. "He's at school in Georgia. And he's crazy hot for a preppy," she whispered in my ear.

I smiled as pleasantly and confidently as I could as we approached the guy called Guy, but once we got to him, all I wanted was to be miles away from this party. Or maybe half a mile away. Like at Indigo Beach, taking a swim.

Guy was gorgeous. He looked like he'd been clipped straight out of a J.Crew catalog—perfectly tousled brown hair, a pretty-boy nose, and a jaw so well-defined it was almost scary. "This is Mia. From Georgia," Corinne announced.

"Hello, Mia from Georgia." Guy leaned against the wall. He caught Corinne's hand and whispered something in her ear, but she snaked out of his grip, fluttered her fingers at us, and then disappeared off to dance.

"You're at school in Georgia?" I asked Guy. He looked past me, still in the direction of Corinne, as if he hoped—as I did—that she would come back and rescue him.

"Emory," he replied.

"Oh, yeah. Atlanta."

"Yeah," he repeated, looking back at me and shooting me a brief, bored smile. "Atlanta."

"Do you like it?" I asked, catching sight of Stacy out of the corner of my eye. She glided past, thinner than a Pop Tart and shimmering in a green dress that stuck to her skin like cling wrap and would have made me look like Eva's favorite floatie. I wondered if Simon would have a hard time seeing her. If he would fall in love with her again.

"I hate it," Guy said, and I turned to look at him. I'd almost forgotten he was there. His voice reminded me of Gen's. It had that same kind of knowing, glassy edge. "I thought I might like the South. Change of pace and yadda yadda." Guy took a swig of his drink, his eyes flicking up and down my frame and then past me. "But it's so slow. It's…I don't know…" he drifted off and shrugged, too disenchanted to finish his own sentence.

"—Tedious?" I offered.

"Exactly."

His eyes sparkled briefly then, as if I'd read his mind. "Want a drink?" he asked. "I brought Scotch."

I considered the offer. The only way to tolerate talking to someone like Guy would be if you got slightly buzzed. "Okay. A little," I muttered, my eyes darting through the crowds, half-hoping for Simon but no longer believing he'd show.

Guy got chatty after pouring me a drink. Even though I didn't feel like talking to him and I hated the taste of Scotch, I didn't know what else to do. Corinne was dancing with Aram; Gen was on somebody's lap; and Beth was giggling and doing shots with a bunch of girls. I was even starting to wish Eva was there, so I could at least pretend to be looking after her, but my parents had taken her out with them this time since Shep had a niece Eva's age staying with him.

"She's amazing, isn't she?" Guy was leering at Corinne, and I followed his eyes, watching as she twirled on the dance floor and pulled flashy moves for Aram, making him pick her up, and then arching her back and pulling ballerina poses. She did it ironically, but it was incredible nonetheless. And she knew it as much as Guy and I did. All eyes were on her.

"She is," I agreed, and in that moment I wondered what it might feel like to be Corinne, twirling around with Aram, everyone watching, everyone either wanting to be her or wanting to be with her.

I felt a tap on my shoulder. Then a gruff voice spoke into my ear. "Daisy."

"Hey!" I grinned and gave Simon a hug. I didn't think I'd ever been so happy to see someone in my life. "You came."

"I did. And you look ravishing, in spite of the fact that you're swimming underneath that sweater."

"I would have worn my skin-tight tube top," I replied sarcastically. "But it's so tiny, I couldn't find it." We smiled stupidly at each other. I complimented Simon on his jacket, a tweed blazer with leather elbow patches. And then we remembered Guy.

Simon extended a hand to Guy. "Simon Ross."

"Simon Ross." Guy cocked his head, a slow smile spreading across his face. "I remember you. You're the kid who went ape-shit last year. Laid into your brother."

I stiffened, but Simon was unfazed. "Guilty as charged," he said cheerfully.

"Hey!" Guy waved over some chiseled randoms who were hovering nearby. "Check it out. Simon from the big rumble here last year. Remember?" Guy turned back to Simon.

"Your brother really clocked you, man," one of the randoms chimed in.

"Ouch!" Guy said. "He here tonight?"

"Nope. He didn't come up this summer," Simon replied lightly.

"Probably good. That way he won't, like, take *this* girl from you... right, bro?" Guy said with a smile.

Creep, I thought, staring coldly at Guy, dreaming I could staple him to the wall just by staring. But Simon didn't let Guy rattle him. "That's right...bro," he confirmed, taking my arm. "And everyone's happy."

"Everyone's happy," Guy repeated, smiling his annoying smile at his two buddies, sharing some kind of in-joke. "Everyone's happy. Yeah, that's a good one. That's wild. I'll drink to that!" he raised his bottle of whiskey to Simon and took a long slug.

By this time a couple of nosy girls were listening in, and one of them was giving me a thorough once-over with penetrating navy eyes, twirling the cocktail glass in her hand. She was a bony, upper-crust type with dead-straight chestnut hair in an angled bob and a strand of pearls so tight across her neck it looked like she might choke. Angela? Alexis? Corinne had introduced me to her. She was from some famous old American family.

"So you're back here for the summer?" she asked Simon, trying halfheartedly to conceal her smirk.

Simon didn't miss a beat. "That's right," he said loudly. "My family is renting Dragon's Lair."

"*Dragon's Lair!*" The smirky girl narrowed her eyes in shock, a hand instinctively moving to her throat as if the idea was enough to cut off all air going through to her windpipe. I struggled to keep a straight face. To this girl, a summer renter was bad enough. But someone actually inhabiting the kitschiest real estate on the island? She looked like she might gag from the thought alone.

"It's such a swell summer pad," Simon deadpanned. "Matter of fact, I'm having a party next Saturday. You're all invited. We have this awesome jungle room. Bring your swimsuits—and snorkels too! There's a whole underground cave system and indoor barrier reef. It's really cool."

"Jungle. Room." The string-of-pearl girl's friend said the words as if she'd swallowed them with wedges of lemon. "Snorkels."

"Later." Simon shot them all his biggest, brightest smile, grabbed my arm, and sauntered away from the scene.

"Watch that fist!" Guy called out, laughing as we walked outside.

"I can't believe that jerk," I began, but Simon laughed.

"Forget him. Do you want to eat? Or we could go back in and dance."

"Maybe we'd better just keep drinking," I muttered darkly. "I'll go get something from someone."

"Just water for me," Simon said. "Or soda."

"You don't want a beer or anything? A *cosmopolitan?*" I rolled my eyes, making fun of the upscale-ness of the party. Like at the last party, there were lots of fancy concoctions circulating at this event.

"Nope. Not a touch of alcohol shall cross these lips."

"You don't drink?" I was surprised. I could feel the Scotch burning in my throat. I'd just given in out of weakness—because I didn't know how else to enjoy the party. But Simon…? He was so much more excessive than me, so much more gung-ho, whether about swimming naked or getting into flaming fistfights over girls. I figured he'd at least be putting a few beers back by now, if not some hard alcohol.

"It's not out of choice. Believe me. But I can't," Simon said as we headed toward the deck.

Suddenly I caught sight of someone on the deck, leaning against the balcony. Someone in a green dress. "Courage," I whispered to Simon as Stacy caught sight of him. I squeezed his arm and then let it go.

"Hi." Stacy looked from Simon to me. If she was surprised to see Simon, she didn't show it. She had a broad grin plastered onto her small-featured face and her eyes sparkled, competing with her glinting strawberry-blond hair in the lamplight.

"Hi, Stacy," Simon replied, not exactly friendly but not rude either.

"It's been a long time," Stacy said softly, walking over and planting a kiss on Simon's cheek. "What've you been up to?" she added, her hand lingering on Simon's shoulder.

Simon stepped back so that her hand fell. "Growing my hair," he replied coolly.

• • •

I'd wanted to stay out there. To give Simon moral support. But I knew he needed his privacy too, so I left them out there on the deck and went back inside. I decided against drinking anything else. If Simon didn't want to drink, then neither did I.

After reapplying my lipstick in the bathroom, I made my way back to the deck. Stacy and Simon were nowhere to be seen. Maybe they'd gone down to the beach? Taken a walk to talk things over? The idea burned me. I hated thinking of Simon talking to that witch after she'd caused him so much trouble and heartache. But what did they say…? Love is blind. Maybe Simon was still smitten with Stacy. Maybe one sweet word and that was all he needed to go right back in.

My throat constricted, and I felt like an idiot standing there. But I didn't want to go back inside either. There was no one in there for me.

"Mia!" Beth slid through the glass doors and threw her arms around me like she hadn't seen me in weeks. She was teetering in her high heels, her eyes red and glittery. Obviously she was trashed. Why else would she try to hug me? "Whacha doing all by your lonesome here?"

"I'm looking for Simon. I went in to get us a drink but—"

Beth interrupted me, shaking her head back and forth, her eyes widening. "Naughty naughty," she said, wagging a finger and straightening up for balance. "Simon shouldn't drink."

"What?"

Beth leaned forward like she was telling a deep, dark secret. "I heard he's like, crazy. He's on *medication*. I think it's to stop him from getting *violent*."

"That's bullshit," I retorted, but Beth bobbed her head vehemently. "Who made that up? Stacy?" I added, folding my arms.

Beth seemed not to have heard me and tottered off, disappearing around the side of the deck.

I made my way down to the beach. Beth's words were stupid, but Simon wasn't there to contradict them. He'd disappeared... and what *was* all of that about him not drinking? Was it possible he hadn't told me the full story? Was it possible he was...*crazy*. Beth's word whispered itself into my ear.

Stop! I shook my head, disgusted to be giving into gossip. I didn't believe it. Not about Simon. But I didn't *not believe* powerfully enough either. What if Simon was just a loose cannon after all, shooting his mouth off around me, acting like we were friends and he didn't care about Stacy, but all the time he was obsessed with her...and maybe with her right this very second?

That's when I saw dark shapes down by the dunes. Stacy and Simon? I definitely didn't want to interrupt them if it was them. But I couldn't help myself from checking. I had to know if it was them. When I got close, I heard Gen's loud laugh. A sigh of relief whooshed out of me. Maybe I'd just stop and ask her if she'd seen Simon.

But as I rounded the back of the dune, I saw something I wished I hadn't. The moon was waning, and it was hard to see in the low light. But I could see enough. Corinne, lying on her back, was making out with Gen, while Guy and Aram looked on, laughing and passing a joint back and forth between them.

"Well, hello," someone piped up from the darkness. "Who's this?"

"Hey!" I said. My voice sounded foreign, as if I were underwater. I couldn't keep my eyes off Corinne. She lay limp as a rag doll, her hands to either side of her, her ribs glowing white as Guy fired up his lighter and sucked on the joint.

"Mimi." Corinne's voice was slurred. Her tiny top was lying on the sand next to her.

Gen rolled off her and shot me a sly look, then grabbed the joint from Guy. "Don't freak, Mia," she said, cocking me a half-smile as I stood there, still as a tree. "We're not lesbians or anything. We're playing Truth or Dare. And personally, I hate the truth, don't you?"

"Mi-mi," Corinne repeated, struggling to lift her head and failing. "You...sweet silly," She broke off, her eyes closing. I could hear her breathing shallowly, and then she moaned and turned over, and I saw what looked like tears streaking the side of her face.

"What's wrong with her?" I demanded, looking from Gen to the guys. "What is she on?"

"What *is* this? Partnership for a Drug-Free America?" Aram said flatly.

"Wrong summer camp, kiddo," Guy snickered. "We don't do s'mores here."

"She's completely out of it," I snapped, shooting Aram a hateful glare as he slid a hand along Corinne's half-naked body. "Maybe you should leave her alone."

"Maybe you should," Guy retorted. Lying there on the dune, he looked the picture of the arrogant, smug jerk that he was. Earlier in the evening, I'd tried to talk to him as he handed me that whiskey. Earlier I might have ignored the open condescension on his face, but this time I stared him down.

"Mia, go back inside," Gen said, in a low, almost-sober voice. "Don't worry. I'll get her back before your parents get in."

My shoulders goose-bumped, but not from the wind. "Is that what you think I'm worried about?" I asked, disbelieving. "Getting in trouble?"

"Isn't it?" Gen challenged coldly.

I wanted to say something back, but I knew it would make no difference. Instead I focused on how to get Corinne out of there. I'd need help, which wouldn't come from these people. But I couldn't physically remove her on my own.

As I considered my options, Corinne woke up, fumbled for her top, and smiled at me like I was an old nanny from some ancient movie, arriving only to spoil the fun. "Mia, is that you?" she asked, blinking wide and running a hand across her mouth.

"Let's go back inside," I said, my heart beating wildly against my rib cage. Corinne's eyes looked so strange, shiny and flat at the same time. Whatever it was she'd taken, she was totally checked out. But after two minutes of failing to convince Corinne to come with me, I left. The scene was just too sketchy for my liking and I was powerless to get my cousin away from it.

I knew I shouldn't be shocked that Corinne was doing drugs other than pot, but I was. And I was disgusted to see her lying there, hardly even knowing who was touching her and not even caring. The blank look in her eyes scared me. But I couldn't help her. She wouldn't let me.

Back at the house, I caught my breath on the deck, my mind spinning. I couldn't forget the way they'd all looked at me as I walked away: half-entertained by me, half-annoyed, like I was a random idiot who had gate-crashed their exclusive gathering.

Barefoot, I walked inside, frantically scanning the room for Simon. The party seemed to have gotten suddenly so much bigger, and I couldn't see him anywhere. I just saw faces, laughing faces, people having a great time all around me. I wanted desperately to talk to Simon. Vaguely, in the back of my mind somewhere, I was aware of a dull pain in my foot. I looked down and saw I'd cut my heel. I must have stepped on broken glass. I was tracking blood across the tiles.

The door opened. I looked up. The parents were home.

• • •

The rest of the evening was a disorienting swirl. My aunt and uncle and my parents were furious. While I'd been looking for Simon and found Corinne instead, the party had gotten way out of hand with empty bottles crowding every surface in the room and people making out on couches. The music was pounding away, and someone had broken one of my aunt's sculptures.

Everyone fled the house in what seemed like seconds. Music was switched off and lights snapped on. It was interrogation time, and only Beth and I were there to answer the questions, though when it came to "Where's Corinne?" I lied and said I didn't know.

My parents kept hammering in how disappointed they were in me. Beth shook her head primly every time her parents said anything, her arms folded, her lip quivering. She gave only the thinnest of answers. She acted sober, brilliantly so, even though I knew she'd gotten plastered. And when her father shouted, she raised her hands to her ears. "Don't shout," she whimpered. "I can't bear it."

Right then, I felt like smacking Beth, and whatever feeling I'd ever had for her, what little bit of remaining fondness for my oldest cousin disappeared. She was so untouchable, her long legs tucked neatly underneath her, a martyrish tilt to her chin. Her father was even struggling to talk quietly. I blinked, amazed that I'd endured her presence for so long without telling her where to get off. She may have put question marks at the ends of her statements, but she'd worked out the answers long before. It was all just a part of her strategy.

By the time Gen and Corinne stumbled in, minus the guys, my aunt and uncle were fuming. Their attempts to get anything from Beth had been blocked by her shrugging, her careful sniffling, her trips to the bathroom to rinse her hands. But they were less afraid of Corinne. Uncle Rufus's face darkened when he caught sight of Corinne's spacey, bloodshot eyes as she edged into the living room, trying not to weave all over the place.

"Where have you been?" Uncle Rufus roared, shaking her by the shoulders. He smelled of alcohol himself. It was weird. I knew the grownups had all indulged in the cocktails through the summer, but I hadn't seen Uncle Rufus out of control before. He was breathing heavily now, and his eyes were bleary and unfocused.

"Look at her eyes. She's on drugs!" my aunt yelled.

"Take your hands off me!" Corinne spat, pulling away from her father's rough grasp.

After that, my parents and I retreated into the background. They were angry with me, but their concern for Corinne eclipsed everything. She looked really bad, her makeup streaked, her hair matted.

"What'd you tell them?" Corinne accused me in a harsh, slurring whisper while her parents argued with each other over what was going on.

"I didn't say anything," I shot back angrily. Why was Corinne turning on me? For one thing, it was obvious she was in a bad way—nobody needed me to tell them that. And for another, I hadn't said anything anyway. I didn't even *know* what she was on, so how could I report it?

"You're all grounded," my aunt declared. "Until further notice. No more parties here—or anywhere else, for that matter."

Beth slunk up to bed, complaining of a migraine, her head held high, high above the scene below.

"Go, Mom!" Corinne sneered. "Parent of the Year." Anger seemed to have sobered her up. But before her mother could reply, Corinne turned on her heel and disappeared up the stairs, closely followed by Gen, who, for first time since I'd met her, looked slightly less than cocky. She'd said nothing during the fight, keeping well off to the side, out of the ring.

Finally my parents let me go to bed, but I was too wide awake to even contemplate sleep. Images from that night—of Corinne and Gen, of Guy...of Stacy and Simon—jostled for space in my mind. It was like someone had emptied a five-thousand-piece jigsaw puzzle into my head and I couldn't sleep until I'd pieced it all together.

I climbed out onto the roof. I was grounded, but I wasn't worried about getting caught. It was late, and, even if anyone was awake, my room was far from the adults' wing. No one would notice me.

As I stared out onto the beach, I caught the movement of a tiny red light, a spidery red line moving back and forth in the darkness. Simon was obviously out there, smoking a cigarette. Making as little noise as possible, I slipped down the trellis and down onto the beach. I walked slowly as I approached Simon, relieved to see he was alone but still mad that he'd ditched me.

"Hi," I said coolly. Maybe I should have stayed on the roof. Or walked the other way. After all, what could he say to me that would make a difference? *Sorry* was an empty word.

"Hello."

I raised an eyebrow. *Sorry* was better than *hello*. Why was he sounding so distant? Where was the instant apology, the backtracking, the explanations about old habits dying hard and love being a hard thing to shake?

I curled my toes in the sand and folded my arms. "Where did you disappear to?" I challenged.

"Me?" Simon sounded surprised. "You were the one who disappeared."

"Yeah, right." My head began to hurt, and suddenly the whole evening rushed back at me in a sharp, shooting pain. If Simon had been out there on the deck, instead of off somewhere having a heart-to-heart or a mouth-to-mouth with Stacy, then I'd never have discovered Corinne. And maybe if I hadn't seen her, I could have avoided the hateful stare she'd thrown my way right before bed.

Tears stung my eyes. Again, I would have given my right arm to blink and be back home in Georgia. Away from all of these people who didn't know how to be. Away from even Simon—especially Simon. I'd invited him to the party. And he'd ditched me the first chance he got.

"I went back in there about a minute after you. I couldn't find you anywhere. I looked and then I came back out," Simon explained calmly. "And then I saw you down in the dunes with that Guy guy and Corinne and her boyfriend. Didn't really feel like joining you. So I figured maybe I'd just take off."

"Oh." I bit my lip as I retraced my steps mentally. Simon and I had obviously missed each other. I'd gone to the bathroom to reapply my lipstick while Simon greeted Stacy. I'd had to go upstairs, since both downstairs bathrooms were occupied. That must have been when he was looking for me. And then he'd seen me down in the dunes...

I shut my eyes. The whole night had been such a disaster, and I began to feel teary again. Then before I even knew what I was saying, I was telling Simon everything, how I'd found Corinne, how our parents had freaked, and how Corinne blamed me for it. "She hates me," I said, feeling a tear spill onto my cheek. "I don't know why I care, but I do."

Simon put an arm around me as we walked down the beach. The wind was picking up, and I wondered whether more bad weather was blowing in. "I want to go home," I told him, leaning into the solid feeling of his arm, which right now seemed like the only solid thing I had. "I'm out of my depth here."

"You're a good swimmer," Simon replied teasingly, but I shook my head.

"I felt so awful tonight. Especially when I figured you and Stacy had gone off—" I stopped. That was saying too much. Now I was embarrassed.

Simon stopped walking. "Stacy?" He laughed. "I spoke to her for one minute, max. Although I did manage to slip in that my family would be returning next year to rent Dragon's Lair." Simon laughed. "That was fun. The look on her face."

"One minute," I repeated.

"I didn't come to the party to be with her, Mia."

"That's okay if you did," I babbled. "I mean, I know you were crazy about her, and it's none of my—"

Suddenly Simon's lips were on mine, a soft kiss. Out of the blue. Out of the darkness.

I broke the kiss, pulling away. I caught my breath, looking away, down to the water. We were only a few yards from Indigo Beach. Simon's hand grazed my hand. I didn't know what to do. I had so much going on in my mind, not least, why was Simon kissing me? We were just friends. It was what we both wanted. Wasn't it? I gently moved my hand away from his.

"I told you I wasn't in love with Stacy. I never was," Simon said quietly. "She's—"

And right then, I did something that took *my* breath away. I kissed him. I leaned in toward him and tipped my face up, pressing my mouth to his.

And as Simon's arms snaked around my waist, I felt the pressure of everything shrink and then disappear. All of the harsh words I'd heard that night, all of the misunderstandings and confusions and embarrassment…everything spun away from me, and all I knew were Simon's hands on my back and his mouth against my own, soft and also not soft, sending little firefly sparks scatting up and down my spine.

Maybe it was the beach setting. Some leftover craziness from the recent full moon added to the emotional roller coaster of the evening. Something irregular had to be responsible, because we weren't behaving logically. It didn't make sense, the way we just fit together. We'd started as friends…or maybe that's what made the most sense of all…?

We moved apart. I didn't think I could trust myself to stand. I could never have guessed the kind of force we would have together. "What are we doing?" I whispered to Simon as he took my hand and pressed it against his chest.

"Swimming," he said to me.

"I don't have my suit." I turned red as I caught the wicked glint in his eye.

"You know my answer to that problem," Simon replied.

I wanted to go swimming with him, to just let go and not care and take all of my clothes off. In a funny way it seemed the right thing to do. It seemed to fit with all of the insanity and hysteria that had colored the evening.

But I wasn't ready. My head may have been spinning, but I hadn't forgotten everything of myself. "I think I should go," I said quietly, as Simon unbuttoned his shirt and I caught sight of his pale, lightly muscled chest.

Simon paused. "Don't," he said, his voice soft in the wind as he caught my hand.

I could make out the sharp edge of his jaw and the broad, straight outline of his shoulders. I wanted to reach out and trace the line of his collarbone. I wanted to stay there with him. I wanted…I was afraid of what I wanted.

"Why can't you drink alcohol?" I blurted out suddenly. I squeezed my eyes shut. The words had seemed to come from someone else. I hadn't thought them through. They'd just tumbled from my mouth. A mistake.

But though in my gut I didn't believe Beth's whispered insinuations about Simon needing medication for mental problems, I couldn't stop myself from asking. Maybe because everyone around here seemed to be off-balance, and it mattered to me to know who Simon really was.

"I'm sorry," I said feebly as Simon started to smile. "I had no right to ask."

"I tried to tell you earlier," Simon replied. "What? Do you think I'm hiding something from you?"

"N-no." I stammered. "I mean, I don't know."

"I can't drink because I'm on medication." Simon folded his arms. "For epilepsy. I haven't had a seizure for years, but I have to be on medication to control it. You can't drink on that stuff. Or at least, I can't. I've tried, and it's awful…"

Epilepsy. Shame washed through me like acid, a bitter burning I could almost taste. I was ashamed I'd doubted him, ashamed too for the flicker of relief that had pulsed through me at the word "epilepsy" when I suppose I'd expected to hear something else, something worse.

Worse? I sneered at my own self-centeredness. Simon had a sickness, and all I'd wanted to know was how it would affect me! A slow, burning second passed in silence. I wished he would say something, shout at me like I deserved. He hadn't gotten angry or even defensive. He'd simply stated facts I had no business asking for but was too insensitive to bypass.

"I'm sorry," I repeated, shaking my head and taking a step back. "I don't know what I—"

But Simon shushed me by pulling me close again and kissing me. *Why?* I kept thinking. Why would he kiss me after I'd doubted him like that? I put my arms around his neck and kissed him back so hard and hungrily I surprised even myself.

We broke apart. "I'm not that complicated, Mia," Simon said, a hint of laughter tugging at the words. "What you see is what you get. Now will you come swimming with me?" He ran a finger along my cheekbone, and my legs turned light and hollow as bamboo.

"I'll see you tomorrow," I murmured, taking a step back. "I really have to go."

"No, you don't."

I squeezed his hand. He squeezed mine back. And then I let go. Too much was happening. Too much had happened.

As I sprinted back to the house, the sound of the waves crashed against the rising wind, and I felt like a storm cloud was gathering in my chest. *He kissed me.* Aftershocks of electricity quickened the rush of blood in my veins. *I kissed him back!* I was excited. I was also afraid.

I slipped into bed but couldn't sleep. Instead I drifted into a light semi-awake state, feeling the free-fall thrill that comes when dreams and memory blend. Half-sensations of Simon's lips touching mine scrolled through my mind on an endless repeat, and, though everything else was a mess, and I knew morning would bring with it angry parents and an even angrier Corinne, I still could not stop myself from smiling.

chapter nine

imon. My eyelids fluttered open. Little sparks leapt through my bones as I thought of the night before. I closed my eyes, daydreaming the kiss a little longer.

But everything fell into shadow as I walked downstairs to the kitchen. Only the clinking of teaspoons punctuated the silence as the family ate breakfast without a word. The air was so sharp with anger that it felt like breathing might puncture a lung. A shard of disappointment nicked me as my eyes fell on Corinne. Her skin was the color of ash and her eyes were as wintry and hard as ice chips as she glared at me from over the rim of her coffee cup.

Even Aunt Kathleen couldn't smile this morning. It felt like a funeral.

I drank my coffee out on the deck. I couldn't let the others squash my secret high. But just the sight of their tense faces had already dragged me down. My happiness receded, remote and dreamlike. Obviously something serious was going down—a lot more than just being grounded after a wilder-than-usual party—and judging by the hostile look on Corinne's face, she still blamed me for it.

Completely unfair. I hadn't done anything to Corinne, so why did I have to take the heat for her bad circumstances? I stared into my mug as Gen stalked out onto the deck. She looked gaunt and hung over, and I braced myself for a snide greeting. Surprisingly, it didn't come.

"Some night," Gen finally ventured and I nodded, tight-lipped, not wanting to say anything to fuel whatever fires were burning around me. "Corinne's parents are flipping. They're threatening to take her back to the city. I think I'd better split soon."

"Take her back?" I frowned.

Gen shrugged. "They think Corinne has a drug problem."

I swallowed, remembering the way Corinne had looked out in the sand dunes. "*Does* she have a drug problem?"

I felt kind of silly asking, but it was an honest question. I just didn't know. Corinne and I were so far from each other. I thought of her lying there, in the dune, with all those hands touching her. A free-for-all. She'd looked half-dead. Like a mannequin version of herself. It made me sick to think about it. But the truth was obvious: I didn't know Corinne anymore. And maybe she didn't even know herself.

Gen smiled—a thin, ironic smile. "Drug problem," she repeated. "It's not like she's doing H or anything. All she did was Ecstasy last night. And some pot."

"Oh," I mumbled. Ecstasy and pot. It sounded bad enough to me, especially if Corinne was making a habit out of it.

"I guess her parents have caught her before," Gen continued. "She's been kind of on probation. But her mom's super-pissed now." Rising voices erupted from inside the house. A door slammed. "It's getting a little *loco* around here for my liking."

"Corinne's got it in for me," I said finally. "I don't know why, because I didn't say anything about her to my aunt and uncle."

"Whatever." Gen took a slug of her coffee. She raised an eyebrow as she caught a glimpse of the shine in my eyes. I bit my cheek hard to keep tears at bay. Being a crybaby over Corinne was bad enough, but doing it in front of Gen?—suicide. I concentrated on peeling flaking varnish from the balcony railing, willing my eyes not to tear up and wishing Gen would disappear.

"Hey," she said in a tone as close to sympathy as I think Gen was capable of mustering, catching me off-guard. "Don't get so emo. Corinne's all over the place. You shouldn't care." She gave my shoulder a brief pat that felt more like a pinch and went inside before I could say anything.

Shouldn't care. Why did I care? Corinne had dug her own grave. Her problems had nothing to do with me. Still, I did care, too much, and not just about Corinne's well-being. Somehow, I hadn't yet managed to make myself less vulnerable to her mood swings. I was delighted by her sudden affection or wounded by her sudden harshness. For some reason, her opinions of me still mattered, even though I knew my opinions of her didn't matter in the big picture of her life, a life so completely unlike mine. A life that didn't have space for me in it anymore.

Shouldn't care. Maybe so. But my face burned with tears, and I felt lonelier and stupider than I had in a long time. *Feel it,* I commanded myself. This was the reward for trying too hard. This was the reward for looking too long for something and someone that was already gone.

I drained the dregs of my coffee and looked out toward Simon's property. I knew where I needed to be.

Except that Mom chose that moment to make an appearance on the deck.

She glowered at me, as forbidding as the cold front hovering offshore. "You girls really screwed up. Honestly, Mia, I thought you'd have some sense and at least try to keep things in check."

"I said I was sorry," I shot back.

"I guess we can't trust you as much as we thought we could," Mom continued in a tone of resignation. "I'm really very surprised at you. I could smell whiskey on your breath. But I want you to know that I didn't tell your father. He's disappointed enough as it is."

"Why don't you just tell him?" I said coldly, meeting her eyes. There was so much disapproval there that it was practically radioactive. And I knew that it would be there for a long time to come, right next to the disappointment that seemed permanently locked into my mother's gaze whenever she looked my way. "Tell him," I repeated. "I know you want to."

"What's that supposed to mean?"

I broke the face-off, looking away and out into the distance. "Nothing," I said. Did she really want me to spell it out? I knew my mother would enjoy letting my father know I was a less-than-perfect daughter. Dad and I were always so together on things. He was always protecting me from her criticisms. My drinking was a ripe opportunity for her to change that.

"Am I missing something here?" Mom's voice rose in indignation. "I said I'm *not* going to tell your father."

So she wanted a medal. That had to be it. She'd probably be reminding me for years to come of what an understanding mother she'd been by not telling Dad I'd been drinking at some stupid party. Reminding me of how lucky I was she didn't punish me further for being at an out-of-control party that wasn't mine to control.

I continued to stare into the distance. I could feel her next to me, expecting me to be contrite, grateful even. But something hard pushed from deep inside me. And it was pushing her away. "Tell him or don't tell him," I said, my voice as flat as the horizon. "I don't care."

Mom sucked in a breath. I was really in for it now. I waited for her to lose it. She paused. And then suddenly, she turned and walked away. Why?

I don't care. I repeated the words. Whatever she was after, she deserved my cold shoulder. I didn't care...so why did I suddenly feel guilty? I put my head in my hands. All I'd done since arriving at Wind Song was think my way into circles that grew ever smaller and tighter, and it was making me dizzy.

"You okay, Meemsy?"

Aunt Kathleen crossed the deck toward me. "Just...waking up," I muttered lamely. There were shadows underneath Aunt Kathleen's eyes and cheekbones, yet she made an effort to smile at me. Somehow, that made me feel worse.

"I'm really sorry about last night," I said. "I feel really bad about everything and—"

"It's not your fault, honey," Aunt Kathleen interrupted, placing a cool hand on my arm. "Beth and Corinne were responsible, not you." My aunt put her arm around me. "Let's take a walk, shall we?"

We headed down the walkway, my aunt's arm resting lightly around my shoulders. "Honestly, I don't know why my girls are so out of hand," Aunt Kathleen mumbled, shaking her head. "They used to be so easy to handle. We've given them everything, but they seem bent on destroying it all."

"Are you going to take Corinne back to the city?" I asked. I wanted to know if what Gen had said was true. If Corinne had really gotten in so much trouble that her mom would take her back to Manhattan for the rest of the summer. Which, I then realized, could mean the end of everyone's summer.

"I don't know how much better off she'll be if we go home right now," my aunt replied. "She can see her therapist more regularly, but I'm not sure that would help. It didn't seem to help last year."

"Therapist?" I hadn't known Corinne was in therapy. Instinctively I thought it was dumb. What kind of problems did Corinne really have? She had a charmed life: perfect family, perfect future, perfect everything. Why wasn't that enough for her?

"I think it will be better if she just stays here with you," my aunt continued. "Maybe with your influence, Corinne will turn herself around and remember that she has a ballet career to think of, which she seems ready to flush away."

My aunt's voice was sharp, full of anger, and who could blame her? But I wasn't sure what use I would be. And I didn't like the thought of being Corinne's "good influence." For one thing, she wouldn't listen to me. For another, it sounded boring—or worse, controlling. At best, as Corinne herself would say, it sounded "tedious."

"Why can't she be more like you, Mia?" My aunt said finally, with a sigh of frustration. "You have a head on your shoulders!" I shuddered, praying she hadn't said anything like that to Corinne. My stock value was low enough.

As we walked, I tried to formulate something to say in Corinne's defense, something that would soften Aunt Kathleen, but I couldn't. I still had that image of her on repeat: Corinne lying there in the sand, with people all over her, so far gone. I could still see the vacant look in her eyes, like someone had scooped her out of her body and left just the shell behind.

"Corinne's had a bad year," my aunt continued, our feet hitting cold sand. "Many dancers lose their stamina at some point in their career. It's understandable. But Corinne's far too young and gifted to be giving up! She's just spun out of control. And I don't know how to help her get her passion back." A wave crashed loudly, colliding with another, smaller wave to send a ripple of spray across the swirling tide line. My aunt sighed heavily. "I thought a summer off would be just what she needed, but—" Aunt Kathleen didn't bother finishing the sentence, her mouth a thin, sad line.

"I'm sorry," I murmured, not knowing what else to say.

"No, honey, *I'm* sorry." Aunt Kathleen replied. "I'm sorry your vacation is turning out this way. I so wanted you girls to have a happy summer again. You must be feeling terrible."

"It's okay." I squeezed my aunt's hand. What an unselfish person she was. Even when she was worried or unhappy, she always thought of those around her and found a way to make them feel happier just for being near her. In that way, she was like the Corinne I remembered from childhood. Always brighter than whatever surrounded her, like a planet among stars.

"What's *that?*" My aunt interrupted my thoughts, shading her eyes and pointing at something ahead. A heap of seaweed and shells. We neared the shape on the flat, freshly washed sand: a giant heart made of seaweed. In the middle, spelled out in clam and mussel shells, was an "M."

My face blazed as I gazed down at the sand.

"Let's see…" My aunt had a mischievous smile on her face. "It's nearest to our house, so it must be intended for someone in it. Now, whose name starts with M?" My aunt elbowed me in the ribs. "Somehow I don't see your dad doing this for Maxine."

I laughed at the idea of my mom and dad being lovey-dovey. It wasn't their style.

"Confess, Mimi." Aunt Kathleen gestured at the shell-and-seaweed heart, her diamond rings twinkling in the sunlight. "Whose artwork is this, and what would I think of him?"

If my mom had asked, I would have squirmed. I doubted she would approve of Simon any more than she had approved of Jake. Besides, Mom and I just weren't natural when it came to talking about love.

But my aunt was someone I could talk to, someone I knew would understand the crazy pins-and-needles I had going on in my gut. She'd understand them better than I did. Because Aunt Kathleen was that kind of person—romantic, exciting, passionate. You just had to look at her to see it. And I'd seen her with my uncle, all through my life.

They were the kind of parents who still held hands when they walked down the beach. The kind of parents who danced in the kitchen to Barry White songs and didn't care if that embarrassed their children. I'd always remembered them this way and always noticed these things about them. Maybe because my parents weren't like them at all.

"Who is he?" my aunt prodded, and, as I thought of Simon, my stomach leapt and fluttered, as if I'd just swallowed a goldfish.

A small smile tugged at the corners of my mouth as I pictured him running around in the early hours, looking for shells and seaweed. Only Simon would think up something like this.

"His name is Simon," I said, my face still red as a candy apple. "He's renting the house next door."

"Really?"

I glanced at my aunt, wondering whether she was thinking about the ugliness of Simon's summer house and if she'd form opinions about Simon because of it. But when she smiled warmly at me, I knew my worries were for nothing. My aunt wasn't shallow, and she wasn't a snob. For all the things she had and the lifestyle she represented, she never demeaned anyone.

"The boy next door." Aunt Kathleen's eyes shone as she tucked a stray strand of hair behind my ear. "Are you in love?"

Love. The word frightened me. I had thought I understood it before. Because I'd thought I had it in my possession. But it was like the time I was a kid and thought I had caught a butterfly in my hands. I was so thrilled. I ran to show my mother. Except that when I opened my hands, there was nothing there. "How can you know for sure?" I asked Aunt Kathleen. "How can you prove it's real?"

My aunt smiled. She looked tired all of a sudden. Old. "Honey, you can't prove it. And you don't know it will last. Love is never a sure thing." Her arm tightened around my shoulders, our feet falling into step as they crunched into wet sand. "All you have is what you feel right now. But that's a beautiful, precious experience. So just go with it."

"But I've done that and I got hurt," I replied. "I can't get hurt again."

My aunt thought for a moment, and then she replied. "The surest way to hurt yourself is to give up on love, just because it didn't work out the first time." She glanced at me, a soft smile playing at the corners of her mouth. "Looking at your face, I'd say the boy next door means an awful lot to you."

Simon. It was like there was a permanent image of him tattooed into the back of my head, burning through all of my thoughts, making my heart skip. But it also made me nervous. What if Simon woke up today and regretted the kiss? Or what if he didn't regret it but didn't want to make a big deal out of it? What if it was a "being in the moment" kind of thing? After all, it was just a kiss. A kiss didn't mean anything. Or rather, it didn't mean *everything*.

It does to him! My inner voice interrupted my doubting self. Simon was an all-or-nothing person. He wouldn't have kissed me if he hadn't really liked me. Right? Except that I'd hotfooted it away from him. Would that change his mind? Would he think I was just too immature to handle being with him?

Whatever he thought, he didn't know the truth. I had never told Simon about Jake, but, in the back of my mind, Jake had been there all along. I had been afraid of getting close to Simon, afraid to open up to him, much less kiss him. But something in me had changed. Since I kissed Simon, Jake truly meant nothing to me. I didn't even feel anger toward him anymore. I didn't feel a thing.

I had let go.

"Aunt Kathleen, I want to go over to Simon's house." I had to see him—and by daylight, where there was no hiding the look in your eye, no hiding what we really felt.

My aunt's blue eyes shone like gemstones as she shot me a delighted smile. "Of course, you *must.*" She winked at me, and we both looked back at the seaweed heart. "What a romantic gesture!" Her voice seemed to carry with it a trace of wistfulness.

"It's kind of a smelly gesture," I joked, watching as a fat fly settled on a bulb of seaweed.

"Mia, I think you still have a chance at having a wonderful summer." My aunt lifted her chin, fixing me with an expression that was both playful and serious at the same time. "Don't let anything or anyone stop you."

• • •

There was no one on the lawns in front of the Ross house, no sign of Simon in the gazebo either. Randomly I wondered how people got their grass to grow out here. How did they mold it to the beach? How did they get it that greener-than-Astroturf color? But I guessed nothing was impossible for rich people. When the sky's the limit, a slab of grass is a piece of cake.

I put one foot in front of the other and tried to look casual, though the more I concentrated on looking casual, the more jittery I became. My thoughts turned gloomy as I tried to relax the muscles in my face and lengthen my stride. I tripped on the walkway, only just managing to not fall flat. Why couldn't I be graceful? Why couldn't I carry myself confidently, like Corinne or Gen or any one of the girls out here, instead of klutzing around without a self-assured bone in my body…

My nervous thoughts kept jumping around. On the one hand Simon had left that seaweed love note for me on the beach. And he had kissed me. But on the other, as Simon had always said, everything was different at night. So would last night seem impulsive and regrettable to him in daylight?

And even if Simon felt the way I wanted him to, was it worth risking a real friendship for the chance of a summer fling? With someone who lived miles and miles away and would either head to business school in the Northeast—or at best, if Simon had his way, all the way to Europe…?

Bad idea. You'll just get hurt.

But my feet kept going.

I squinted at the glare coming off the deck of Simon's house. From the outside, the place was eye-blinding white tile and chrome, and shone back at me as shiny as a cruise ship. I had been here only once, years before when we'd attended the Marty Hollis Hairy Butt barbecue. But the house had been almost entirely redone, and it was now a weird flying saucer shape. From here, it was harder than ever to imagine Simon in it.

"May I help you?"

I jumped. A rail-thin woman on a deck chair shot me a wan smile from behind her sunglasses. I hadn't even seen her. A glass of iced tea rested at her elbow, and she had red hair, I noticed, like Simon's.

"I'm looking for Simon. I'm Mia. From next door," I said.

"Oh!" A ripple of pleasure skittered down my spine as recognition registered in her widening smile. Simon's mother had heard about me. "Simon will be happy to see you, Mia," she said, standing up from her chair and walking back inside the house to call him. "I think he's painting in his room."

While Mrs. Ross went inside to get Simon, I took in the surroundings, a mishmash of architectural styles posing as something ultramodern. Below the deck and to the side of the house was a kidney-shaped swimming pool with statues of nymphs as fountains and mosaic tiles around the sides. That was new and must have cost a fortune to put in.

From the deck, I caught a glimpse of the house inside. Marble floors, everything white and shiny and sterile, somewhere between a doctor's office and a Greek tomb, with fluted columns everywhere. It didn't take a connoisseur of beautiful buildings to see that the house was a mess. An expensive mess. But more than being architecturally disastrous, the house just looked so cold. I wondered how the family inside it could relax in it.

I did like the pool though. It was tacky, but it was kind of amazing, the mosaic tiles shining with gold leaf. Maybe Simon would suggest a swim.

But he didn't look like he wanted to as he came out onto the deck.

"Hey," he said.

"Hey." I swallowed. Simon looked serious and kind of embarrassed. Was he embarrassed about me? Was he weirded out that I'd come over? In the clear light of day, was Simon's inner, rational voice telling him he'd made a mistake?

But just then Simon's eyes crinkled into a smile and he broke his unusually long silence. "I'm glad you came," he said softly. "I'm—"

Before he could finish, a loud voice split the air. "Karen!" the voice boomed, a similar gravelly voice to Simon's. "Where's the goddamned lunch! Christ!"

Simon flinched, a slight movement, but I caught it and caught him meeting his mother's gaze as she pasted a bright smile to her face. "Coming, dear!" Mrs. Ross replied. "I'm just meeting Simon's friend, Mia!"

Simon closed his eyes then, and I knew he wished his mother hadn't said anything. She directed her smile toward the living room and then back at us. Something about her smile seemed remote controlled—as if it didn't come from her but from somewhere else. Someone else.

I expected to see an ugly, ogre-like man as a dark shadow crossed the living room and the figure of Mr. Ross emerged. But he was handsome in a thickset, very masculine way. He had silver hair and wore a pink sports shirt with a Polo logo emblazoned on the pocket, crisp khaki pants, and soft loafer-type shoes as thin as leather gloves. He looked like he was about to go and play golf. But I knew from Simon that he still hadn't been invited to play on the coveted links of Southampton Club.

176

But if Mr. Ross wasn't powerful out in Southampton, it was clear he was a powerful man in his own life. He oozed confidence and shot me such a dazzling smile I felt like I must have misheard the angry snarl that had come from inside only moments before.

"Very nice to meet you, Mia. We're neighbors, I take it?"

"Yes," I replied, shaking the hand he offered. "I'm staying with my uncle and aunt."

"I think we met them at a benefit last year, didn't we, honey?" Mr. Ross said smoothly in his deep voice, turning to smile at his wife for confirmation. He had steel-gray eyes, I noticed, darker than Simon's but with that same marble-flecked intensity. Except in Mr. Ross's eyes there was a hardness—something calculating, intimidating. Looking into his eyes made me want to look away.

"We should all have a get-together, shouldn't we, Karen? We've been a bit reclusive since we got to the beach," Mr. Ross said to me with a chuckle. "But I'm glad Simon's been sociable."

Simon, like his mother, kept silent. When Mrs. Ross disappeared and then returned with a tray of ice tea, I could see Simon start to fidget. But Mr. Ross had me deep in conversation, asking me about where I grew up and what my college plans were. He seemed pleased when I told him I was interested in oceanography. "A girl with direction. I like that," he declared loudly. "You'll stay for lunch?" Mr. Ross asked, but it was more of a statement.

"No, we're heading out. For a picnic," Simon replied. "To Georgica Pond." He was improvising, but as I looked over at him, I caught his smile. I knew it occurred to him then that what he'd proposed was actually a great idea.

We said our good-byes and walked around the side of the house, exchanging a look of relief to have escaped. As we approached the garage, two expensive new cars stood waiting, parked outside. But Simon marched right past them and into the garage. Inside stood the same antique-looking, butter-yellow convertible I'd seen him in that one time on Dune Road.

"My dad bought it at a car show in Sag Harbor. He must have had sunstroke, because for once he bought something that's easy on the eyes. I'm not allowed to drive it. It isn't even road worthy yet. But—" Simon's eyes gleamed as he patted the hood of the car, "—this baby is going to Georgica Pond. She's been out a couple of times already. She can handle it."

"How's your father going to get it back to Minnesota?" I asked. The car was beautiful, but it was old too, and clearly wouldn't make a trip halfway across the continent.

"Yeah, right?" Simon shook his head. "That guy. He's all about buying. He has to spend money or he doesn't feel right. I don't know. He'll probably FedEx it back home in a jet."

"Is it licensed?" I ran a hand across the car's polished leather seats, picking up a faint smell, like perfume and smoke and sea spray mixed together.

"Just get in." Simon shot me a devilish grin, and I slid into the passenger seat, trying not to picture Mr. Ross when Simon got back from our road trip in his special new car. If it even made it back.

"You're going to get into so much trouble," I said as Simon started the engine, but he just looked at me and laughed.

"That's Mia. You're always living in the future. One step ahead."

"What do you mean?" I asked as the car purred to life.

Simon reached across the driver's seat and lightly stroked my cheek, still holding that devilish grin. "Welcome to the now, Mia. Sit back and enjoy it."

And with that he screeched onto the main road.

Within minutes I didn't care at all—not about Mr. Ross, not about what was waiting for me back at Wind Song, not anything—and Simon seemed not to care either. He looked relaxed, his gray eyes light and clear, his hair blowing and curling against his cheekbones. I stole sideways glances at him.

With each profile view of Simon, a jolt went through me. I had kissed him! He had kissed me! And now we were out on a road adventure. Okay, we were only going a short distance, but it felt like the whole world was being left behind and it was just us and the wind and the sun peeping out from behind the clouds now, transforming the day from gray to sunny.

"Here's an idea," Simon said, slowing for a traffic light. We'd spent a comfortable period in silence, with nothing but the sound of the wind rushing past us, towns like Southampton, Watermill, and Bridgehampton flicking past as we sped along the highway.

"What?" I asked, as we waited for the light to change.

"Let's not talk about our families for the rest of today. Not my father. Not your cousins. Nobody."

"I can do that," I replied. Our eyes met in the rearview mirror. Simon gave me an approving nod. And then we both stared ahead at the road that rushed toward us like a long, black ribbon.

. . .

"I do not live in the future," I said, slamming my car door. "I can live in the present just as much as you can."

"Really?" Simon quipped as he led me through a tangle of green foliage and out to the water of Georgica Pond. "Because for a second there, I could have sworn I read your mind, and it was working over the probabilities of the car making it back home today."

"Shut up. You're ruining my enjoyment of the moment."

We came to a clearing of trees framing a view across to still, blue water. "And how is your moment now?"

I paused, gazing out at the pond. "I think I'm having an epiphany."

We both laughed.

The pond water was still and beautiful. After the pounding surf of the Atlantic, swimming in Georgica would be like lying down on a cool, round mirror. But I liked the quiet of it, the flat calmness stretching out beyond and around us, rimmed by trees that camouflaged mansions. Ahead, sailboats bobbed lazily. From across the water came the jagged drone of a motorboat. A water-skier trailed behind, crisscrossing the pond's surface. Everything was baked gold by sunlight.

I spread a blanket and unpacked our picnic. We'd stopped to pick up bread and cheese on the way, and some Twizzlers and soda. I tried not to be self-conscious as I pulled off my cutoffs. Simon took off his T-shirt too. I acted like I wasn't taking in the sight of his broad shoulders, his pale skin that suited him. Simon lay on the blanket. I stayed sitting, sun warming my bare back. After a few minutes I relaxed, leaned back on my elbows. I was getting brown, I noticed, glancing at the curve of my shoulder. Summer was going by fast…

Georgica Pond is the biggest tidal pond on Long Island, separated by a thin strip of sand from the beach. The water is kept fresh by ocean water and springs feeding into the pond. The last time I'd been was with Corinne and our dads, years ago. We'd caught small crabs and tossed them back. We'd taken swims in the navy water…But the past and even the future drifted away as I felt the sudden warm graze of Simon's fingers lightly encircling my left wrist. He pulled me down to the blanket, and I looked up through the trees at the sky, patches of light blue crosshatched by the green of leaves.

"The light out here…it's like nowhere else in the world," Simon murmured, rolling onto his stomach to gaze out at the pond. "Do you know there's a color of paint named after this light? It's called Hamptons Blue. See how the light here almost looks like it has ripples in it? It's like there's water in the air."

I rolled onto my stomach too. "There is water in the air," I explained as Simon's fingertips made soft circles on the inside of my wrist, causing my pulse to flicker. "There's a reason the light here is different," I continued, trying to keep my voice even. "It's because of the combination of seawater and the high concentration of all the ponds out on the Island. These bodies of water create bands of light that make it seem like the air is vibrating. But it's really all about reflection and refraction."

"You really like to define everything, don't you?" Simon shook his head. "That scientific mind of yours. We have to get you a lobotomy."

"What's wrong with science?" I challenged. "Don't you like to know the way things are?"

"Even science isn't an exact science," Simon countered. "There's chaos theory. There are things that don't make sense at all. Like quantum physics. That stuff is completely out there."

I was stunned to hear these words from Simon. I'd been puzzling over these concepts all summer, but I hadn't shared my thoughts with him. "I know," I replied. "But still…" I finished lamely. I couldn't stop myself from looking for the facts, analyzing everything around me, even as I knew that what you thought was true and reliable might not be after all.

"Take me for instance," Simon continued. "I see the light, and I just think it's beautiful. And that's all there is for me. Just the beauty of it. You can't explain it scientifically, it just *is*—a beautiful, strange light."

"That's too poetic for me."

"What's wrong with poetry?"

I smiled. "Too romantic for me."

"Oh, that's right," Simon murmured with playful sarcasm. "I forgot. You're not a romantic."

"You said it."

"Even in romantic situations?" Simon's moved his fingertips from my wrist and up the inside of my elbow to my shoulder.

"Someone's got to keep their feet on the ground," I murmured, unsteady as his fingertips trailed fire across my collarbone and back to my shoulder.

"What was it you said before, when we had our first talk on the beach?" Simon tipped his head back, trying to remember. "Something about romantics and how they set themselves up for failure?"

"I said it was better to be a realist." I shivered as Simon's fingers followed the curve of my shoulder blade and moved down my spine. "Romantics are always—"

He cut my words off with a kiss. "—Disappointed?" he growled teasingly, lifting his head and placing a finger on my lips. I tipped my head toward his again, kissing him back, a long sweet kiss…it seemed to stretch and warp time.

Finally, we broke apart, rolled onto our backs, and lay there, side by side, looking up through the trees. I closed my eyes and breathed, to lengthen the moment, as if time really was an elastic band you could pull to extend it. A twinge pinched at my heart because even in moments like that, there's a part of you that's already sad—a part of you that knows the moment is already on its way to being gone, because nothing truly perfect can last.

At least not yet. Not until scientists figured out how to stretch time. I thought of telling Simon about Einstein's theories of time dilation. Of how if you could move fast enough, you could actually slow down time itself.

But talking would only spoil what I had right now. This was as close to pure happiness as I had ever known in my life: managing to have a whole conversation just by being next to the person you want to be with and eating too many Twizzlers. I had never thought that love would be in such small details, that it would feel so familiar even though it was new. I'd thought love was this wild, unknown thing that rushed at you and swept you away. And there was a part of love that was definitely like that, but it wasn't everything.

Some piece of me broke away like a balloon let loose, and I drifted up and imagined looking down at us from above—two figures lying in the middle of a great, green forest, water at their feet and blue sky above and beyond. There was just us, our bodies shrinking and telescoping away, smaller and smaller, the higher up I went.

Just us. In a circle of green and blue. And it was perfect.

chapter ten

The day after the trip to Georgica, Gen left.

"Snap out of it. At least they're not sending you to rehab!" she joked to Corinne. "Get that girl to pick up her lip," she instructed Beth and me, leaping into her car. "If she mopes like that, her glands will swell."

And then she left, smiling her million-dollar smile as her sports car screeched down the driveway.

Corinne didn't say a word. She just stood there, looking sullen.

The parents had gone to a winery on the north fork of Long Island, leaving the three of us and Eva to say good-bye to Gen and amuse ourselves for the rest of the day. I swallowed as Corinne marched back up the stairs, no doubt to sequester herself in her bedroom. If she would just talk to me…Or if I could just talk to her. But who was I kidding? I was last on her list of confidantes. And right now she wasn't talking at all.

"I'm hungry," Eva whined as I stood in the hallway, trying to figure out my next move.

"Then get something from the fridge," I snapped. "You're a big girl."

Eva rolled her eyes and strode off to the pool. As I watched her flouncing over to a deck chair and flinging herself into it, I wondered what sort of person she would become. Would she grow up to be spoiled and moody and troubled like Corinne had turned out to be? Eva showed all the signs of it now. But Corinne, at Eva's age, had never been bratty like Eva. So maybe Eva would be worse than Corinne, Gen, and Beth put together. A truly creepy thought, and very possible.

I grabbed an apple and wandered out to the deck where I could be alone to daydream, transporting myself away from Wind Song to a new secret happiness called Simon Ross. Not even Corinne and Eva could corrupt and ruin that. Yesterday had been so perfect. After Georgica, I'd had to endure only a few hours of the family before I slipped up "to bed"…and then climbed out the window to meet Simon at Indigo Beach.

I took a bite of my apple. New secret happiness. Last night tumbled forward: Simon had kissed me in the water, his arms around me in the dark…I'd needed him to hold me tight. Everything else was antigravity, my usually grounded thoughts smothered by free-floating bliss. Hard to imagine that just a few days ago we were just friends…

But were we ever just friends? I was sure of only one thing: what I felt for Simon was so strong it frightened me. Maybe I should slow down. Take a step back. But I didn't know how. And I didn't want to.

"What are you doing today?"

Startled, I turned to see Corinne gliding through the open sliding doors and onto the deck. "Not much. The beach, I guess," I replied, looking her over with neutral eyes.

Corinne lit a cigarette, and, for a while, we said nothing and just looked out at the ocean. It was a gorgeous day. The beach looked like it had been swept clean, and the water sparkled, flecked with white-caps far out to sea where the wind was strong.

"I'm sorry, Mia," Corinne said, keeping her eyes distant, in line with the horizon. Her tone was flinty, a little grudging. Still, I was surprised and grateful she'd come to make peace. But I reminded myself of the recent past, of how being eager to be Corinne's friend wasn't necessarily the way to my own happiness. Corinne was tough on those who really cared about her. So a little distance was a good thing. For all I knew, she'd cloud over in a matter of minutes anyway.

"It's okay," I said with a shrug.

"I know you didn't rat me out to my parents." Corinne continued, turning to me with apologetic eyes. "I was wasted. It was unfair of me to take it out on you."

"No big deal. Really." I bit my lip. I wanted to say more. I wanted to ask Corinne why she got so wasted all the time and why she would pick a guy like Aram to be with, when he obviously had no respect for her. I wanted to ask her about her supposed boyfriend, Alessandro. He still hadn't called her back and I'd seen her pause at the phone, looking sad. Did she care for him after all? But if so, why was she toying with Aram? I wanted to know why she no longer talked about ballet or seemed to care that she'd failed her audition. I wanted to know why she seemed so bitter toward her mother, when she had the best mother on the face of the earth.

But I kept my mouth shut. There was too much distance between us. Too much to expect Corinne to open up to me.

Corinne sighed loudly, stubbed out her cigarette, and leaned over the balcony, resting her weight on her thin arms. Ballerinas look so fragile and fairy-like. They seem so delicate, their movements so effortlessly graceful, but they're incredibly strong. And right now, my cousin looked so innocent and pretty in a melon-colored summer dress with tiny shoestring straps. But if you looked in her eyes, you could see she was tough and jaded. I just didn't understand how she'd gotten that way. She had the world at her feet, and anything she could ever want she could have, unlike the rest of us ordinary girls who could never hope to be even half as exciting or magnetic as Corinne.

Why did she seem to swing from being the naturally happy and fun-loving Corinne I had known to the morose, checked-out person I'd seen her morph into? Was the change something she could do deliberately, flick on and off like a switch, or was the cold, flat look in her eyes the result of something beyond her control? I didn't know, but I tried to imagine something in Corinne's exclusive and lavish world being beyond her control. I couldn't come up with anything. Or anyone. Corinne had so many talents, not least, the ability to make people love her, even when she wasn't likeable.

People like me.

"Are you shocked by me?" Corinne asked suddenly, turning to look at me. "You must think I'm a total mess."

Instantly the image I longed to forget came to mind: Corinne lying in the sand with Gen kissing her drunkenly. How could I answer without incriminating myself? If I said I was shocked, she'd judge me for judging her or call me a prude. If I said I wasn't shocked, that was a judgment of her too—and an obvious lie, revealing spinelessness I would no longer accept in myself.

"It's none of my business what you do," I said carefully, picking at the skin of my apple.

"But I asked you, so I've made it your business," Corinne retorted.

"We live in different worlds," I replied evasively, knowing I sounded lame and high-handed.

"You're right. We do," Corinne turned her gaze back to the sea. "I guess I've always been jealous of you, Mia. Did you know that? Maybe that's why I can be so mean."

I stopped peeling my apple. Was she joking? Corinne jealous of me? In a parallel universe maybe, where everything was the opposite of what it was here on Earth. "Jealous of what?" I asked. "What do I have that you don't?"

Corinne hugged her thin arms to her chest as the wind picked up, goose-bumping her smooth, tanned skin. "A happy family, for one thing," she said softly. I thought I saw tears glittering in her eyes. But she looked down and away.

"Happy family." I blinked, trying to digest what Corinne was saying. Happy family? My parents worried about money; my mom was always fighting with my dad and seemed miserable. I wasn't close to my mom…Eva was a brat…what was there to be jealous about? Granted, my family wasn't that bad. We were just normal people with normal family troubles.

But Corinne didn't need normal. She had everything she wanted and more. She was a gifted ballerina. She looked like a Maybelline commercial. Her parents adored and spoiled her. And they were crazy about each other. It just didn't make sense. Surely Corinne could hear how ridiculous she sounded?

"You know, I've often wished I could trade places with you. Have your parents instead of mine," Corinne admitted with a rueful smile. "Sounds awful, I know."

I shook my head. This was too much. "You have the greatest mom of all time, Corinne. And if you don't realize what a charmed life you have, then you're blind and insane!" I caught a breath, surprised by the bitter strength of my words. But she'd asked for it. And I'd been waiting to say those words for a long time.

"I guess the grass is always greener," Corinne replied with a half-smile. "It all depends on where you're looking from. Know what I mean?"

I blinked a few times, waiting for my anger to dissolve. "I guess," I answered stiffly. Maybe up close, Corinne's life had those "everything is relative" kinds of problems that just don't seem like much from where I stood. But I still couldn't figure out what she saw in my life that she could possibly be jealous of.

"Your mom, though…she's the ultimate. She lets you do whatever you want. And all your life, she's been proud of you. Whenever she calls my mom, she always talks about your dancing and how great you are. My mom…" I swallowed, trying to keep the hurt out of my voice. I didn't want Corinne's sympathy. I just wanted her to get it. "My mom's not proud of me. She wishes I were more like her. More like Eva. Or you."

Corinne laughed then, a dry, low laugh. "Not everything is what it seems. Take me and *my* mother. She's been pushing me since the day I was born. I always had to be perfect. Look perfect. Be a dancer. Be the *best* dancer."

I frowned. This didn't tally with my reading of my aunt at all. I'd always seen her as Corinne's biggest fan, unselfishly dedicating herself to helping Corinne follow the passion she was born to.

"I thought you *wanted* to be a ballerina," I responded, wondering if Corinne was just playing me, if the note of envy in her voice was just an act. On second thought, I knew Corinne wasn't happy and that her ballet career was shaky. *Corinne's had a bad year.* "I thought you loved dancing," I said.

"Maybe once." Corinne shrugged. "Maybe not. I don't know. I have nothing to compare it to. Ballet is all I've ever known." Corinne looked at me then, straight in the eye, her small features quivering. I knew she wasn't messing me with me. "It was my mom's dream that I become a dancer," she said. "Not mine. It's not like you, with your love of the ocean and all that science stuff you're into. You've always known who you are, Mimi. I'm the opposite. I got told who I was…and I'm not sure that's who I really am."

My head spun. What Corinne was saying seemed so unreal. At the same time, I'd had hints all summer that her and Aunt Kathleen's relationship was troubled. And maybe it had always been. Really, what did I know? I'd only seen my aunt and cousins at holidays when I was just a kid. Maybe my aunt wasn't the perfect mom I'd always imagined.

But even if Corinne was right about her assessment of her mom and herself, she was still dead wrong about me. *You've always known who you are, Mimi.* Was she hallucinating? I gripped the balcony as if for extra support against the internal tidal wave crashing through me. My head hurt, too many contradictory thoughts smashing into each other, each one making the other seem like a misinterpretation or a pack of lies. Maybe the truth lay somewhere in between it all. But for now I was floating with nothing to hold onto. Like being in water but falling through it because you didn't know how to swim.

"We definitely have a lot of catching up to do," Corinne said in the silence. "But I don't think now's the time."

I followed her gaze to see a figure striding up the beach. Tall, thin. A loose white shirt billowing in the wind. Red hair.

"Here comes your man," Corinne said. "I should disappear."

My man? How much did Corinne know, or how much had she guessed about our relationship? As Simon came closer, my thoughts shifted: I remembered all the mean things Corinne had said about him in the past. I felt protective. But then I recapped what Corinne had just told me, and, as her sun-strained eyes looked from Simon to me, I saw something like longing in them. Like envy but without malice.

Was it really possible that Corinne wished she were in my shoes? That she was unhappy in her life of luck and privilege and opportunity? That even though she'd spent her whole life dancing to applauding crowds, she felt sad and lonely? A bolt of sympathy kicked through me. Right now, Corinne looked sad and lonely. And I sure as hell knew how that felt.

"You don't have to go," I said, stopping her with a hand on her arm. "I mean, we were talking."

"Don't be silly," Corinne laughed, but her laughter sounded forced. "You have better things to do. Go have fun…don't worry about me. We'll talk some other time."

"You sure?" I asked doubtfully. "I mean, are you okay?"

"Definitely." Corinne shot me one of her blazing smiles. I smiled tentatively in return, searching her eyes for more information, but she looked away. She waved as Simon strolled up the walkway. "Catch you later," she said to me, and then she turned and went back inside the house.

• • •

I forgot about Corinne as I walked down to the water with Simon. Instead I absorbed the thud of the waves backing the gravelly tones of Simon's voice as he talked about a painting he was working on. He still hadn't let me see any of his art. His paintings were all "works in progress," he'd said in an offhand tone. "Like me."

"There's one I think you'll really like," Simon chattered excitedly. "I think I have something. I'll show you when it's done."

"I bet it's brilliant," I said, but Simon shook his head vigorously.

"Brilliant is all about doing something new and groundbreaking. I'm just trying to capture something I think is beautiful."

"It's hard to make something beautiful," I argued. "It takes talent."

Simon shrugged. "It doesn't matter. I'm having fun. That's all I care about right now. Just trying to get the light down the way I see it. Learning how to use my eyes…"

"I have a favorite painting," I said. "Not that I know anything about art. But there's this one." I hesitated, wincing as I remembered

Jake in the High Museum of Art making fun of the piece that had struck a chord in me. "It's called *Green Sea*."

Simon nodded. "Milton Avery. I love that painting."

"You know it?" My heart leapt. It's not like *Green Sea* was the *Mona Lisa*. It's not like everyone would have heard of it, much less loved it.

"*That* is a brilliant painting," Simon replied. "It looks so simple. It's the kind of painting that makes people say, 'I could do that.'"

"Or 'My dog could do it,'" I added quietly.

"Except those people who say that stuff? They didn't do it. That's the point." Simon's eyes glittered. "It's easy to make fun of art. Much easier than actually making it."

At that moment, I knew Simon was right for me. This time I wasn't infatuated. I wasn't fooling myself. I wasn't wishful thinking myself into it. It wasn't a trick.

It was real.

Simon carried on talking, his gray eyes bright and dreamy the way they looked whenever he talked about painting or old jazz. And I felt lucky he wasn't paying attention to me as much as to his own thoughts. My feelings were almost too much for me. I didn't think I could bear to share them. I looked out to the curling waves spilling over into Indigo Beach and watched the water swell and collapse.

I was so happy, so afraid, so happy. Afraid. Even though I was standing on dry land, I felt seasick.

"I brought oranges and marshmallows," Simon informed me, indicating the messenger bag he'd slung over his shoulder.

"Sensible choices," I joked as we spread our towels. I watched a gull swoop and dip, but even the placid scene in front of me—the gull carving lazy turns in the air, the blue water, the sky studded with small, fluffy clouds—not even that postcard picture of tranquility could squash the fear inside me…the fear of giving your heart to someone, of being unable to control what happened to your own feelings. But people did it all the time. I had done it once before. And I was about to do it again.

"Your aunt has invited my family over for a barbecue on Friday." Simon's voice pierced through my internal monologue, and I smiled tensely.

"I know." Yet another thing to freak me out, only three days away. What if my mom was standoffish to Simon's family? And then there was Simon's dad—he was obviously a live wire. I knew Aunt Kathleen was just trying to be nice and do something for me, but I was dreading it.

"Don't worry. I'll be on my best behavior," Simon joked.

I turned and looked him square in the eye. "I'm not worried about you. I'm worried you'll hate me after you meet my family."

"Ditto."

"I met your family," I replied, taking Simon's hand.

"For all of five minutes."

I traced my fingers over the crease lines of Simon's palm. "Yeah, well. None of them has anything to do with us."

But neither my words nor even Simon's hand closing over mine could calm me. It was everything: the approaching dinner, my fears of letting myself tumble into something I couldn't control, and the disturbing things Corinne had told me, things she'd only hinted at. I knew there was more to come.

I stared down the beach, at odds with the landscape, with its gentle dunes marked with wooden fences—a classic Long Island image. "I always used to think those were picket fences," I said sadly, pointing at the wooden fences lining the dunes. "You know. Like pretty property markers. To me they were a big part of my whole image of the Hamptons—lovely summer homes with picket fences."

"They're not?" Simon frowned.

"They're there to prevent erosion."

"Who told you that?"

"My aunt." I sighed, running my free hand through the sand, picking up a handful, and then opening my fist so the sand spilled back down to where it came from. "The dunes are in danger of disappearing because of all the development out here. That's what happens when you build on sand…"

"Sand castles," Simon said as he followed my gaze. The shapes of large houses marked the dunes all the way up and down the beach, as far as the eye could see.

"I wish I hadn't been told." I said, suddenly feeling heavy. "About the picket fences, I mean."

"They're still nice to look at," Simon reflected.

I smiled. "Yeah. They are," I said after a while. "I guess they still are."

Simon tipped my chin up with a finger. His lips met mine, his hands trailed down my back, and the hard knot in my stomach loosened. All my worries splintered into pieces and drifted away on the wind. The only thing I knew was what was really there: Simon's hands warming my skin, the sun shining in flecks of copper-gold on his hair, and his deep, urgent kiss, taking everything I had and turning it into some kind of liquid fire.

I kissed him back with everything I had. My kiss was a wish in itself, a wish that as I made it seemed like it could come true: the moment stretched, and I went with it, almost believing it would never end and I would never have to worry about anything again.

Almost.

chapter eleven

*W*e spent the whole night out here once when we were little. Remember?" Corinne emerged from my bedroom window and perched on the roof outside, her long legs tucked underneath her in a crouch. She looked like a marsh heron, thin and watchful.

"Yeah, I remember," I said, leaning back against the shingles. "But our parents came and got us after we'd fallen asleep."

Corinne laughed. "I forgot about that."

I looked out at the dark water, smiling as I remembered Corinne and me, so many years ago. We'd been determined to camp out on the roof. It was flat and big enough to be safe, but our parents had come and gotten us anyway, worrying we would be cold or would wake up frightened. I remembered my dad carrying me in his arms through the window and putting me to bed. I'd always loved it when I was little and Dad would carry me. I wondered if Corinne remembered that feeling too.

"It's really nice out here," Corinne said.

We sat in the stillness, watching the flickering light of an airplane as it cut through the sky. It was after eleven; our parents had gone to bed; Beth was playing music in her room; and usually I'd be out here looking for Simon. But not tonight. I'd thought I would try to talk to Corinne and find out more about what was on her mind. Maybe it wasn't too late for us to connect.

"Do you really think you have an unhappy family?" I asked after we'd spent a few moments in silence—not an awkward silence, but the kind of silence that builds to important things that need to be said. "Your childhood always seemed idyllic to me."

Corinne gave a dry, hollow laugh. "Idyllic," she said. "Well… not since I was old enough to know what my parents' marriage was really like."

"What's it really like?" I asked warily.

"Daddy had an affair years ago, when I was still a kid." Corinne's voice seemed to hang in the air. "I remember them fighting, and I remember him leaving for a while. I found out about it years later."

The revelation shocked me so much I could barely process the words. "How?" I bit my lip, expecting Corinne to shoot me down at any minute.

But Corinne seemed eager to get it all off her chest. "When I found out my mother was having an affair, she used my father's affair as an excuse for hers."

My breath caught in my throat, and I sat as still as a statue, uncomprehending. Aunt Kathleen too? Having an *affair?* I pictured my aunt and uncle holding hands, tanned and glowing and beautiful, the way perfect happiness looked.

Or was that just an illusion? *You're not exactly Mother Teresa, and we both know what I mean.* Now I was beginning to understand the angry conversation I'd accidentally overheard between Corinne and Aunt Kathleen weeks earlier.

"I think Mom has stopped seeing her…boyfriend or whatever," Corinne said. "So maybe my parents still love each other. If you can call it love. But I don't know. Maybe it's too difficult to get divorced when you have a lot of money. Too expensive and complicated…"

"It seems so, so—" I stumbled. I was stunned.

"—Hard to believe?" Corinne finished.

"Yeah."

She sighed. "They put on a good act. Especially Mom. She's been acting like everything's fine for so long I don't even think she knows the difference anymore. You see, to Mom, everything is appearances. It's all about the performance, about *presentation*." Corinne let a hand drift into the air to echo her point. Then she let her hand drop. "But you can't keep that up forever."

I leaned back, looking up into the darkness of the night sky. Above us, hazy pinpricks of stars made dim appearances through the clouds, and I stared at them fiercely. They were the only fixed point of reference I could latch onto. Over the course of my vacation, it had begun to seem to me like everything I took for granted was really just a myth. The things and people I believed I knew so well were turning out to be the opposite of themselves, of what I'd thought they were. Even me. Moving this way and that, trying to be different…

But it's not all bad, I told myself, thinking of Simon. A few months ago, if someone told me I'd fall in love with a boy this summer—the summer when I'd most wanted to forget the l-word—I'd have said no way. But now here I was, allowing it to happen…

One positive new discovery couldn't cancel out a negative one, though. My aunt and uncle had fooled me. And worse, if Uncle Rufus and Aunt Kathleen—the golden couple of our family—had ended up in a bitter, disloyal marriage, then what did that say about love? Funny, as I stared up at the stars, I also knew that some of them weren't even really there. They were just echoes of stars that had burned out long, long ago. Like Aunt Kathleen and Uncle Rufus.

"Let's go down to the beach," I suggested suddenly. I couldn't sit there anymore. I didn't want to think. "This way," I instructed Corinne, showing her how I swung my legs down onto the trellis and then jumped to the sand.

"Impressive," Corinne remarked with a hushed laugh. "Apparently you've done this before."

"I'm an old pro."

Corinne slipped down the trellis and landed next to the deck without so much as a light tap.

"You must weigh one pound," I remarked after her silent landing.

Corinne laughed in the darkness. "That has nothing to do with weight. It's just ballet training," she said. "The illusion of weightlessness."

As we passed the dunes, walking toward the water, I took a deep breath. There was something I wanted to do. "Have you ever been swimming at night?" I asked Corinne.

"Are you crazy? I'd never swim where I couldn't see my legs."

"I thought you were so adventurous," I teased as we looked out to the water's edge, listening to the hiss and suck of small waves breaking onto the sand. "It's low tide," I added. "Come on."

"You've gone in the water at night?"

"All the time," I replied. "With Simon," I added casually, unbuttoning my cotton shirt.

"Skinny dipping with Simon! *All right!*" Corinne laughed. She shimmied out of her designer jeans and threw off her T-shirt. "So you *have* been getting up to some mischief this vacation. What's that expression? Still waters run deep."

"Not really," I admitted, reluctantly. I liked the idea of Corinne thinking of me as a free and adventurous spirit, but I was still too full of the old me to lie about it: I hadn't skinny dipped all the way with Simon. I'd been too afraid to. I was nervous about skinny dipping with Corinne, let alone Simon.

But as we ran toward the water, our hair streaming out behind us, the thrill of the ocean ahead, my misgivings floated up and away, leaving me as light as leaf. *The illusion of weightlessness.* Corinne grabbed my hand, and, as the water came at me in the darkness, the world seemed like a place where anything was possible and everything was forgivable.

• • •

I was a fish. Dipping and diving, unrestricted, nothing between the water and me. That's what skinny dipping felt like.

After my first skinny dip, I didn't think I could go back to swimming in my suit at night. It was like I'd forgotten my body, become something else. But at the same time, there was a familiarity too. I'd come out of the water with a sense of myself that had been missing for a long time. It wasn't some huge epiphany; it was more like when you find something you've misplaced for a long time: a favorite shirt, maybe with a few holes in it, but it's the comfiest one you have and nothing bright and new could replace it.

After that, the idea of a suit seemed so ridiculous. I had my own waterproof skin to swim in. But stripping down with Simon near was too much. I'd never been naked in front of any guy.

"But I can't even *see* you," Simon prodded as we sat at Indigo Beach, well past midnight. I'd told him about my naked swim with Corinne the night before, and he was determined to get me to skinny dip with him. "There's not even a moon tonight."

"You have good vision," I retorted, snuggling back against Simon's chest, his arms in my lap. I'd brought a blanket, knowing we'd be out here for a while. Simon shifted until he was lying on his elbows, my head moving to rest against his taut stomach: a perfect stargazing position. Where I live, the sky is often really clear, and I'd spent a lot of time mapping out the stars with my telescope. But you can't beat stargazing out at the beach, and on this night it was cloudless, the stars so bright I could see not only the Big Dipper and the other usual suspects, but also the constellations of Cassiopeia and Lyra. I even fantasized that I could see black holes.

"Do you know what a black hole is?" I challenged Simon as we lay there.

"That would be the state of my father's bank account these days," Simon retorted. "Or did you mean the other kind?" he joked. "Those big holes in the universe that can suck you in if you happen to be floating past on your way to another galaxy?"

"They're not really holes," I said, looking up into the dark, moonless sky. "They're actually the heaviest objects in the universe."

I told Simon that black holes were stars that had collapsed and died. And that they weren't empty at all but the densest form of matter known to exist.

"So they're the opposite of what they're called."

"Yeah…" I trailed off. "Except that things fall into them. And once something is caught in a black hole, it can't escape. A black hole keeps everything trapped inside, even light."

"Like you," Simon said softly.

"What's that supposed to mean?" I angled my head so that I was looking up at him, at the dark lines of his face.

"You're beautiful, Mia. But you keep all of your light inside. You don't let it show."

For a moment, I didn't say anything. *Beautiful.* The word stunned me. It had so much force. And then I felt embarrassed for wanting it so much. "I don't know what you're talking about," I babbled. "And I didn't know you were so corny," I said, lightly knocking Simon's chest with my fist.

"There's nothing corny about comparing someone with a black hole."

"I guess not." I smiled and shifted my gaze back to the sky. *Beautiful.* I could almost touch the word; I had coveted it for so long. Even Jake, who had paid me plenty of compliments, had never used that word with me. Hearing it made me realize just how much I'd wanted to hear it. Its absence had burned a hole in me for so much of my life that I'd stopped expecting anything different.

"I'm not withholding anything from anyone," I said, after a while. "What you see is what you get. I'm not…" I trailed off. I was thinking about Corinne. And Gen. And Stacy. All those confident girls who outshone me.

"You *are*," Simon growled in his hoarse voice. His voice was so sure, so full of belief that I wanted to kiss him. "But you hold back. And that's okay." As Simon's lips met mine, I turned in his arms until my hands were at his neck, my fingers in his thick hair. "The rest of the girls out here are just shooting stars," Simon whispered into my ear. "They're on a crash course to nowhere. But you, my lady friend, you're a black hole. You've sucked me in, and now there's no escape…"

Simon crushed my laughter with another heady kiss, and now I felt like a shooting star, burning in a dizzying rush of light, heading for…who knew? How could I know where I was going? I only hoped it wasn't a crash course to nowhere.

But I did know my trip had to end soon. The summer was slipping by fast. Soon enough, Simon and I would be miles away from each other. Could we keep it together so far apart…?

"You're a heavenly body," Simon murmured teasingly, interrupting my doom-filled thoughts. "A celestial being. You're a—"

"Let's go skinny dipping," I interrupted him, surprising myself with the words.

"Really?" Simon placed his hands on my shoulders and, even in the darkness, I could see him struggling not to look eager but instead concerned and respectful, the struggle more endearing than even the concern. "You're sure?"

"Yeah," I lied. "But don't look while I take off my clothes." And before I could chicken out, I stripped and ran down to the water, Simon's footfalls pocking the sand behind me.

I dived in, the shock of the dark coldness as exhilarating and frightening as swimming naked with a boy I was in love with. A boy I would soon be separated from. Simon hollered as he splashed noisily behind me. I stayed low in the shallow water, as usual. This was far enough for me.

"Can I kiss you?" Simon asked, swimming up to me as I lay with my back to the sky. "I promise not to get too close."

"Kissing is close," I replied, half-laughing, half-terrified as I felt his hand on my wet shoulder, slipping down my back. "I'm still getting used to the naked thing."

"I can't see anything," Simon said.

"Liar," We drifted deeper into the water, my heart thumping. "Just a little farther," Simon said. "That way you'll feel safer."

It seemed almost funny. I was trading off one fear—going too deep into dark water—by replacing it with another—being too exposed. I stopped Simon from pulling me out farther. "You can see..." I took a deep breath and stood up. The water skimmed my hip bones, the warm night air enveloping my shoulders and chest. "You can see me," I finished. "I know, because I can see you." Simon's slender body made a pale outline against the dark air, his broad shoulders and chest in front of me, coming closer. I shivered, but only partly from cold.

"Objects in front of you are warmer than they appear," Simon teased, taking my hand and placing it on his damp chest. "You look like a mermaid," he added, drawing me closer. "You're so beautiful."

I did feel beautiful, if beauty is a kind of fearlessness you feel in the simple fact of your own skin. I inhabited my own body like there was nowhere else I wanted to be. Because there *was* nowhere else that I wanted to be. I closed my eyes. I felt lucky to be me. A simple moment. But getting there had been hard.

Simon brought my hand to his lips, kissing my fingertips. A bolt of heat charged through me, and I stepped closer to him, closer, my toes pressing into the sand beneath, until we were shoulder to shoulder, and then, skin to skin, our bodies pressed against each other and locked together in a salty kiss that felt like a shower of stars. Finally we pulled apart.

"Look!" I stared as the water around us turned bluish-white. Maybe the stars I'd felt had really tumbled out of the sky and dropped into the sea…I was so woozy, the explanation seemed possible. The water around us was lit up: a curling wave zigzagged with stripes of light, glowing like it was carrying a tide of fireflies.

"What is that?" There was wonder in Simon's voice. "Who spilled the DayGlo paint?"

"It's phosphorescence," I said. "Small sea animals glowing in the dark."

"I thought I was the only animal who glowed in the dark around here," Simon joked as the glittery wave broke ahead of us. "This is magic," Simon breathed.

"Define magic," I deadpanned and then I laughed. "Kidding," I said. "It is magic." It was. I'd seen the luminous glow of plankton before, but only once when I was much younger. I had no idea it could be so bright. It felt like the moment had been created just for us.

Was it possible for love to intensify in a matter of hours? It was like an electromagnetic force field around us, and I could swear he loved me too, though neither of us said the word. We just held onto each other until a wave crashed over us and we ran out of the water and onto Indigo Beach. As we ran, our footprints filled with light, marking a path in the sand as if to illuminate the way to the water.

We stopped and looked at the sinking phosphorescence where our feet had imprinted the sand, and then we turned and looked at the waves rising behind us in ripples of light. We stood still as the water seethed and glowed, and then we ran back to our clothes, holding hands like we'd never let go, like nothing could ever force us apart.

chapter twelve

So am I going to like this guy?" Dad asked as we walked along the shoreline early the next morning. A light fog hovered above the sea, and the sand was wet and new, a blank slate, so that the only marks on the smooth sand were the fresh prints made by our feet.

"You'll like him," I replied. I knew Dad would. If I was happy, he would be. "I hope Mom's nice to him," I thought out loud, dreading the idea of my mother cross-examining Simon or looking his parents up and down for signs that they weren't "well-bred." I just wished she could be more like Aunt Kathleen—at least in public—more generous and easygoing, less class-conscious. I knew Aunt Kathleen would be nice to Simon's family no matter what.

But thinking about Aunt Kathleen also produced a sliver of pain inside me. I still didn't know what to make of her. Corinne's stories seemed so alien to me: her mom being pushy and overly ambitious about Corinne's dancing. The affair. I loved my aunt…but I also knew Corinne wasn't lying. I just wished she were.

"You should cut Mom some slack," Dad said as we paused to look at a large, curly whelk shell that had washed up on the shore.

It looked perfect until I picked it up and saw that it was only half intact. "She only wants the best for you."

I frowned, dropping the shell. "I haven't done anything to Mom," I replied defensively. Mom and I had barely spoken since the post-party tension. We'd been careful around each other, but that was all. Thankfully, we'd hardly been in the same room together, which suited me just fine.

"She wishes you would share your life more with her. That's all," Dad said as we wandered along the tide line. Obviously Mom had put him up to this. This was some stunt to make me feel guilty.

"You confide in your aunt. She was the one who told your mom you had this new friend." Dad stopped and fixed me with his kind brown eyes, a trace of concern flickering through them. "It hurts your mother that you aren't more open with her."

I shrugged, annoyed, struggling for words that would appease my dad. "It's just…" I trailed off. How could I say it nicely? "It's just that Aunt Kathleen understands more," I said, groping. "She's more the type you talk about romantic stuff with."

My own words fell a little flat on my ears. Love. Romance. I was no longer sure that Aunt Kathleen was the right person to talk to about these things anyway. But I still thought she understood me better than my own mother ever could. After all, Aunt Kathleen had been young and romantic once. Long ago, maybe, but still.

Dad cocked his head and smiled faintly. But he didn't say anything for a while, until we reached the Southampton Surf Club. In front of the small, low-roofed wooden structure, a long row of empty chairs glistened with moisture in the foggy, early morning light.

"If anyone's a romantic out of those two, it's your mother, Mia."

I pictured my mother with the crease lines of worry and frustration that always seemed to tug at her eyes, her mouth so often curved in disapproval, unless she was looking at Eva, or occasionally—occasionally—when she and Dad got ready to go out for dinner. Then she sometimes looked happy, or as close to happy as she could get.

I used to watch her putting on her lipstick for these evenings, touching her perfume to her pulse points. Chanel No. 5. As a kid, it smelled like anticipation to me. Like restaurants with candles on the table and stemmed glasses filled with ruby-red wine the color of Mom's lipstick. I still remember the way I used to stand in the doorway and watch Mom prepare at her dresser, watch the way she smiled when she skimmed lipstick across her lips…she had her softer moments, but romantic? More romantic than Aunt Kathleen? No way.

"Do you know that your mother had all sorts of wealthy high-society men who wanted to marry her when she was Miss New York?" Dad said as we paused near the lifeguard tower. "The family was broke then, and your mother had been used to the finer things. But she chose me. Just a guy from Georgia whose family owned a hardware store." He ran a hand through his thinning hair. "That's romantic."

"I guess," I replied. But I was still thinking of Dad's earlier words. *All sorts of wealthy high-society men who wanted to marry her.* Men like Shep?

Dad's smile faded and he turned serious. "I probably shouldn't be telling you this, Mia. But your aunt…" he gestured emptily into the air. "She chose your uncle mostly to advance herself. I knew Kathleen then, and she was a hard woman. Don't get me wrong…she was always a lively, warm person, and she always had that special kind of charm. But she was tough too.

"She was never a romantic. She wanted the good life, and she married your uncle as a strategic move. I'm not saying she didn't care about him, but that love had a lot to do with the life he could give her—the life she'd grown accustomed to and which her family could no longer afford."

"How do you know what she wanted?" I shot back angrily. I'd heard enough about my aunt. I didn't need Dad stripping down what little I had left of her to admire.

"Because she told your mother," my father said quietly. "Kathleen and Rufus are…having problems. Your mother has been trying to convince your aunt to work it out, but it's possible their marriage may be over. I've been telling your mother to stay out of it, that she can't save a sinking ship, but she's a romantic…" he tossed me a weary half-smile. "She's gotten herself in an emotional spin over all of this. You know Mom—she always takes everything so hard."

As I digested Dad's words, a hot flash of shame ripped through me. I saw Mom's tense eyes looking at my aunt, unspoken troubles lurking in her body language all summer long. I had assumed Mom was just being jealous and irritable. I'd never in a thousand years have imagined she was worried about Aunt Kathleen.

"I'm sorry to burst your bubble," Dad sighed, putting an arm around my shoulders as we turned back for the house. "But I think you're old enough to know the truth. Or at least, as much of the truth as any of us can figure out..."

I nodded, but I couldn't speak. What else would be thrown at me this summer? I'd spent my life hero-worshipping my aunt and Corinne, golden people in a golden family. Now that the truth was out, I didn't know what to think. Everyone was a stranger. *What's so great about the truth, anyway?* I thought to myself bitterly. *I didn't ask for it.* Maybe illusions should be left alone. Because without them, everything looked broken and ugly.

I looked out across the ocean at a small white sailboat gliding past. I thought of what Corinne had told me when I'd first arrived, about yachts cut loose by owners who could no longer afford them. Something once treasured now dumped behind a dune or abandoned in the reeds to rust.

What a strange summer.

"Dad," I started nervously, licking my dry lips. He'd always adored Mom. He'd never wanted to see her faults. Even now, he called her a romantic. And maybe she was. But maybe this time, it was someone else who made her heart beat faster. "I think you should ask Mom about Shep Gardner," I said quickly.

"Shep Gardner?" Dad seemed amused. As though he hadn't even thought about handsome, wealthy Shep. Mom's "beach buddy." The man who made her eyes shine. Who made her put on her fanciest pashmina to attend a barbecue at his palatial beach house. But we were all guilty of ignoring the warning signs when it came to people we loved. Also, Dad hadn't seen the way Mom and Shep had fallen into each other's arms that night on the deck when they'd reunited after so many years.

"I think being here is bad for Mom," I mumbled, stumbling over how to tell Dad that I feared he was in deep water and swimming with sharks. "I think this place…Aunt Kathleen and what's happening with her. It's having an effect on Mom."

"What's that got to do with Shep?" Dad asked cluelessly.

"Dad!" Did I have to spell it out? "Mom's crazy about him. They're really tight. From long ago."

"I know," Dad replied.

"And you're not bothered? Or threatened, even?" I was astounded. Was even my trusty old dad turning into some kind of jaded sophisticated type?

"I'm not threatened by a gay man," Dad said mildly. He put his arm around my shoulders. "Shep's a dear old friend of your mother's, but that's all. He's a great guy, really. I think you'd like him."

And suddenly I started laughing. Really hard. Right through Dad's explanations of Mom's old friendship with Shep, of how she told Dad that, as a teen, she used to go as Shep's date to parties and events, because back then he was still in the closet. I couldn't believe it. And yet, suddenly so many of the puzzle pieces in my head fell into place.

"Your old man's not as out of it as you think," Dad teased. "My gay-dar's better than yours."

"So tell me, are you and Mom becoming alcoholics?" I joked feebly as we made our way slowly toward home, my arm linked through my father's, my head leaning against his shoulder.

"Not yet, honey." Dad chuckled. "How about you? I thought I smelled whiskey on your breath the night of that party."

I froze, but Dad didn't seem concerned. He was still smiling. "I'm not worried. You don't really like whiskey, do you?" he asked.

"No. But give me another month out here..."

I was kidding, but as we retraced our steps, a cold heaviness settled in the pit of my stomach, as if I'd swallowed a rusted anchor. The faces of my family in scenes from long ago whirred in the back of my mind like old home movies. Corinne, Aunt Kathleen, and Uncle Rufus seemed like actors, playing parts in a play that I had always thought was real life. Tears stung the back of my eyelids.

But Simon and me, we weren't a lie. That part of the summer was real. More real than anything else I knew. And now, with so much else seeming so doomed and so hopeless, I knew I had to hold on to Simon tighter than ever. No matter what.

• • •

Late that night, I stood by my dark window. I flashed my flashlight three times. From up-shore, a needle of light pierced the blackness, flashing three times as I knew it would. My heart kicked. I had dark circles deeper than potholes under my eyes from all the late nights out with Simon. But I was running on adrenaline, my eyes glued open, my insides twisting into sailor's knots as I slipped out the window and climbed down the trellis and onto the walkway. On the beach, everything—the crash of the water, the damp night air on my skin—felt louder and more alive, the way things feel when you're half-dead from no sleep.

I ran toward Simon and together we walked to Indigo Beach. Once we were there, I didn't think twice as I slipped my shirt over my head and kicked off my pants. This time, wading into the water, I wasn't nervous as Simon placed a hand on the small of my back. I felt warm, calm, the warmth spreading through me until I turned and pulled Simon toward me in a fierce kiss that said everything I wanted him to know.

I knew the vacation wasn't going to last forever, and neither of us wanted to dwell on what our lives might be like when we left each other. But the here and now was up for grabs, and I wasn't about to let it slip away.

Bold. Living in the moment. Only a few weeks ago—or was it days?—I'd been careful, cautious. But now I felt like I'd just busted out of a cocoon, a new creature with the power of flight. *Who'd have thought…?*

I shrieked with laughter and splashed Simon, the two of us rolling in the water. Naked at two o'clock in the morning. Yet I couldn't imagine being anywhere else. Or with anyone else. If I felt a little crazy, it was balanced by an absolute faith that I could trust Simon. By being my most vulnerable self, I had unlocked a secret part of me for him, and now there was a trust between us that couldn't have been there before. Yet another contradiction that I had learned. I thought about that—how if I hadn't been vulnerable to Simon, I couldn't have gotten so close to him. You need to take risks to end up feeling safe with someone, which seems to be totally illogical, when you start to break it down. But it's true.

As we sank to our towels, I touched my fingers to Simon's face. I didn't need more light to see by. I could take his expression on faith, and I knew there was love there for me. He pinned me down, and his chest against mine was a weight and also a lightness, a delirious shock that made me feel completely calm.

"You trust me, don't you?" Simon whispered, pausing between kisses.

I nodded. I wasn't afraid. I closed my eyes, but not before I caught a glimpse of the North Star, the only Northern Hemisphere star that doesn't ever appear to move with the night sky. If you were looking for it, it would be in exactly the same place every day, no matter what time of year or where you stood. And it was right above us. I smiled.

"What?" Simon asked, making small teasing circles with his fingertips on my rib cage.

I inhaled sharply. "I just feel like I know exactly where I am." I pointed up at the sky, and Simon moved partway, twisting to follow my finger. "See the North Star?"

"Also known as Polaris," Simon added. "Don't look so surprised. I've watched PBS before."

"I'm impressed." I laughed, and we both looked up at the brilliant point of light. "It doesn't move when the other stars move. I like that."

"Don't you move either," Simon growled teasingly, and my smile got squashed by his lips. As our kisses increased in urgency, my eyes slowly closed so that all I knew was what I could feel: a million tiny dots of pure light burning inside me, through me, from my skin to what felt like my soul. And then I was just drifting with the sky... weightless and directionless. I never wanted it to stop.

chapter thirteen

*D*rifting. The next day I was still drifting. I'd been dreaming about Simon, and on waking up, I daydreamed about him, preferring to keep my eyes closed from the harsh daylight that sliced into my dreams. It was too bright in my room. But I couldn't stay asleep forever.

I forced my eyes open and sat up. My hair was caked with salt. The night rushed back to me as I yawned. I covered my face with my hands, a part of me automatically contracting in disbelief as I relived the night before, picturing us as we lay together on the beach.

I stretched lazily and flopped back onto my bed, my mouth twisting into a naughty smile, my stomach giving a little kick as I thought about me and Simon…the way he'd made me feel…I closed my eyes and lay back against my warm pillow, wondering how I would get through the day without thinking constantly of him. How would I walk and eat and talk to my family?

Don't think, just be! I commanded myself, a dizzy smile forming on my face.

Simon Simon Simon Simon Simon Simon Simon Simon Simon Simon Simon Simon. It was useless. If I wasn't blushing brighter than a fire truck and thinking dirty thoughts about him, I would be staring at the wall, not concentrating on anything except the constant rewind and fast-forward of my mind: back to me and Simon, and forward to me and Simon when we could next be alone together.

I jumped out of bed humming and sleepily headed for the shower. Only when I was back in my room, toweling my damp hair, did I glance over to the clock on my nightstand. *Whoa.* It was almost noon. The house was quiet. They day had long since begun, and I was still in dreamland. Not that I minded.

Maybe I'd take a walk over to Simon's. Maybe he'd show me his paintings now if I just showed up. I could twist his arm. I grinned.

I looked different these days, I noticed, studying my face in the mirror as I brushed my hair and put on lip balm. My eyes looked different. Brighter maybe. It was hard to tell exactly what the new me had that the old me didn't have, but it was there, like an aura, invisible but still present. I liked it—

"I hate you!"

I froze. It was Corinne. My hairbrush hung in mid-air as I heard her footfalls. She rushed up the stairs and into her bedroom, followed swiftly by another set of footfalls.

"You've given us no choice, Corinne," Aunt Kathleen said firmly. "You have nobody but yourself to blame for your behavior."

"You just want to get rid of me!" Corinne spat, followed by a string of convulsing, angry sobs. "You're sending me away to an institution!"

"It's an alternative school for challenged teenagers," my aunt said soothingly. Corinne howled with what sounded like a strangled laugh. I could hear everything. Obviously they thought I was long up and out of the house; they hadn't even bothered to close Corinne's bedroom door.

"You can do your dance training at Bard College," Kathleen continued. "The school is very accommodating."

"That's all you care about! My stupid training." Corinne wailed.

"Please, darling. The school wants to help you get on track. We all just want you to be happy!"

Corinne's anguished sobs and my aunt's attempts to soothe her were more than I could bear, so I got out of there the only way I could escape unnoticed: I flung open my bedroom window.

As I moved farther away from Wind Song, I tried to empty my mind by focusing only on what was in front of me: it was a bright, sizzling day, unpleasant to be on the beach, unless you were going for the grilled lobster look. I put on my sunglasses and kept walking.

Simon's mom was out by the pool when I arrived at their house. She looked tired too, shooting me a faint smile from behind dark glasses. "Go on upstairs, Mia. He's in his room," she said. "And we'll see you tonight," she added as I crossed the deck.

"Great," I replied.

Mrs. Ross replied with another of her watery smiles, the kind of smile that managed to be both brave and timid at the same time. I got the feeling she'd rather crawl into bed than have a barbecue with all of us. *And maybe she's onto something there,* I thought, climbing the metal spiral staircase to the upper floor of the house. With my family being so touchy, the closer it got to the barbecue, the less it seemed like a good idea.

• • •

Simon only let me in once he'd had a chance to hide his painting. "I'll show you when it's finished," he insisted. "You'll have a private showing of my Southampton series!"

"Can't I just take a peek?" I stared at the canvases lining the walls, turned in so I couldn't see them. The one I particularly wanted to see stood on an easel facing the closet.

"When I'm done. That one is a special one," he added, as I stared at the back of the easel. "I've been working on it since before we even met."

I walked slowly around Simon's room, inhaling the scent of oil paint and turpentine. Tubes of blue paint oozed in the heat. Jazz music tinkled in the background. We smiled dumbly at each other, and then Simon closed his bedroom door and pulled me into a hug, running his hands down my back and across my hips.

"Hello," he said again, into my hair.

"What's this music?" I asked, in an effort to seem normal in spite of the fact that Simon was maneuvering me toward his bed, making my heart stutter.

"*Kind of Blue*. Miles Davis."

We lay on Simon's bed, and he kissed my neck. My eyelids drooped and closed at the sensation of his warm mouth at my throat. But I couldn't completely go with the moment. "Don't you like the music?" Simon asked, stroking my hair from my face, sensing something. "This track, 'Blue in Green,' is my all-time favorite."

"It sounds like sadness," I said, with a small smile. "It's beautiful, though."

It felt good being there, Simon's weight half on me. Safe. But I was sad too. I stared out beyond Simon's shoulder, out to the open window where a light breeze blew the curtains inward. Through the window was a small tree, and I watched as a rush of wind snapped up one of its leaves, tugged it, and took it away, out of sight.

Though it was a bright, hot day, it felt like summer was ending. The wind felt like fall. Or maybe it was just me, always looking forward and back instead of just being still. I had managed to suspend myself the night before, but now that carefree feeling seemed far away.

The music ended and the room felt empty, as if someone had just left.

"My aunt and uncle are sending Corinne away to a boarding school," I told Simon, shifting onto my side.

"She might like that," Simon replied. "Zero parental supervision."

"I don't think so," I added ruefully. "I don't think she'd like that," I amended, wondering if, after all, getting her parents' attention was part of why Corinne was acting out. Clearly my aunt and uncle had been wrapped up in their own problems...

Would they get a divorce? I wondered. Tears stung the back of my eyelids, and I chided myself for being so emotional over this. Even if my aunt and uncle did get a divorce, did *I* have to take it so hard? They weren't my parents after all. But the thought was still heartbreaking. It changed the way I saw my childhood, and, at the same time, made me feel nostalgic for it. Or for what I'd thought it had been.

There was something else weighing on me, something even more difficult. Saying it would make it worse, and Simon and I had this unspoken pact not to talk about the fact that what we had right now wasn't going to last forever. I looked up into Simon's eyes. Soon we would head back to our separate parts of the country. It was too hard to talk about, but I couldn't send the thought back to the dark place where it had come from. Not with those beautiful gray eyes right above me picking up bits of extra sun from the room and reflecting it back at me.

Simon studied me from underneath his long lashes. "Don't be sad," he said quietly his eyes searching and thoughtful, like he was mapping my thoughts. "I can see you fretting about the future." He ran a fingertip across the line of my chin. I turned my head. "But you don't know how it'll all work out." Simon continued in a serious voice. Then he cocked his head as a new song started up. "Only Miles Davis knows."

A trumpet melody rose and fell like breathing in the background as I intertwined my fingers with Simon's, his mouth coming closer to mine. I wondered if the music's beauty had to do with its sadness. And if any of us would be back here next summer…

Don't think ahead. Stay here… Simon's warm lips found mine and I closed my eyes. My dark mood tried to pull me back down, but Simon's kisses took over, and, before long, everything else faded.

chapter fourteen

*W*hat a wonderful meal, Kathleen."

Simon's mother smiled as my aunt brought a huge platter of grilled Atlantic salmon to the table. We were eating on the deck. I'd helped make the mango-chili salsa and a salad, but I'd been mostly silent in the kitchen. Because of all I had recently learned about Aunt Kathleen, I was upset at her and couldn't be my usually chatty self.

And yet, watching her arrange food on the table and beaming at all of her guests, my heart warmed. Kathleen would always be my aunt. I would always love her. And she was showing her love for me by making a beautiful meal for Simon's family even though she had her own problems. Uncle Rufus had left for the city earlier in the day, called back to work for something important. I'd seen Uncle Rufus and Aunt Kathleen talking next to his car; I'd seen the strain on their faces. But Aunt Kathleen had come back inside with a smile on her face. Whatever was going on, she wouldn't let it spoil the evening she had planned for Simon's family and ours.

The dinner had begun well enough. Simon's dad, who was very talkative and charismatic, engaged my dad in conversation about business. This left Mom and Aunt Kathleen to talk to Simon's mom.

Mrs. Ross was quiet but seemed grateful to be around women. And Mom was making a big effort.

I'd been a little freaked when she introduced herself as "Maxi" instead of Maxine to the Rosses—Mom's sanitary-pad nickname has always disturbed me, especially since she's never seemed to get what's wrong with it. But I knew Mom was trying to reach out to Simon's parents. Still, she wasn't completely at ease with them. I'd seen her eagle eye flickering over Simon's father's bright golf shirt and large gold pinkie ring with the diamond chip in it. It was hard for her to come off as warm and open like my aunt. They're kind of like me and Corinne, I realized, as I watched Mom and Aunt Kathleen together. One of them was naturally more relaxed than the other. And as I looked at them, I couldn't help hearing my father's words in my mind: *If anyone's a romantic out of those two, it's your mother.* The idea still seemed wild.

"The countdown is on," Simon remarked, following me as I went back to the kitchen to refill the lemonade pitcher. "How long until my father gets overheated or says something tasteless?" he added. "I say we bet on it. Pre-sunset? Post?"

"Maybe he won't," I said, and then Eva was at my elbow, clinging to me and looking for attention. "Stop tugging at me," I scolded her. "You're going to make me drop something."

"Siiiimon," she sang out, being deliberately irritating. "Are you Mia's *boyfriend?*"

"Evie!" I glared at her as she flashed me a saucy smile.

"Yeeees, Eeeva," Simon replied, ruffling Eva's hair. "I'm Mia's *boyfriend.*"

Eva's eyes lit up, and she darted off to the deck, no doubt to seek a bigger audience. And although I was annoyed by her, my cheeks flushed with pleasure. I stole a glance at Simon. *Boyfriend.* This time, the word wasn't just something I wanted. This time, the word really fit.

"I hate cooking," Beth whined as we walked into the kitchen. Even fed up, she looked incredibly gorgeous—in a silky red-and-white striped dress that would have made me look like a beach umbrella. She wrinkled her nose, gingerly nudging a scallop onto a piece of foil. For once, my aunt was making all of us girls pitch in (maybe lingering punishment for the party?), and I couldn't help laughing as I watched Beth's face.

"God, I need a cocktail or something," Corinne moaned from her perch at the kitchen counter, where it was her job to shell sweet peas. "All this family time is making me thirsty."

But she smiled at me and Simon. I knew Corinne was glad for my sake that we were having this barbecue. Ever since our skinny dip, Corinne and I had somehow gotten over an invisible barrier. We'd left a lot unsaid, but somehow we had an understanding. I knew Corinne was unhappy, but she made sure I didn't dwell on it. The few times I'd tried to talk to her, she had waved me off and encouraged me to be with Simon.

"Dinnertime," my aunt called out. We all drifted to the table and piled our plates.

As everyone munched happily, I relaxed. Things were going okay. Good food solved a lot of problems.

Simon made witty conversation, but I could see the small muscle in his jaw flickering when Mr. Ross took a deep swig of his drink. I scooched closer to Simon, pressing my knee against his to remind him we were both in this thing. If our families did embarrass us—if they got too loud or made the wrong comment—we'd get through it.

Smooth, superficial conversation (and plenty of wine for the grown-ups) helped us through dinner and on to dessert. While Aunt Kathleen heaped raspberries and kiwi fruit into bowls and the fathers discussed deep-sea fishing, Mom started asking Simon about his future. "You'll be a senior next year. Any plans for college?" my mother asked, lifting a spoonful of raspberries to her lips.

I froze. I'd been waiting for this. The third degree. And Mom wouldn't like the answer. Simon's vagueness wouldn't impress her. What I loved about him—his lightness, the fact that he didn't take himself too seriously—would not sit well with her. Mom had a traditional approach: men had to be serious and leave the lightness to women.

"Well, Mrs. Gordon, I'm not really much of a planner," Simon replied, as I handed him a bowl of fruit. "I think planning is overrated."

"Overrated?" My mother looked nervous. *Here we go.* I could just picture the lecture I would be receiving later that night. *Dilettant... too laid-back...*

But Simon seemed undeterred by my mother's expression. If anything, it made him more eager to explain his theories on life. "I don't feel ready for college. Maybe someday. But not now." I put down my spoon.

Simon continued happily, unfazed by my warning looks. "I really love to paint. I want to learn by experience. Go backpacking through Europe. Take menial jobs, see and paint in all the places that produced Picasso and Vermeer and Titian and Rembrandt..."

Simon's eyes sparkled. Mom hadn't moved an inch. "I'm only seventeen, so I figure I should just take it as it comes. You know?"

No, I answered silently. *She does not know.* This was the person who had been planning Eva's career since birth, grooming and coaching her for a glittering future.

"Yes, I think I *do* know," Mom replied, nodding vigorously. "I always wanted to spend a year or two in Europe, experiencing the street-theater culture of Paris. Perhaps not with a backpack *per se* but…"

I was blown away. I sat back, my eyes riveted on my mother, a piece of kiwi lodged in my throat. Mom looked bewitched. She was totally taken by Simon, lapping up his every word, her eyes shimmering.

But I guessed I ought not to be so surprised. Simon had that effect, an ability to make you excited about things you'd never considered before.

"Our son is a dreamer, Maxine," Simon's father stated, interrupting my mother's own dreamy Euro-fantasy. Evidently he'd overheard the conversation. "But the reality is set. Simon will go to Wharton for business school."

"Maybe we shouldn't talk about this now, Dad," Simon said stiffly.

"Simon doesn't like the idea, but we can't always do what we like," Mr. Ross said, his voice light but strained.

"We can if we support ourselves while doing it," Simon replied evenly, but his father shook his head.

"You can do whatever you want after college. But family traditions must come first." Mr. Ross looked from Simon to my mother. "Our other sons are both Whartonites."

"Family tradition is a wonderful thing," Mom chimed in, apparently impressed by Simon's family's lofty connections. Or maybe she was just being polite and trying to ignore the tension.

"Tradition?" Simon quipped. "I think that word implies more than one generation."

Simon's father struggled to retain his composure, anger flashing on his face. "Our oldest is in the navy now," he said proudly. "Rising rapidly through the ranks. A place like Wharton builds all the necessary life skills, no matter where you go from there."

"It seems Simon just wants to take his own initiative, George," Dad broke in. I was surprised. My mild-mannered dad hardly ever said much, and especially not when there was friction between others. "Sometimes you just want to carve out your own path. I didn't do that. I went into my family's business. But my wife was a free spirit," he added, smiling at Mom.

"Business school is an excellent foundation for anything. It teaches you how to use your head," Simon's dad continued, refilling his wine glass.

"You mean like all these business people who've been losing everyone's money and eviscerating our economy?" Simon shot back.

The table fell into a hushed silence. "You don't have a clue what you're talking about!" Simon's father barked. "And it's a privileged kid who learns the word 'eviscerating.' How do you think I pay that private school tab, son?" He took a deep slug of his wine.

"I would have killed for the opportunity I'm giving my boys. But—" Mr. Ross shrugged—"when everything's handed to you a platter, there's no respect. No sense of obligation. At least that's what we're finding with our youngest!" He chuckled, but his laugh was empty of humor.

"Dad, let's change the subject. We're being very boring." Simon's tone was casual, but I could tell he was embarrassed and upset. I also thought I saw something else in Simon's eyes. He was afraid of his father. Their eyes locked across the table in an extension of some private angry conversation.

"You'll see, son. Business school isn't what you think it is. I'm all for the arts." Mr. Ross turned and addressed the table in general. "I own several pieces of world-class art myself. Matter of fact, when we were last here I purchased a drawing by Jackson Pollock." He smiled at the table. "But a boy who spends his college years painting in cafés?" He shook his head, his gaze resettling on Simon. "Not after everything I've put into your education."

"Who's Jackson Peacock?" Eva asked. For once, not even my mother answered her.

"Oh yeah, the Jackson Pollock," Simon said lightly, scooping fruit onto his spoon. "Don't you keep it in a safe?"

"It's too valuable to hang," Mr. Ross retorted.

"Too valuable to hang." Simon repeated the words softly, under his breath, but his father smacked his hand on the table.

Everyone froze at the loud smack of Mr. Ross's palm. "When are you ever going to learn to keep your mouth shut?" he growled.

"I don't know, Dad. You never have," Simon replied quietly.

"Hey, why don't we go to the beach while the parents have coffee," Corinne suggested loudly, her voice falsely bright. She sprang to her feet, looking from Simon to me to Beth.

"Okay," I answered quickly and stood up to gather plates.

"Let me take your plate, Mr. Ross," Corinne chirped in a sugary tone. I took Mrs. Ross's plate. During the entire conversation, she'd said nothing. Her eyes seemed sad but also distant, like she was somewhere else entirely. Simon mumbled something about getting some more lemonade, but when we got to the kitchen he was leaning moodily against the refrigerator, his mouth curled at a dejected slant, his eyes vulnerable and furious at the same time.

"Have a beer," Corinne suggested, whipping a six-pack of Sam Adams from the fridge and sneaking three.

"He can't drink," I replied automatically, but Simon took the beer.

"One beer won't kill him," Corinne remarked, grabbing her beach bag. "Let's split."

. . .

"I'm coming!" Eva shouted, trailing after us as Corinne, Beth, Simon, and I trudged into the dunes. "I'm allowed!"

"Of course you are, Evie," Beth said, just a hair before I tried to tell Eva the exact opposite. But I didn't really care. My concerns were with Simon, with the defeated slump of his shoulders and the deep burn of anger in his eyes. I hoped maybe we could take a walk alone so he could vent about his dad, get it out of his system.

But Simon seemed to prefer lying in the dunes, sipping on his beer and watching the light fade to the gold-pink of sunset, his mouth set in a tense line. I wondered if the beer would interact with his epilepsy medicine, but I didn't dare say anything. He was clearly too upset to care about that for now. And though he tried to smile when I laid a reassuring hand on his shoulder, his jaw clenched.

"I'm sorry it got like that, Mia," Simon apologized. "I shouldn't have let it."

"It's not your fault," I replied gently.

We watched Eva and Beth walk down to the water. "My father... I've done *everything* to get him to drop this Wharton idea."

He shook his head miserably. "All my life he's tried to control me. He'll be breathing down my neck until the day I die."

"Have you ever shown him your paintings?" I asked softly. "Maybe he just doesn't understand—"

"He never will," Simon interrupted, planting his beer in the sand in frustration. "He's a total meathead. He has all these fake manners he's learned over the years, but he's a boor. *I own several pieces of world-class art myself.* He doesn't care about his collection. To him it's just money. An investment. My father appreciating Jackson Pollock! What a joke."

"Just tell your father to go to hell. You don't need him to go to Europe or anywhere else," Corinne spoke up. We both turned. I guess she'd been so quiet we'd forgotten she was there. She tapped her cigarette ash into the wind, where it drifted and disappeared. "If it's what you want, you shouldn't let anyone get in the way of it," she added with feeling.

I smiled at her. But she looked away from me, staring down to the sand. "I mean, whatever," she added, absently. "If we were in a movie, that would be the right line for me to add. But what would I know? I have no burning desire to go anywhere. I just know where

I *don't* want to go," she muttered darkly.

"No, you're right," I said, looking first at Corinne and then over to Simon. "You have to ignore him."

Simon nodded. "I'm taking off when I'm done with high school," he said, his words heavy with determination. "He can't stop me," he added.

"No, he can't." I squeezed Simon's arm, but I could feel the tight pull of his body. I wondered: *How far would his father go to keep Simon under his thumb?*

Corinne got up and walked to Beth and Eva at the water's edge. We watched silently as they built a sand castle. I leaned back on my arms. A sliver of crescent moon hovered in the sky. Simon followed my gaze.

"Don't you think the moon looks like a bitten-off fingernail?" he mused. "When I was a kid, I thought God was some nail-biting giant. He worried so much about all of our earthly problems that every few weeks he chewed his thumbnail off and spat it into the sky."

I smiled. "Do you still believe in God?"

Simon frowned, considering. "I believe there's something out there…Maybe I'll be disappointed if I die and I'm proven wrong." He shrugged. "But that's beside the point."

"That *is* the point," I countered. "If you believe in something and you're proven wrong, then it was a waste of time. You were fooling yourself all along." I bit my lip, wishing I hadn't sounded so negative. Simon didn't need a doom-filled discussion from me right now.

But instead of depressing him, my words did the opposite. "That's not true. Believing is never a waste of time." Simon looked at me intently, his eyes flickering. "Even if you're wrong, you could have been right. Take me, with my painting. I don't know if I'm any good. So maybe I shouldn't try because maybe I'd be setting myself up for disappointment. But it's like you looking for old coins on the beach. Whether you find any or not is for bonus points—it's the search that counts. It's the belief that they might be out there."

There was so much conviction in Simon's voice that I wanted it too. But I couldn't believe in God because, when it came down to it, I was driven by facts. I wasn't a person of faith. Very few people really are, I realized. But Simon was. It was in everything he did and said: some kind of glow I'd never seen in anyone else.

"But how can you believe so much, when everything around you…?" I trailed off, an image of Simon's father coming to mind, his stern, steely eyes, his determination to make Simon follow the course he'd laid out for him. I thought of my aunt and uncle; I thought of Corinne, how everything and everyone seemed a symbol of something that had failed. Even if there was something noble about having faith, it still hurt when you lost it.

The sound of a breaking wave echoed across the water. "I have doubts. I get afraid, same as anyone." Simon's eyes glazed over. But then they refocused and he smiled at me. "Nothing is for certain. Except maybe one thing."

"What's that?"

"If you don't have any dreams, then they won't come true."

Simon leaned against me and I shifted, putting my arms around him, drawing him closer. Holding him in my arms felt right and certain—as true as Simon's words. I rested my cheek against his hair. I didn't understand all the convoluted arguments that raced through my mind, thoughts about faith and proof and how it all fit together. It didn't matter.

Putting yourself at risk...that was the only path to anything meaningful. The biggest risk was in *not* taking a risk. I was starting to see that for myself in a whole lot of ways: if you kept your light inside of yourself too long, it might burn out altogether.

● ● ●

"Dubious family, but Simon is lovely—such a charmer, and such charisma!" Mom remarked after the barbecue.

I smiled at her. Though I didn't want to admit to myself how much it mattered, what she thought of Simon did really matter to me. Of course, if Mom had thought Simon wasn't right for me, I would have just ignored her. It wasn't her choice to make. But she liked him. And I was happy about it.

"His father is awfully hard on him," my aunt said as we stacked the dishwasher. "You'd think he'd be more in tune with his children, but it seems he's all about himself."

"Funny, that," Corinne remarked coolly, gliding past her mother on her way to the fridge.

An uncomfortable silence hung in the air.

"I'm exhausted," Beth said to no one in particular.

There was nothing more to say. We finished up the dishes and went our separate ways.

• • •

Alone in my bedroom at last, I closed the door, looking forward to some alone time. But muffled, angry conversation drifted in through my open window as Corinne and my aunt argued in Corinne's room. I turned up the volume on the CD player, but I could still hear them underneath the music, underneath my thoughts. Until Mom peeked her head around the door.

"That was an interesting evening!" she declared brightly, closing the door behind her. Suddenly I pictured Simon's father's face: his angry eyes, his harsh words.

"It wasn't boring," I joked feebly, wishing she hadn't come in. Mom had been on her best behavior all evening, but I had a feeling she'd be unable to resist a quick heart-to-heart with me, chock full of judgments about the unsuitability of Simon's family and the problems of the newly rich.

"Simon's got a very striking face," Mom volunteered, coming to sit on the edge of my bed. "He's handsome in an old-fashioned way."

"I think so."

Mom smiled. "He has a strong chin. A good chin is very important."

"Yeah." I had to smile too. "I agree."

I twisted my hands in my lap, waiting for a pointed comment, a warning, a loaded observation.

Instead, Mom ventured timidly: "What I like most about Simon is what I saw missing in Jake."

I looked up, surprised. "What do you mean?" Before, I would never have wanted to hear Mom's opinions on Jake. But now I could handle it. And I was curious.

"Trustworthiness," Mom replied, taking my hand in hers. "I can see he really cares about you, Mimi. You can trust him." She patted my hand. "That's a rare quality. I saw it in your father when we first met. I knew he was the real deal." She kissed my cheek and headed for the door.

"Mom?" I said as she walked away.

"What?"

"Thanks."

"For what?"

A lump appeared in my throat, like I'd swallowed a bird's egg. "I don't know." And I didn't know exactly. But I thought of what Dad had said. About how Mom had loved him so much she'd dropped everything for him. And about how she'd been hurt that I hadn't confided in her about Simon. For what felt like a long time, I looked at my mother, at the clear blue of her eyes, the small lines creasing the skin around them. She cocked her head at me, a hand on the door handle.

"You're tired. I'll leave you alone now."

"I'm glad you like Simon," I said softly.

Mom paused, turned back to me, and then waved good night. She gently closed my door, and I listened as her footsteps clicked down the hall and into silence.

I lay back on my bed. If there was hope for me and my mother, then maybe Corinne and her mother would figure it out too. I took deep breaths letting all the bad feelings seep out of me. But I couldn't help fearing Corinne would have some kind of meltdown. Or that her family was falling apart. What if this was the last time our families ever spent time together?

The thought was too alarming. I let it just drift, drift away...

• • •

A light but insistent tapping on my window. The flick of a lighter—on-off, on-off, on-off. A red glow in the window pane.

Bleary-eyed, I staggered to the window, smiling sleepily at the dark shape of Simon silhouetted behind the glass. I didn't know what time it was. Had I drifted off for only a few minutes, or was it already early morning?

"Shh," I giggled as I opened the window wider for him to climb in. "You'll wake everyone."

"I came to say good-bye," Simon said into the darkness of my room. "I'm leaving."

"You're what?" I turned on my bedside lamp and glanced at my clock: 1 a.m. I was wide awake now. "What happened to your face?"

"I'm getting out of here," Simon said in a low voice.

"Going where? What—?" I reached up a hand to touch the side of his cheek. His cheekbone was swollen, the skin a deep red. His lip was split.

Simon caught my hand halfway to his face. "Don't," he said fiercely.

"If you're going somewhere, I'm going too," I said firmly, pulling on a pair of jeans in the low light.

"You don't have to," Simon growled. "You don't—" he stopped, and I saw tears glittering in his eyes.

I pressed my hand to his chest. "Shh," I said in a soothing voice. "Go back outside. I'm coming."

My heart thudded as I threw on a sweatshirt, grabbed my flashlight, and climbed out of the window. I didn't know what was worse, seeing Simon's cheek and cut lip, or seeing the tears in his eyes. I edged along the roof, my knees suddenly shaky. My throat felt dry and sandpapery as I shimmied down. Simon was waiting for me at the bottom, his hands jammed in his pockets.

"What's going on?" I whispered anxiously.

Simon grabbed my hand and led me not down to the beach like I'd expected, but up around the front of the house and down the long gravel driveway. His father's yellow car was badly parked outside the gates of Wind Song, half on the shoulder of the road, half in the road itself.

"Where are we going?" I slid obediently into the passenger seat, my eyes flicking to a duffel bag perched on the backseat.

"I don't know. Anywhere." Simon wiped his eyes roughly and stared straight ahead as he gunned the engine.

My throat constricted. I could see the outline of Simon's swollen cheekbone in the light shining from the lamps in the driveway. The corner of his mouth was a bright raised edge of red, and his eyes were wild and skittish.

"Did your father—?" My question hung in the air. Simon's silence was confirmation. Anger sliced through me in a blinding flash. I was right to have seen something hard in Mr. Ross's eyes the very first time I met him. But apparently he was more than just tough: he was cruel.

"Let's get out of here," Simon said gruffly, turning on the car lights. "You with me?"

"I'm with you." I felt sick to my stomach, but I didn't want to show it. The empty shock in his damp eyes made me want to cry. He didn't look like himself at all.

Simon pulled out onto the road. "I just need to drive," he said, pumping the accelerator. "It doesn't matter where, so long as it isn't here."

Instinctively I gripped the door handle as Simon veered onto Dune Road. I bit my lip as the speedometer climbed. And then the car came to a screeching halt.

"Oh. I forgot." Simon uttered a dry laugh as our headlights illuminated a triangular warning sign: Dead End. We'd arrived at the Shinnecock Inlet, and we couldn't go any further. The car puttered to a standstill, and Simon gripped the steering wheel and hung his head.

"What happened?" I prodded him gently.

He rested his head on the steering wheel. "I asked for it." He looked up to the sky, closed his eyes, and sank back into his seat. "My comments about business at dinner were bad enough, but it was what I said about his art collection that really got him. My dad was so pissed with me for showing him up in front of your family. I told him he'd done it all by himself. That he was just a crass idiot trying to buy his way to respectability, and any Wasp could see that a mile away. You don't say that stuff to my father. Especially not when he's loaded."

"Ouch," I said quietly. "At least you were gentle," I added, my voice teasing in an attempt to downplay my anxiety. I didn't want to upset him even more.

Simon half-smiled, lit a cigarette, and stared off into the darkness. We couldn't see much beyond the headlights, but you could feel the water out there in the bay. It had a presence, as though it were alive.

In the background, somewhere out to our left, the distant clap of waves from the Atlantic beaches echoed through the night.

"I wanted to hit him back," Simon said, turning to look at me, his voice trembling. "But I couldn't. I don't know if I was afraid. I just couldn't. And my father just looked at me then, Mia. Like I was a piece of dirt. And he said if I was a man, I'd hit him back."

"That's such BS," I muttered, reaching out to take Simon's hand. But he kept gripping the steering wheel, as if he was going somewhere.

"I don't know…" Simon trailed off. "Maybe he's right."

"He's wrong," I said fiercely. "He's a bully."

"I'm a coward."

"That's a stupid word. And it's not true either."

"It is." Simon sighed, ran a hand through his hair. "But I'd rather be a coward than a jerk-off like him—"

"Don't!" I said gently, laying my hand on Simon's arm. "You're beating up on yourself now."

Simon was quiet for a moment and I could see the shine of tears in his eyes, though he kept his gaze fixed straight ahead. "I told him I hated his guts. That he made me sick," Simon sniffed and wiped his eyes impatiently with the back of his wrist. "And then I left. I wanted to run away, you know? To get away from him. From this place…And here we are—" he looked at me again, flashing me a rueful smile. "In a dead end."

"We could turn around," I suggested. "We could still try."

Simon shook his head. "It doesn't matter. We won't get far." He laughed hoarsely. "Not in this old clunker. This is style over substance. Not a good bet, in the long run."

I put my hand up to Simon's head, and this time he let me thread my fingers gently through his hair. "We could go swimming," I suggested.

"Yeah?" Simon took my hand and folded it between both of his. I shot him my best seductive smile.

"What are you bringing that for?" I asked as Simon grabbed his duffel bag off the backseat.

"I'm not going home. I'll spend the night on the beach."

"Don't be stupid. You can stay with us."

"Oh, yeah," Simon replied with a sarcastic grin. "Your family will really love me when they find me in your room tomorrow morning."

"I can set you up on the couch in the living room," I argued back. "There's plenty of room."

For a moment, Simon said nothing. "No," he said finally, his voice low and quiet. He kicked a loose piece of gravel, and we listened to it skitter away into silence. "I'd prefer they don't see—" he broke off, gesturing somewhere in the direction of his face.

"Simon," I said softly. "Please—"

"Hey," he interrupted loudly and deliberately, pointing at a driveway to the left. "That's Dragon's Lair!" The house was hidden, a curved driveway and thick hedges keeping it from prying eyes. But the mailbox—shaped like a dragon's head—was a giveaway. "I guess we'll be using their beach access," Simon added, gesturing at me. "Come on."

We moved down the dark driveway, our feet crunching on gravel. "Trespassers will be mauled," Simon joked as we rounded the last bend of the driveway. The mansion rose through the darkness, up and up and up, its crazy proportions suggesting a movie set sooner than a home that actually belonged to a human being. In a high corner of a ghostly tower, a single square of light shone through from a room.

"I think there are gargoyles coming off of those turrets," Simon whispered.

"And *I* think you secretly love this house. You just don't want to admit it because it goes against your mantra of impeccable taste at all times," I teased in a hushed voice as we stood there gawking.

"There is something bizarrely cool about the place," Simon admitted. "It has a kind of weird, surreal power."

"I think it's creepy," I murmured, tugging on Simon's hand. "Let's get to the beach before someone finds us."

Simon turned his head, his eyes gleaming. "Not yet," he said quietly. "I have a better idea. Let's break in."

"Break in?" I repeated dubiously. "Why?"

"Why *not*? That's the question, Mia. When will you get that?" Simon replied cheerfully.

"So *why not* just *not* look for trouble? Have you ever thought of that?" But I'd spent enough time with him to know that when Simon got an idea in his head, it was pointless to try and go against him. In that way, he was like his dad.

"We can look at the shark tanks. The underwater grotto. See if all those things really exist. Come on. It'll be fun!"

"There are probably people in there," I countered. "There's a light on."

"You told me yourself they couldn't rent it out this summer, much less sell it," Simon argued. "Your aunt told you, right?"

"There must be a caretaker," I said weakly.

"A light on in a window. That doesn't mean anyone's in the house."

"How did we become friends again?" I joked as Simon pulled me toward the mansion. But even though I was definitely *not* pleased to be going into that house, I was also glad that after the awful events of the night, Simon seemed like himself again.

"I bet the caretaker's fast asleep, stashed in some cottage on the grounds," Simon said as we poked around the stone walls of the house looking for an entrance of some kind.

"I bet the caretaker's stashed *inside* the mansion," I said to Simon.

"Let's find out."

Simon walked up to the huge front door. It was made of metal, like some medieval relic. Maybe it was a medieval relic. The door had, of course, a gigantic knocker shaped like—what else?—a dragon's head. And in the dragon's head, a glowing red button.

"This would be the doorbell, I presume." Simon pressed it, and, from deep within the house, we heard the strains of organ chords, like a riff from some medieval monk hit.

"Cute," Simon pronounced.

"That was smart," I whispered sarcastically. "Now what?"

"Now if someone comes, we pretend we're looking for a party and have the wrong house. If no one comes, we know the place is empty."

No one did come, and we spent the next half hour crawling around the castle, looking for a way in.

"Open sesame." Simon's eyes lit up as he spotted a half-open basement window.

He climbed in and stood still for a moment. "See?" he whispered triumphantly. "There's no alarm. They know no one wants to steal anything from here. They probably can't *give* their stuff away. They're probably hoping for a burglar."

"They probably have a serious *silent* alarm system," I muttered, gingerly climbing in through the window after Simon. "Like lasers or something," I added, but Simon seemed not to have heard me.

"Pass me your flashlight." He swept the beam across the room, revealing three large washers and driers. "Interesting," Simon said. "I guess dragons have a lot of laundry…"

After a few minutes of fumbling around in the laundry room, we made our way up to the top of the stairs and out into a hallway.

"Check it out," Simon murmured as we padded through big, echoing rooms. "I told you no one was in here."

Our mouths dropped open like trapdoors as we wandered through the cavernous interior of Dragon's Lair, the flashlight picking up either empty, vault-like rooms or the sinister shapes of sheet-draped furniture. It was like walking through a tomb or a museum that had been closed for renovations.

"Come on," Simon whispered.

I paused, hanging back outside the big, dark shape of a door. I was still scared someone would come and find us any minute. I didn't want to go deeper inside the house. What if we couldn't find our way back out? But Simon pushed against the door, and it swung open, saloon-style.

"Bingo!" Simon shone the flashlight ahead. The beam picked up what looked like a wall of rock and a long, deep, rippling pit that curved into a wide circle underneath the high point of the rock wall.

"Let's get some more light," Simon said, fumbling around the edge of the wall. "Maybe here…abracadabra!" With a click of a switch, the room was bathed in an eerie, fluorescent glow that seemed to come from the pit itself. Now we could make out the inner contours of what must have been the indoor lagoon, built on fake rocks. Except it was drained of water and empty, the underwater light illuminating not tropical fish and electric-blue water but gray concrete instead.

"Wow…" Simon shook his head and made a face. "Preposterous!" he mumbled, holding his hands up over his face in an exaggerated version of his horror.

"Oh, it's so *you*, Simon. You love it," I joked.

Playing along, Simon turned to an imaginary broker. "A marvelous water feature," he said loudly, gesturing at the "lagoon." "What's your asking price again?…Only twenty mill? We'll take the house!"

Simon stepped around the lagoon. He crouched at the edge. And then he jumped in.

I ran to the edge, alarmed at the hard slap as he landed on the concrete floor. "You okay?"

"I'm king of the castle!" he shouted, holding his arms wide as he straightened up. "And you, my dear, are queen."

I giggled and positioned myself carefully on the rim of the lagoon, my legs dangling over into the emptiness. We looked up at the giant wall of rock. I could imagine a waterfall splashing down, its rushing sound filling the room.

But as I lingered on the edge of the dry pool, my laughter drained away. Seeing this strange room incomplete and abandoned made me feel sad. "You have to admit, the guy had vision," I reflected. "It's an ugly vision, but it's his own."

As I spoke, Simon explored the lagoon. He touched the walls and took running jumps, attempting to climb the curves, his pale skin glowing in the neon-blue of the pool light.

"He had guts," I mused. "At least he knew who he wanted to be, no matter what anyone else had to say about it."

"But it didn't get him anywhere," Simon murmured. "I mean, he went bankrupt trying to express himself. So much for living out his dream."

Simon lit a cigarette and sat down. He rested his head against a curving wall, his purplish bruise glowing in the fluorescent light. He took a long drag, the smoke drifting up in a gray-blue plume around him.

"But yeah," he said, looking around the room and nodding, a wry smile—half-grimace from the pain—spreading across his face. "There's something to be said for bucking the system. And this guy definitely stuck a poker up the snooty collective Southampton ass, right?" Simon chuckled into the emptiness.

"I wish I could hate my father, you know?" he said suddenly. "It would make everything easier if it were just pure hatred I felt for the asshole. If I didn't care what he thought about me at all."

"He's your dad," I said simply.

Simon stood up and began pacing. "The old man thinks he's a great one too. And that getting me set up in that stupid school is the best thing he could do for me." He sighed. "But I can't hate my father. In his screwed-up way, he thinks he's helping me. It's because all of his life, he had nothing. People looked down on him for being nothing. He came from nothing. Everything he's done, he's done out of self-determination."

Simon walked to the base of the waterfall and leaned against it on his palms, craning his head as he looked up, as if he expected the water to come down onto his head. "A self-made man." His voice echoed, a hollow sound reverberating off the concrete and fake rock. "But somehow he's forgotten that there's something good about determining your own path," he added with a tight smile, drawing the cigarette to his lips. "The apple doesn't fall far from the tree with me and my father. But he just sees me as a troublemaker. The black sheep."

I didn't know what to say to make Simon feel better. I didn't have any answer—not about Simon and his father, or about what it meant to be yourself in this world and what sacrifices were worth making to get somewhere. Instead of offering lame words of consolation, I held out my hand to Simon, and he helped me down.

"We haven't been swimming yet." I wrapped my arms around Simon's waist. "Let's get out of here."

"But we could swim where we're standing," Simon protested, running a hand down my back and pulling me closer toward him. "In this lovely lagoon."

I smiled. "It's breathtaking," I said sarcastically. Still, the pit was pretty impressive in its own strange way, more so now that I was standing inside it. The rocks glinted in the underwater pool light, their shapes and contours rising like cave walls around us. It was spooky and tacky at the same time, but it was also kind of beautiful. "Hey," I added, spotting black mesh built into the walls in regular intervals. "I think there are speakers in here."

"A little music would be nice." Simon pulled me tighter and grabbed my hand, his cigarette dangling from his lips. We began to dance a little, just a small shuffle across the floor. I started giggling again. Simon stopped and pulled an iPod from his pocket. "I almost forgot. I do have music." He climbed out of the lagoon. "If I can just find the system," he muttered, opening a cabinet built into the wall.

Minutes later, music filled the room. "*Kind of Blue*," I said, as Simon climbed back down to join me.

"Not anymore," Simon joked, sliding his arms around my waist. "I'm happy now."

As Simon's lips found mine, heat surged up through my body. I giggled, almost losing my balance. Was I dizzy from the kiss or because we were still dancing, turning together in an empty fake lagoon?

I didn't know, and I soon stopped caring because Simon's fingertips were now tracing the line of my T-shirt at my waist and his mouth had moved to the gap between my neck and my shoulder. His hand snaked in under the cotton, and, as his bare hand touched my skin, moving up to stroke my stomach and then my ribs, a delirious spinning pleasure shot through me. I felt the scientific truth of my body—how we are ninety percent water and hardly solid at all.

"Enjoying your swim?" Simon asked, his voice husky.

"Water's a little cold," I murmured.

Simon took my hand and led me out of the lagoon and the blue light. We climbed the stairs built into the side of the pit. We moved through the doorway of the cave-like room and into darkness, the glowing tip of Simon's still-burning cigarette now the strongest light around.

I grabbed my flashlight from the back pocket of Simon's pants and clicked it on as we moved silently from one dark room to another.

"There," Simon said, as the beam of my flashlight picked up the white sheet-draped oblong of what looked like a gigantic couch near a big picture window. "Definitely room for two," Simon murmured, pulling me down on top of him as he sank onto the couch.

"Hold it." He twisted on the couch and balanced his half-smoked cigarette on the floor, the glowing tip pointing up.

"Careful," I said softly, as he pulled me on top of him. "I don't want to hurt your lip." But Simon seemed to need kisses more than caution.

"Thanks for being here with me," he whispered. I pulled back, taking in the sadness and exhaustion I could make out in the deep recesses of his eyes and the swell of his bruised cheek. "Everything feels so bad. Except for you."

I softly touched Simon's face, and he moved his hands onto my hips and then slowly up to my shirt. I closed my eyes and thought I could hear the blood pulsing through my veins, drumming in my ears in a rushing sound, like when you hold a seashell to your ear and imagine you can hear the beat of waves.

Simon pressed his body against mine, his fingers tangling in my hair, and I wondered whether any of this was real—in this strange dark room that felt as if it had been dreamed up by a set designer. Maybe I *was* inside a dream…except that it had a sharp, too-real smell inside of it.

"Stop—" I whispered to Simon, stiffening in his arms. "What's that smell?"

Simon looked questioningly into my eyes and then his eyes widened. "Jesus!"

"Fire!" I yelled, springing back off the couch. Simon jumped up, and the two of us stared for a split second, shocked, as the white sheet of the couch arced and brightened into a glowing crescent of orange flame.

"Shit!" Simon said. He stamped on the edge of the burning sheet and ground out the remains of his cigarette, which had caused the sheet to catch fire.

And then he started laughing. And for some reason, so did I. "Get some water!" Simon ordered, still stomping on the sheet, while I just stood there, watching and giggling, somewhere between hysterical with laughter and just plain hysterical.

"Sorry!" Though the scenario still seemed weirdly funny, I snapped out of my stupor and grabbed the flashlight. The sheet had begun to smoke, and the flames had spread to the couch. I bolted to action, pushing into rooms, looking for a bathroom, a kitchen, some source of water. I pushed open two doors. More empty rooms. On the third try, I found a sink. I turned the faucets on, but nothing came out.

"Water's off!" I yelled, running back to the couch.

"I think I got it." Simon had dragged a sleeping bag from his duffel bag and was smothering red flames with it. I started to cough as the smoke rose around us. Simon had put out most of the fire, but flecks of red and orange still sprang from the sheet, licking the fabric of the couch. He went at them with the sleeping bag.

It smelled awful in there. I longed to open a window, but I thought oxygen might fan the dying sparks back to life.

"Is it out?" I rasped, half-laughing, half-hacking from the fumes.

"Almost."

And then we both froze. A high-pitched beeping sound pierced the air around us.

"Shit!" Simon said.

"Smoke alarm!" I stated the obvious, rooted to my spot on the floor. Each shrill beep drilled a hole in my skull. Someone would surely be on their way to find us. Still, I was grinning foolishly at the event. And at Simon too, stumbling around with his sleeping bag, snuffing out small flames and laughing.

"Hurry!" I said, grinding my heel into the smoldering edge of the couch. But though the flames were almost out, a patch of carpet had begun to glow red against the darkness.

And then we heard it. A deep scraping sound. The front door.

"Who's there?" a deep, muted voice called out. Faint. We still had time but not much. Someone was most definitely inside the house. Soon they would make it to our floor.

"Come on!" I hissed at Simon as he jumped on the burning carpet, extinguishing a circle of crimson, a shower of sparks kicking up around his feet.

"Get out of here!" he ordered me in a loud whisper. "Go! Now!"

"But what about—?" I stammered. Now I was really panicking. Simon would get caught if he didn't drop what he was doing and run.

"Go *now!*" Simon urged in a hoarse whisper. "I'll find you later!"

I stood there, mute as a pillar.

"Mia!" Simon hissed. "*Go!*"

I did what he said. I ran. Or rather, I slipped away. Down into the dark hallways, feeling my way along walls and trying to map out the rooms I'd been in, the sound of footsteps coming closer. Someone was climbing stairs beneath me. My eyes had adjusted to the dark, but the house was so big, I wasn't sure where I was.

The footsteps disappeared. My heart crashed in my chest as I crept down a corridor. Had the person gone...or would I walk right into him? The thought terrified me. All I wanted was to get out of that house. What had we been thinking? Now what had been so much fun seemed like the worst idea in the world. The house felt alive, like it was a big hand holding me in its grip, refusing to let me out.

A light went on at the end of a passageway. I held my breath, clamped my teeth so hard together I could feel the roots in every one. I was still in shadow, protected, but for how much longer? I blinked. I could see a stairwell ahead, or what I prayed was a stairwell: a curving blackness.

But even if those were stairs, was it too late to make it down? I kept my eyes on the end of the passageway, waiting for the dark shape I knew would come. It was as though the volume in my head was turned up, so even the slightest sound—my hand moving across the plaster wall, my own breath—seemed deafening. *Footsteps?*

A moment passed in numb anticipation.

Nothing.

It was now or never. I took a breath and inched toward the stairs. I grasped the balustrade and eased my way down. Still nothing. I was in the clear.

I stumbled down the stairs and found myself in the laundry room. The sight of the open window flooded me with cool relief. Our way in would be my way out.

Outside I sank to the grass, almost deliriously happy to be in the open air, away from menacing footsteps and the acrid smell of smoke. A post-adrenaline drowsiness combined with a thick, smoky feeling deep inside my lungs. I had to concentrate on breathing deeply, letting the fresh salt air sweep through me.

Once I could breathe and think normally again, I went from calm right back to panic. Simon was still in there. What if the fire had spread? What if he was in real danger? *He is not,* I told myself sternly. The fire had been small. The caretaker or whoever it was that had answered the smoke alarm would surely have found a fire extinguisher.

Logically, I knew my fear was irrational. But I knew I wouldn't feel okay until Simon came out of that house. And from where I was, I couldn't see anything, no sign of the fire, no sign of Simon or anybody else. The stillness was disturbing. The house was a vault, sealing Simon in.

I moved behind the bushes and positioned myself at a spot where I could see the front door of Dragon's Lair. I waited.

It was so quiet. My legs began to cramp from crouching. Minutes dragged by. Finally, a sound: the crunch of gravel followed by the filmy whiteness of headlights sweeping down the driveway and across the dark doorway to the house. A fire truck had arrived.

I gulped. The sight of the truck suddenly made things more serious. It wasn't a big-city fire truck, but it was still a fire truck bleeding deep-red through the darkness.

What were we thinking?

Three men got out, wearing helmets. The static of shortwave voices cut through the air. A shuffle of footsteps, and the men were inside, dark shapes sliding into the house like shadows. I swallowed hard. My throat was completely dry, lined with smoke. Again, I was plunged back into stillness and silence.

A cricket started up, keeping me company with its low whirring buzz, and a pang of gratitude welled up in me for the sound. And just when my legs didn't seem like they'd hold up through the razor-sharp cramping, the front door of the mansion opened, the dark rectangle opening to reveal grayish-blue light. Several shapes spilled out of the house. Flashlights painted white lines in the night. Voices dipped and rose in excitement and anger. One of them was Simon's.

Yes! It was only when I exhaled on hearing Simon's voice that I realized I'd been holding my breath, waiting for him to get out of the house, digging my fingernails into the palm of my hand.

Simon's voice floated in snatches through the air, something about "sorry" and "homeless." He sounded cheery, theatrical even—being Simon, he was no doubt enjoying the thrill and ridiculousness of his situation, spinning a very complicated, elaborate lie for the benefit of the fire department or whoever he was talking to…But my relief at hearing Simon seeped away as doors slammed, the truck chugged to life, and soon he was gone along with them.

I was alone. Even the cricket had deserted me. It was time to leave.

• • •

Wisps of fog drifted in off the ocean, a coolness all around. Walking home from Dragon's Lair across the beach, I was grateful for the salt scrub of the air stripping away the smoke from my hair and clothes. I hugged my arms to my chest, a gnawing unease settling over me. Whatever happened with the authorities and Simon would be bad enough, but I knew the real trouble would come from Mr. Ross. By now, they'd probably called him in.

I broke into a run.

I dreaded the inevitable: Simon's father would hit the roof when he discovered what had happened. *Simon will talk himself out of it,* I tried to reassure myself as I slipped through my window and stumbled into bed. But the words sounded false.

chapter fifteen

"Well, good afternoon, Sleeping Beauty," Dad said, fixing himself a glass of lemonade in the kitchen. "You sure slept in."

It was one o'clock. I'd woken up groggy and disoriented, sheets twisted around my feet. Bad dreams I couldn't remember disappeared when I sat up but left me with a nagging feeling of doom.

"Did Simon call?" I asked anxiously. "Or did he come by?"

"Not that I know of," Mom replied, slicing tomatoes at the sink. "How about washing your face before lunch?"

But I was out the door already and racing to the beach. Corinne and Beth lay like tiny dolls way off on the dunes, but I averted my eyes and picked up my pace. I didn't have time for them now. A bead of sweat trickled down my back as a fluorescent sun beat down. It was so hot that not even the ocean breeze felt cool. The day seemed bleached of color, the gray of the sky bleeding into the gray of the sea.

I cut across the walkway of Simon's house and headed across the lawn instead. It was quicker that way. I walked around and past the swimming pool area. No one was out. The glass sliding doors to the outside deck were closed, the curtains drawn. The pool chairs lay in a neat, still row like sleeping people. The blue water was so flat and undisturbed that it looked solid.

Nerves jangling, I circled the house, running through all of the awful scenarios of what might have gone down between Simon and his father. I stared at the glaring white columns flanking the front door, and I thought I heard voices coming from inside, but I couldn't be sure. I rang the doorbell and waited.

A minute passed, and I had a sudden, horrible suspicion that the Rosses had gone, just picked up and left Southampton altogether.

But the dull click of footsteps broke the hot silence, and Mrs. Ross opened the door.

"Hello, Mia," she said tonelessly. Her face looked drawn and sleepy, like she'd been woken from a coma.

"Is Simon here?" I asked, a tremor in my voice.

"You can't see him," she said. "I'm sorry. He's busy with his father."

I swallowed and searched Mrs. Ross's face for information, but I could see she just wanted me to leave. "Is everything…is he okay?" I said, my voice faltering. "He's okay, right?"

A ripple of something broke through Mrs. Ross's impassive face. "You shouldn't be here, Mia," she said quietly. "This isn't a good time. Simon is in a lot of trouble."

From behind the door, I now clearly heard the angry staccato of Mr. Ross's deep voice.

"Please let me come in, Mrs. Ross," I said anxiously. "Maybe I can explain to…you and…Mr. Ross." My eyes darted past her, trying to see in, my mind leaping with strategies I wished I'd thought of sooner. Maybe I could convince Simon's father that I had set the fire. After all, he couldn't exactly deck me in the jaw. "It's not all Simon's fault," I added, looking back toward Simon's mother. "I was there too."

The lines around Mrs. Ross's pale eyes softened, and she looked at me with sympathy and some flicker of familiarity. Maybe she'd tried to cover for Simon too when he got in trouble. And maybe she knew it was useless. That's what her face seemed to say. It would explain why she always looked so tired. Maybe she was tired of fighting. Maybe she'd given up.

"Mia, you really must go home now. I'm sorry." As she retreated into the foyer, I took a step toward the still-open door. She might have given up. But I was only getting started.

"When can I see him?" I pressed. She touched her neck nervously, and then her hand fell away. It was freckled with thin, light blue veins crisscrossing her wrist. Somehow, just looking at her hand made me feel sorry for her.

She looked at me for a fraction longer, considering. "My husband is going out this evening at seven," she said. "You can come back then. Simon's not supposed to go out or receive any visitors, but if you come over just for a short visit…"

"Thank you," I said.

"And don't worry," Mrs. Ross added, shooting me one of her tremulous, watery smiles. "Simon is fine. He's in trouble, but it's not as bad…as you think."

"Thank you," I repeated. My heart lifted a little, and I held Mrs. Ross's gaze until she broke it and softly closed the door. I was so relieved standing there that I had to take a minute before walking home. *It's not as bad…as you think.* Mrs. Ross evidently knew I was worried that Simon's dad had hit him again. Obviously he'd held off. I knew I'd still be tense until I saw Simon again, but knowing he hadn't gotten into a physical argument with his father eased my biggest fear. At least for now.

• • •

The afternoon passed with the speed of a glacier, minutes seeming to stretch into hours into…forever. I lay on my bed, unable to sleep or go out and swim. I played music, leaving the same CD on repeat over and over. I didn't care what I listened to. I wrote in my journal but couldn't focus my thoughts.

Outside, the sea glittered horribly, shining like aluminum foil. The air crackled with the threat of a thunderstorm. But it didn't come. Four p.m. finally rolled around, and my mother knocked on my door. "Don't forget about tonight," she said.

"Tonight," I repeated. "What about tonight?" As I asked, I remembered: a family dinner at a clam shack in Watermill. I squeezed my eyes shut.

"We're leaving at six," my mother said.

"I can't!" I said sitting up on my bed and running a hand through my tousled hair.

"Can't?" My mother folded her arms.

"I have to see Simon."

Mom frowned. "You saw Simon last night, Mia. Tonight's a family night. I told you about this days ago."

I shook my head impatiently. "Mom, please. I have to see Simon. I can't go."

"Yes, you can," Mom retorted, her shrewd, china-blue eyes giving me a thorough once-over. "What's the matter with you?" she added, a note of concern creeping into her voice. "You look exhausted. You got up at one. What time did you get to bed last night?"

"I'm fine," I answered evasively. "I just don't want to go out tonight."

"Perhaps you've had too much excitement lately," Mom remarked. "I think an early night will do you a world of good."

"An early night," I repeated. "Yes. That's great. So I'll stay home."

Mom and I locked eyes for a long second. I looked away first. She was on to me. "You can come and have some dinner. We won't be home late."

"Mom!" I bleated. "I can't. I *have* to see Simon. Please."

"You can invite him then." My mom studied me warily as I squirmed on my bed. "I think that would be all right."

Invite him? He was grounded. His dad was only leaving the house at seven.

"He can't come," I said sulkily.

"And I'm sure you'll live until you see him tomorrow."

I flopped onto my bed and stared at the ceiling. I'd have to wait until late that night to slip off and talk to Simon. Things had gone from bad to worse.

• • •

"So I read in the *Hampton Daily* there was a fire at Dragon's Lair last night," Aunt Kathleen said to the table as we sat on the patio of the clam shack. "Accidental, it seems."

I almost choked on my garlic bread, but I kept my eyes firmly on the red-and-white-checkered plastic tablecloth. I knew if I so much as looked up, my face would be redder than the lobster on my aunt's plate.

"A fire? That's an act of God, not an accident!" Mom joked.

"The house wasn't very damaged," Aunt Kathleen replied, a note of regret coloring her voice. "Just a little furniture. Some kid broke in. Apparently he was squatting there or something."

"Squatting in an abandoned castle," Uncle Rufus chimed in. "Only in the Hamptons…"

I kept my eyes on my plate and my ears open, hoping to pick up more tidbits about what had happened. Would Simon have to go to court? Had the police charged him with anything?

I toyed with a crab claw, listening, but the conversation drifted on to other things. More agonizing hours would have to pass before I'd get the scoop about the fire and what was going to happen to Simon. *Not long*, I told myself, but I knew it would feel like an eon before I was clear of this evening and free to climb out the window.

"Are you eating those?" Dad gestured at my crab legs. I blinked, the bucket of seafood in front of me coming into sharp focus.

"Go ahead," I replied, giving the bucket a push in his direction. For once, I didn't feel remotely excited about eating seafood. And my spirits sank even further when I realized that soon enough my parents and my aunt and uncle would discover that Simon was responsible for the fire at Dragon's Lair. This was a small town, and news traveled fast. The great first impression he'd made on them would soon be out the window.

Or maybe not, I told myself desperately, trying to cheer myself at the thought of my mother and aunt throwing their arms around

Simon and thanking him for trying to destroy Dragon's Lair. After all, the summer had taught me that the impossible was possible, hadn't it? But the thought faded as quickly as it had come. Nothing good would come of this. Nothing.

• • •

A distant but threatening rumble of thunder accompanied our drive back to Wind Song after dinner. The heat was finally breaking. But it was only once everyone was in their bedrooms for the night that the storm really began. Lightning blistered the sky in a strobe effect. On the horizon, crackling white fingers reached down into the water.

On any other night, I would have loved this, the sky all bruised and churning, bolts of lightning, the steady beat of rain on the roof. But I felt more desperate than ever as the first sheets of water slanted down, deafeningly loud on my window pane. If it didn't stop, how would I get out there and talk to Simon? And even if it did stop, would he go out on such a wet miserable night to look for me?

I liked to think I knew the answer—that, of all people, Simon wouldn't let even a terrible storm come between us. But I was unsure as I stood by my window, waiting for the weather to quiet down. Maybe Simon was upset and angry and needed to be alone. Maybe, too, he'd heard from his mother that I'd stopped by earlier and was supposed to visit in the evening. Yet I hadn't showed up, so maybe he was also upset with me. I didn't know. I just stared out at the storm. Waiting. And then I saw a flash of light.

At first, I just thought I was seeing some light effects from the storm. But by the third flash, a delicious surge of recognition rippled through me: Simon still had my flashlight from the night before. And he was sending the signal for me to come out and talk, flashing three times across the beach toward my window.

I grabbed the plastic hooded windbreaker I used for sailing, slipped out of the window, and climbed down the rose trellis. It was still raining, and the storm hadn't cut the steamy humidity. Simon walked toward me, switching the flashlight on and off as I made my way onto the beach.

"Where have you been?" he asked. "I've been watching all night for your window light to go on." He wasn't angry, though, and midway through my rushed apologies and explanations, he folded me into a hug.

"You're okay?" I murmured into his soaking jacket. "I've been so worried…"

He pulled away, shone the torch up to his face, and grinned. "Worry no more." His cheekbone was dark with bruising from the night before. But the swelling had gone down. "I'm fine. He laid off me this time." He looked up as the rain began to sprinkle harder. "Let's go sit this out in the gazebo."

As we made our way across the sand to Simon's house, he filled me in on everything that had happened after I'd escaped Dragon's Lair. The caretaker had come. Simon had managed to put out the fire by then. Once the firemen arrived, there was nothing for them to do, so they took Simon to the police station. After first spinning a tall tale about being a drifter, Simon eventually spilled the truth. And the police contacted his father.

"Dad went ballistic at first, but he had to keep it in check in front of the cops."

"Are they going to charge you?" I asked.

Simon laughed dryly we hurried into the gazebo. "Nah. They called the owner this morning. My dad's buying him off. Paying in full for all damages. And probably a chunk extra to have Dragon Dude drop the whole thing."

Simon slid onto a bench and let out a long, low sigh. "I'd rather have had community service than have my father bail me out, but I didn't have a choice. It was all done without me."

"So it's all fine then? I mean, no one's prosecuting you? What about your dad? What's he going to do?" My questions came out in a rapid-fire rush.

Simon looked out at the sea from underneath our shelter. It was dry and dark where we were, but flickers of lightning still streaked across the water, illuminating the gray-green waves for an instant before plunging them back into darkness.

"Dad's furious. Breaking and entering. Destruction of property. What did he call me...?" Simon chuckled as he remembered. "Oh, yeah. A *bohemian anarchist* on a *road to nowhere*. But you know what's weird?" He looked at me, a smile playing at the corners of his mouth. "I'm not afraid. He's trying his best to hide it, but I frightened *him* this time. He's mad at me, but he won't lay a finger on me again. I can see it in his eyes. There's guilt there."

"There should be."

"The cops asked me what happened to my face. My dad was right there, and I could tell he was nervous. I said I tripped at Dragon's Lair. I couldn't see in the dark. That's what I said."

"Must have been pretty intimidating with your dad in the room."

But Simon shook his head. "No. I wasn't afraid of him. Somehow I couldn't rat him out. It didn't feel right."

"But, Simon, he hurt you!"

Simon kept shaking his head. He was impatient with me, excited. "It doesn't matter anymore, Mia. Listen to me! Something's *changed*. I'm telling you. My dad's still talking the tough talk. But I know he won't hit me again. Not ever. I don't know how to explain it. Maybe it's because I didn't rat him out. Or maybe he got freaked when I disappeared last night.

"Whatever the reason, I can feel he knows in my own way I won't back down. I might not hit back, but I won't let him push me around. My dad's finally getting it! He can't change me. No matter what he does, he'll never make me into something I'm not."

"Be careful, Simon," I retorted, picturing Mr. Ross from the night before as he explained Simon's obligations to his family tradition. *We can't always do what we like.* Simon's cheekbone was less swollen today, but it was still bruised.

Simon shrugged. "Don't worry. I got off light. I'll be punished, but that's all."

"So you're grounded. Like forever," I said. "And you'll be broke for the rest of your life paying off some claw-footed couch. Is that it?"

"The couch is toast." Simon laughed again. "And there are some serious holes in the carpet. And, of course, he's threatening to send me away for senior year to some military boot-camp high school in the sticks where I can *get some discipline*." Simon shook his head, smiling. "But he won't. It's all talk. He's just saving face."

I looked at Simon warily. His eyes shone. Heavy rain drummed on the gazebo's roof. I sat still, trying to digest his words, searching his face for some sign of anxiety, but he looked so different from the person who had knocked on my window only the night before.

"Maybe I'm imagining this change in my father," Simon said softly. "But even if I am…His threats can't bring me down. I feel free. I'm not afraid."

Simon pulled me closer to his chest, resting his chin on my head as he looked out into the darkness. The rain slowly turned to more of a drizzle, pattering through the silence. I felt his heart beating through his jacket. "You're really okay?" I whispered. "You'd tell me if…?"

Simon stroked my hair, and I could feel the warmth of his gravelly laugh as it moved up through his chest. "You know what's so crazy? All my life, I've been the wimp in the family. The epileptic kid. Never the tough one. Always pissing my dad off because I'm not what he wanted. Not sporty and straight down the middle like my brothers.

"But somehow, being that kid is starting to pay off. It's almost like the harder it is to be yourself, the more you're prepared to fight for it. I'll make it to Europe or wherever it is I want to be next year. But I won't be going to Wharton. Not ever. My father will have to accept that. And who knows? He might even be proud of me one day."

A bright, blinding sheet of lightning turned the night suddenly into a snapshot second of broad daylight, the deep crack and boom making me jump. Simon tightened his arms around me.

"Wow!" His voice was full of wonder. "It's like pure energy in the air. I feel like if I lit a match, the whole world would go up in flames."

"Or if you dropped a cigarette butt," I joked.

He tickled my ribs in answer as another loud crack of electricity made me squirm. "Isn't this incredible?" Simon was feeding off of the currents in the air; I was a little afraid of the excitement. "Have you ever gone swimming in a storm?"

"No." I sat up and shook my head. "Definitely not. I hope you heard that loud and clear."

"Come on." Simon maneuvered me into his lap and wrapped his arms around my waist. "Are you telling me you really don't want to? Think of how warm the water will be. The water's always amazing during a rainstorm. Even better if there's lightning. It'll be like a Jacuzzi out there."

"Still."

"Do you know how rare it is to be struck by lightning?" Simon scoffed. "It's like shark attacks. They're about as likely to happen as…well, getting struck by lightning."

"Why can't you just watch? You can never just watch." I asked, sighing as I leaned back into Simon's chest, gazing ahead into the darkness to where I could just make out the light patter of sprinkling rain.

"If you haven't been swimming in a storm, you haven't lived. I swear, Mia, it will blow your mind." In the distance, another fissure of lightning slit the sky, creating a purplish aura around the bolt of white light.

"You haven't told me what your punishment is," I said to Simon. "Tell me. I feel like there's more."

"I'm leaving in three days. We're going back home."

Three days?

The words went right through me. Stunned, I shook my head. I'd thought we still had weeks together. My eyes filled with tears, and Simon leaned down to kiss me on the cheek, a soft kiss, like a whisper, which only made the tears come harder.

"He can't make you go home," I choked.

"I have to go, Mia," Simon's voice was soft, resigned. "It's going to cost me all my savings to pay for the fire damage. And if I'm going to go away next year, I'll need more than my job during the school year. I'll need to start working it off ASAP."

"You have to stay." I sniffed. "It's not fair."

"I have to go," Simon repeated quietly. "My father's had enough of summer anyway. Everything's collapsing at work."

"You can stay with me. My aunt would let you."

"I wish I could." Simon's voice was firm, yet tinged with regret. "But I don't have a choice. And you know, I have to prove to my dad that I am responsible," he added, lifting his chin. "I don't want him to think I'm just a bum. Because I'm not. I'm not some slacker spoiled brat. I'm happy to work this one off. It was well worth it," he added, smiling.

"Three days," I whispered in disbelief.

"I'm not through with you yet, lady," Simon murmured, kissing my other cheek. "Don't cry. I'm still here." He pulled me tighter toward his body and rested his chin on my shoulder.

"But you're leaving," I said. "You're leaving me."

"I'm not leaving you." Simon tipped my chin up, his eyes blazing. "I'll be with you. I don't know how or when. But we'll figure it out."

"You'll come back?"

"Shh." Simon put a finger to my lips. "Let's just be here now. Just be here with me." His voice was fierce and thick. "Please, Mia. I need you to be happy. I'm happy. I'm with you. We're right here. Together."

I mashed my lips together in a tight line. I knew if I kept blubbering, it would only be worse for both of us. Simon needed me to be brave, more than anything.

"You promise I won't get struck by lightning out there?" I muttered, stifling a sob and swiping the back of my wrist across my eyes.

"I promise," he said.

• • •

My nerve endings felt naked and raw as we ran down to the ocean, tossing our clothes aside. A yellow moon parted a big swirling cloud, peeping through. The moon dropped back behind the cloud, and then reappeared, glowing to compete against the smoldering sky. I shivered, cool drops of rain pelting me, fear and excitement mingling. But the minute my feet touched the water, a pulsing warmth suffused my ankles. I wanted to throw myself in.

"Oh, my God!"

I tensed and then froze as a white curtain of lightning illuminated the ocean. The surf was huge and breaking closer to the shore, foaming white-capped peaks lurching forward.

"Don't choke on me," Simon pleaded, grabbing my hand.

Water lapped at my shins. I inched forward, yelping as we dipped suddenly down a steep sand embankment and into waist-deep water.

But the sand floor curved back up, and soon we were standing in the shallows again. Raindrops lined my eyelashes, and an intoxicating mixture of salt and warm air swirled around me, drawing me forward.

"Right here is good!" I shouted, stopping thigh-deep.

I turned around just in time to see lightning flickering like the flash from a giant camera, revealing the beach houses, lighting up roofs and bedroom windows and the clouds beyond that gathered in stretches of gray and white. It was amazing. The longest, most powerful, most violently beautiful storm I'd ever seen. And being out there in the warm water, rain sprinkling my damp hair and shoulders, was like nothing I'd ever imagined, much less experienced.

That's when I finally truly understood why Simon had wanted to be out there—why he always chose to be close to the edge. Knowing that at any moment light could reach down from the sky and burn right through us, knowing we were swimming in the ocean, the largest electrical conducting surface possible—made being alive feel *more* alive.

Every cell in my body seemed to buzz, and I clutched Simon's hand, a current passing between us and through us, all around us. I knew that the surge I felt couldn't exist anywhere else or with anyone else. The ocean was an extension of the pulse moving through me—even the smallest waves felt electric, hypnotic, seeming to coax me to stay in the water, to stay in the moment. I had no fear. I wanted to stay like that forever. In the middle of a storm.

The moment passed. The lightning ended. We stood in the silent blackness. The show was over. My eyes stung with salt.

"Whoa," I laughed as a small wave broke against us in the shallows, slapping at our legs and sucking the sand back with it. "I'm getting out."

"I want to catch a wave in."

"It's rough," I said.

"Yeah, it is." Simon agreed, dragging his feet toward me, the hiss and suck of water at his shins. "Don't worry," he said, pulling me into a salty kiss. "I'm not going out far."

"You better not," I said. "Because you'd be crazy."

"I'm not crazy." Simon kissed the tip of my nose.

"Could have fooled me." I tipped my head for more.

"Not crazy." Simon kissed my nose again. "But I can't not take a wave in. There." He indicated the shallows immediately in front of us. Swirling in front of an underwater sandbank, the shallow water had its own mini-reef. The waves breaking there weren't huge, but if you bodysurfed them, they were big enough to carry you all the way in.

I trudged up the sand to where we'd left our clothes. I got as far as putting on my damp underwear before I realized I'd be better off leaving off the rest of my sopping clothes and going home in only my underwear and windbreaker. I smiled to myself in the darkness. Only a month ago, I'd never have walked home half-naked, even in the middle of the night.

I ran my hands through my hair and squeezed water from it. My body felt rubbery, scrubbed by salt and water. My scalp itched with sand. I wondered if I could sneak a shower back home without alerting the whole house…

I wished Simon would hurry up. I peered uselessly into the black ocean. He should have come out by now. Fear flickered, but I dismissed it. Simon had no concept of when it was time to call it a night. I'd probably have to drag him out of the water...I dropped my windbreaker and grabbed my flashlight instead.

"Simon!" I called, standing at the water's edge, scanning for him through the blackness. "Hello?"

A muffled shout came back to me, and I trained my flashlight beam in the direction of his voice. I smiled as he waved and ducked underwater. I jiggled my foot impatiently, keeping my flashlight beam fixed on Simon's dark head as he swam toward the shore.

But after a full minute had passed, I realized he wasn't getting closer to shore. If anything he was moving backward. "Simon!" I yelled. "Come on!"

That's when I heard him, heard the word he'd been shouting, heard it rise only just above the level of the rushing water. "Help!"

My body turned to ice. Blood beat in my ears as I willed my trembling hand to stay steady, to keep the beam of light focused.

And then I smiled. Thinly. Simon's idea of a joke. This was a typical Simon move. There was the time he ducked under the water to bump up against me like a shark, and the night he crept out of the water when I wasn't looking, just to freak me out. I folded my arms. No night was a good night for playing wolf, but especially not tonight, the tide high in the rain.

But Simon was in a shallow place, too shallow to pretend to be drowning.

"Get out!" I yelled, as Simon's torso emerged from the water, and he waved his arms at me. This prank was so not funny. I set my jaw tight. I hated being gullible. I'd always been gullible. But this time I wouldn't give Simon the satisfaction. I beckoned impatiently with my hand. He seemed to float backward, apparently not yet ready to give up his fun. I would really lay into him this time...

He went under.

A coldness filled me slowly, moving from the center of my chest out to my limbs. Recognition. Instinct. Somehow, I knew then that Simon wasn't joking. Something was wrong.

"Simon!" I yelled, whipping the flashlight back and forth. Nothing. The green-black of seawater. A film of rain crisscrossing the beam from my flashlight. Water. More water. Nothing else.

A loud rushing filled my ears, the sound of my blood, or adrenaline, amplifying itself in my eardrums, mingling with the rushing of the water. I couldn't think. Panic locked my joints, rooted me to the spot. Only the beam of my light moved, sweeping jerkily left and right, up and down, searching.

Yes! A dark circular shape, a smear of pale skin as Simon surfaced. Relief, warm as blood, snapped me out of my shock. There was a lull between waves, and the water swirled menacingly in a dark, snaking channel pulling back from the shore. But I could see Simon and he could see me.

"Help!" he shouted again, hoarsely, his face white against the dark water.

I could think again, and one word pounded through my brain: *riptide.*

"This way!" I shouted, pointing to my right. "Swim sideways!" I knew Simon had to get away from the path of the current, swim parallel to the beach. I'd been told this repeatedly every beach vacation of my life. "Across!" I yelled.

But he couldn't hear me. Or else panic had gripped him too tightly. I could see him struggling to pull forward, his shoulders lifting out of the water, his head bent, a curl of white water encircling him as he struggled against the grasp of the tide.

Don't fight it! I heard myself shout, but I couldn't get the words out. I knew it was insane to think I could even help Simon, standing there in the dark rain, trying to shout above the sound of the ocean as it fought to suck him back. I was having trouble even keeping the flashlight's beam on him, my hand shaking like a leaf. The beam was powerful, but it was just a thin line. No match for the darkness of the sea.

A long, terrible second seemed to bend, warp, stretch forward and back, and loop around itself as I gazed out at the water, at the struggling shape pressing forward, arms forward and striking the surface. Maybe he felt he was moving forward. But from where I stood, it looked like he was pinned to the spot, stuck like the moment itself. Like me. Unmoving.

A swell came in and lifted Simon up. And then he was gone.

My flashlight dipped wildly back and forth, my eyes straining to see. I'd lost him. I arced the beam, spiraled it, circled around and around the same spot—or was it the same spot? It was just ocean, endless dark ocean, and then my heart began to overtake everything, the thud, thud, thud painful against my chest.

"Simon!" I screamed. My voice sounded strange. Like it was coming from someone else. No answer. Not even an echo.

Breathe. I squeezed my eyes shut. I needed to fill the white noise around me, the rushing silence of water. I issued hard commands to myself. I could save him. But I had to focus. *Wake up. Move. Go. Run.* There was still time.

I ran.

My feet matched the pounding of my heart, and the rest of me disappeared. I was flying and not flying, above the sand and sinking into it. I could feel every cell in my body, but I also couldn't feel it at all. And I was fast but not fast enough. *More.* I drove energy down into my calves as my bare feet pummeled the sand. I had to move faster.

And then I was nearing Simon's house, but I knew I couldn't stop there. Some clear voice coming out at me through my numbness reminded me that Simon's father was not home, that he had gone to the city...And his mother...I saw her tired smile and fragile, veiny hands. I could not go to her...

I need help...need help... I said it like a mantra as I sprinted toward Wind Song. I ran until I couldn't breathe, and then I stumbled and started sobbing, and suddenly I thought of Simon's big hands and his nose. His perfectly imperfect nose. *Don't stop...don't cry.* I had to get to my dad, to my uncle, to someone who could help.

Help...hurry...help...hurry... the words drilled through me as my feet left the sand and pounded across the wooden walkway of Wind Song.

"Dad!" I screamed, but nothing came out as I banged on the sliding door of the deck. I was gasping for breath. A stitch burned at the side of my ribs like a line of fire, and my throat was thick and swollen. "Dad!" I managed to croak.

Lights and voices. And I managed somehow to tell them something, but not fast enough. Confusion. A slowing down. More lights switched on. Someone was fetching me a robe…But there was no time, and I had trouble swallowing, had trouble breathing right and formulating words.

"He's at Indigo Beach!" I managed to say finally.

"Where's that?" I heard someone say. My mother? My uncle?

I forced myself to breathe.

"Help him!" I yelled. And then I was out the door, running across the sand again, running into the darkness, feeling air rush through my teeth, my lungs, my dry and closing throat…

"He's there!" I sobbed, pointing out into the blackness as I stumbled near the water's edge, my sailing windbreaker shining where I'd left it, bright orange like a flag, and then I started to sink into the sand.

chapter sixteen

I like to think I really do remember everything just as it happened. I know I don't. Of the rest of that night, I know mostly what I've been told. But I do remember the sun coming up. From the night search, I also remember the pattern of light made by the coast guard's lights sweeping up and down the water. And the horizon. I stared at it until it brightened into morning. I told myself that if I stared at the horizon without blinking until the sun rose fully, Simon would be found.

I must have told myself other things. Bits and pieces floated into my memory afterward, and they didn't make sense. They were strange images bumping up against promises I made to God and the universe, even though I didn't believe in God, and the universe didn't listen to some girl's prayers: *If we find him I will never again… If we find him I promise to…*

Some parts are clear, like photographs, like scenes from movies: someone talking on a cell phone, Simon's parents appearing. His father's face ashen, his gray eyes wild and terrified.

—*What's going on here? Where's my kid?*

—*George, he may be all right. There's a buoy nearby, and we think it's possible the tide brought him around to…*

My father and my uncle apparently helped in the search, took a motorboat out. I don't remember that. I don't remember who was with me either, not for most of that night. Only a blur of faces and voices and standing with a blanket someone had wrapped around me. And the constant suck and sigh of the sea. But there was no peace in the sound. It was hollow. Relentless.

They'll find him. I remember telling myself that, over and over, not believing it, but then Corinne's hand was clasping mine and that's when the sun came up. The sand was washed with pink, and it was so beautiful that right then, I think I did believe. I think we all did.

• • •

And they did find him. His body washed ashore a half mile down the beach. We were still standing at Indigo Beach when the news came in. Simon's father broke into loud, hacking sobs, and I remember seeing his knees buckle. His wife had to help him stand up. I'll never forget seeing him like that. It sliced right through me. I can still picture Mr. Ross exactly in a yellow sweater and plaid pajamas, his eyes red and dead-looking.

My memory cuts out after that. Apparently I went into shock or came out of shock, because I became hysterical and they had to call a doctor. He injected me with something to stop me from screaming.

In the days that followed, my parents told me it was not my fault that Simon had drowned. Simon's parents told me it was not my fault that Simon had drowned. The storm had brought on an unusually strong riptide. It was an accident, that's what they said.

Not your fault. The words sounded true, sounded false, were meaningless. None of it mattered anyway. He was dead. Nothing and no one would ever bring him back. Least of all me.

GEORGIA

chapter seventeen

"Coming?" Dad asks.

"In a minute. You go ahead. I'm just finishing this page."

Outside our bungalow on Tybee Island, Dad and Mom are waiting for me. Eva is flirting with some surfer even though she's not yet eleven, even though the reason she's here in Savannah is so that I can look at schools. Though I don't think I want to go to college in my home state. I want to try something different. Maybe North Carolina. The beaches out there are wild and unspoiled. And they're different from the ones up north, so I won't feel constantly reminded.

It might sound strange to say that I still love the ocean when it took away from me the only other love of my life. But having lost the one, I can't lose the other. Because if I did that, I would lose myself, the Mia that Simon knew. And then we'd both be gone.

• • •

Two days after Simon drowned, I flew back to Georgia with my mom, and my dad drove the car back home with Eva. I watched Aunt Kathleen and my cousins recede from view as Mom and I were driven to the airport. I pressed my hand to the car window. I wanted to wave, but it seemed a lot of effort.

They looked so sad huddled on the driveway. Pale and worn. So different from how they'd looked when I'd arrived. *So long ago,* I'd thought to myself as I watched them shrinking into the distance and remembered the way they'd looked when we'd first arrived at Wind Song. Glowing. Radiant. Perfect.

On the airplane, my hand felt cold in Mom's, and her eyes barely left my face for a moment. I saw the fear in them and I wanted to reassure her, to tell her I was okay. But I was numb. I couldn't speak. I didn't have the words.

I didn't start my junior year along with everyone else. It took me two months to set foot outside of my house except for short trips to a therapist. It took much longer for me to feel even a little bit normal again. I had a lot of counseling. And I had two parents staring intently at me every single day, for months and months and months, until I thought I might go crazy from that alone.

Everyone was very careful around me. Maybe that was the strangest part. Even Eva acted solemn and well-behaved when she was near me, like some kind of impostor Eva. It was so quiet around the house. That's what I remember most. The sounds of empty rooms when you sit in them during the day while everyone else is out in the world. Smells of lemon polish and the loud tick of the living-room clock. The hum of the garage door.

Sometimes I'd lie on the couch and remember Simon holding me on the beach, right before we went swimming in the storm. *Be here with me now…I'm happy. I'm with you.* He had been happy. And fearless. About his dad, about everything. It's bittersweet to remember that. But so far, the bitter hasn't managed to cancel out the sweet, though there was a period of time when I wasn't so sure.

In those first months, when I felt weakest and angriest, I'd try to think about Simon's courage. He'd had a lot of courage. Maybe too much. He taught me to take a step forward even when I can't see what's in front of me. He believed in taking chances, in going toward the center of things, no matter how rough it got. That's what he was all about. I like to think he left some of that courage with me, even if I wish I could rewind and take some of it away from him. But you can't do that. And when I want to, I make myself remember the feel of the rain on my skin as I stood in the water and watched the storm.

My parents had questions for me after it happened, questions and hesitant rephrasings. The Rosses wanted to know if maybe I'd misremembered something. Maybe Simon had been drinking that night and had had an epileptic seizure. Maybe he was angry and unhappy. Maybe this, maybe that. His parents wanted proof, a reason that did not have to do with weather and randomness and a kid who wanted to get too close to a rainstorm. They wanted something defined, something they could understand. Something that made sense.

I knew better than to look for it.

I told my parents what they needed to hear, and I made sure they let Simon's parents know that he had felt okay about them, about everything, and that he had been perfectly sober that night and happy about his future. Beyond the facts, I didn't talk about it. Not for a long time.

Nowadays, I talk about Simon. I want to remember everything about him forever. So I write about him. It's easier than talking out loud. It's also more permanent—a way of keeping a record. I've always had a good memory, a good head for facts—although when something is behind you, it changes when you try to capture it in words. The past is slippery that way. I know all about that. And even the present is hard to pin down. You think you know everything that's happening around you. But you can't always see clearly when you're standing right there in the picture.

Still, everything about that summer feels fresh and clear. And when I read my journals, it's as though I'm still sitting in my room in Wind Song, writing. My room smells like wild roses and sea. Sunlight flashes through net curtains and falls on the wide wood planks of the floor. I only have to close my eyes and I'm there.

It's been almost exactly a year now. I'm seventeen years old. I'll be a senior soon. I'm starting to think about colleges. It helps to have something to think about. I still think I'll end up majoring in oceanography, but I don't know for sure how it will all shake out. You can only take steps toward the future you want. It's not guaranteed to be there.

This is why you have to live inside each beautiful or terrible thing as it happens to you, because the present may be all you've got. And if there's more ahead, then the present is where you can really shape your future. Simon made me realize that. If you stay on the sidelines of the here and now, then your future will only ever be a pale version of a dream you never had the courage to experience.

That's my positive spin. Some days I can roll with it. Some days I can agree that it's better to have loved someone and lost them than never to have loved at all, or however the saying goes. Some days I know there will be another day when I can put *Kind of Blue* on my stereo and listen to it again. But on bad days, I think I never will. On bad days, I just miss him.

Nighttime is the hardest. My bad dreams are beginning to fade now. Most nights I can sleep without being haunted by memories and regrets that swim to the surface of my mind. But some nights I dream of Simon struggling against the current. I dream of cuts in the sandbar from the riptide—gashes in the sand like lashes from a whip.

Other nights I could swear that I am back there in the water, and it's beautiful, pulsing with electricity, the sky purple and lit up. I wake up shivering and lie there in my sheets waiting for the sun to come up, tears sliding down my cheeks into my pillow. In those moments, it's like it just happened, only half a breath ago.

And sometimes I wake up drenched with relief and high on some kind of joy, knowing that we saved him and now everything is going to be all right.

Then I realize I'm only dreaming. It's like the opposite of a nightmare. You jam your eyes shut when you wake up so dreams can come back to soothe you from the nightmare of what's real.

• • •

"What do you think of Tybee?" Mom asks, threading her arm through mine. I smile at her. Her hair has gotten grayer recently, and she's let a few natural wisps show. It suits her.

"It's nice," I say truthfully. "It's a nice beach." *It's not Indigo Beach.* It's hard not to think of the place Simon had named. And maybe Mom knows it, because she presses my arm close, tucking it under hers as we watch as Eva skips ahead and Dad stoops down to examine something at the tide line.

Mom and I have gotten closer in the last year. We'll never completely understand each other, but we know each other better now. The gap between us has shrunk. I never thought I'd need her so much. But without her, I doubt I'd have made it through the year.

We walk along the sand, and my eyes drift over to the water. I often wonder where it is, the message I sent out to sea…

• • •

The spring after Simon drowned, I went back to Long Island. There had been a memorial service for him in Minnesota, and his mom had written to mine. But I didn't want to even hear about it. Not then. It took months for me to want to say good-bye, and, though a huge part of me didn't want to go back to Indigo Beach, I also knew I had to.

It was a cool day and the beach was empty. My parents were with me. As we walked, I tried not to look at Wind Song. It stood empty as a washed-up seashell. My aunt was in Europe teaching at a French culinary academy; my uncle was in Manhattan; Beth was at Vassar; and Corinne was at her school in upstate New York. Everything felt scattered and sad and forgotten like the cargo of a shipwreck. The smell of summer was gone. It was too late for that particular sweetness of wild roses and sea grass. Or too early.

There was another reason the house felt empty—because there was nothing in it. Not a trace of my family remained within the walls of Wind Song, and a For Sale sign hung forlornly from a post in front of the driveway. My uncle had lost a lot of money. Other people's money too. They'd had to sell the house. It wasn't just that they could no longer afford it, but also, according to Mom, Uncle Rufus wasn't popular in Southampton anymore.

When Mom told me about the house, I remembered walking with my uncle down to the marina at his club the summer before. There was the frosty greeting from Uncle Rufus's friend, William. At the time, I'd thought Dad and I were the reason for the cold shoulder, because we didn't belong there.

It had never occurred to me that my handsome, charming, wealthy uncle might be the one this man didn't want to see. But though Uncle Rufus and Aunt Kathleen lost a lot of their fortune, their lives still went on. For wealthy people, I guess there's always money somewhere…

As I walked closer to the tide line and away from Wind Song, the scent of new sand and salt water rushed to meet me. I breathed it in, a familiar sharpness lingering. The smell of water. The cut-glass light. *Hamptons Blue.* That mellow softness of summer, the varnished golden haze I'd always known, was gone, but the spring sunlight was clear and shimmering. And when I waded into the icy cold of the ocean at Indigo Beach, I felt a flicker of something good. Not happiness exactly, but maybe the memory of it, some distant cousin of happiness.

In my hands, I held a bottle, and in the bottle was a message for Simon. It had taken a long time for me to want to do something to remember him because it had taken a long time for me to understand that he was gone. I'd struggled with my letter. And finally I knew. Those three simple words I'd never actually said to him. I know he knew it, but it felt good to write them down, fold the paper, and put it in the bottle. It was a note, a love letter, just three short syllables in ink.

I hesitated at the water's edge. I used to look for treasure the ocean had given up; now I would be giving a treasure up to it. The glass of the bottle couldn't protect the note for long. The water would seep in, even if the bottle didn't break on the rocks. The water would seep in and wash the words away.

But it was not the note that counted so much as the writing of it. Just because it wouldn't last forever out there didn't mean it hadn't existed. That's why I was there. I was there for a moment. And because of a string of beautiful moments spent at that very same place, moments I would keep inside me wherever I went.

Deep breath.

I looked out to the ocean, to the glittering water. I threw the bottle in, as far and as hard as I could. *The light that burns twice as bright burns out soonest.* I don't know where the words came from, but they welled up in my heart—heavy, and also light as an echo. I swallowed them back and watched a wave catch the bottle. And then it disappeared under the crush of white foam, not a parting gift but a souvenir. Because I wasn't saying good-bye…I was promising to always remember.

My parents were waiting for me when I came out of the water. "Ready?" Dad asked.

"Yeah," I lied. And then we turned and walked away.

• • •

"I heard from Aunt Kathleen," Mom tells me as we walk along Tybee Pier. "She's back from Europe. She and Rufus are trying to work it out."

"Do you think they will?"

"I don't know."

We say nothing for a while, and I think about Corinne, about the email she just sent me. She finished her junior year at the alternative boarding school. *It wasn't bad*, she wrote. *I got really into yoga there.* She's returning home to Manhattan, but she's not returning to her dance program. *I want to be a yoga teacher now. Mom's adjusting, but it's hard for her.* Corinne sounds good, centered. I'm glad. She deserves to be happy.

Beth, meanwhile, has dropped out of Vassar and has gone off to cooking school in Provence, the same school where my aunt teaches every year. It makes me smile to think of Beth at cooking school. I can still see her beautiful face scowl in disgust as she poked at a scallop the night of the barbecue with the Rosses.

I don't hear from Beth much, but I know she's probably still the same, like one of those beautiful sea anemones that store venom in their soft folds, beneath the pale glow of their tentacles. I'm sure Beth will keep going through life trading on the vulnerable exterior that hides the toughness of who she really is. For Corinne, it's the opposite. Or at least, that's how I see it. But maybe they'll surprise me. People change.

Gen surprised me: After Simon died, I got a sympathy card in the mail from her. It was really heartfelt and didn't sound like her at all. Which made me appreciate it even more. She'd sent it while on location for some independent movie about a bunch of naked zombie women who terrorize a frat house. I look forward to renting it.

As I walk along the beach with Mom, the sky turns a soft, mother-of-pearl pink. Like so many times before, I try to turn my mind away from that summer and think instead about what might lie ahead. New faces, new chances. I can't see them yet. But I'll take them as they come. I won't let them glide past.

Mom still keeps in touch with Simon's mom, and a few months after he died, his mom sent me a big package. I knew what it was, but I wasn't ready to open it. I stuck it under my bed for a long, long time. I couldn't bear the thought. And then one day, I dragged it out and ripped the packaging open. It was a square canvas, about two feet by two feet. Before I turned it over, I remembered how Simon had looked when he told me he was working on a special painting. His gray eyes had been excited and faraway. *I'm just trying to capture something I think is beautiful.*

I had felt, for the first time in my life, fearless and beautiful around Simon because that's what he saw, just as I saw it in him. Clichés are corny, but they become clichés because they're true. And here's one I know to be true: *Beauty is in the eye of the beholder.*

As I learned that summer, so are a lot of things. Everything and everyone is only how you perceive them to be. If you're looking up at someone on a pedestal, they seem impossibly high, impossibly far. If you're looking down at someone, they become small and unimportant. There's no complete truth. There's only the way you see it, the way you remember it.

Here's how Simon remembered it:

He used thick strokes of a palette knife to smooth blocks of color into an abstract flatness. But there's a recognizable quality to the painting too, or what Miss Elliot, my art teacher, calls "figurative"—you know what you're looking at.

Everything has been distilled down to its essence: the gold of sand, a deep sea-green for the water, moving into blue. Above, a flat, turquoise stripe of sky. In the foreground and bottom left, two triangles of dune. Between them, two pale arcs—the suggestion of knees—and then the sand meets the ocean, its colors so true that your eyes sink into its dark-blue depths…and rise up as the blue lightens to teal-green and into the swell of a wave.

In the middle of the wave is a figure, arms up, caught mid-leap: a strip of flesh-tone, a squiggle of dark hair, two navy swimsuit lines crisscrossing the figure's back. It's me.

It's a simple painting, but simple is hard to do. It's more than the colors and the balance of the composition. It's more than just a painting of a beautiful seascape. Simon has captured something fleeting: a perfect, happy moment. Within the stillness of the painting, the swimmer diving toward the wave is the moving center. In a few strokes, Simon has caught a feeling: that feeling just before a wave breaks over you, that pure summer energy.

He never got to finish it. There's a section of the ocean and sand that isn't filled in, a blank white staring out through the painting. I think I know how Simon would have completed it—just adding more water, more sand, leaving the landscape empty except for the tiny figure in the middle and the knees of the viewer peeping out between the dunes. But the fact that I don't really know holds me, and I often find myself staring at the gap in the painting.

He might have added in another figure. Maybe a smudge of towel on the beach…I like staring into the hole in the image and wondering what would have filled it. There's even a drip mark on the white of the canvas in that unfinished section. That casual drip makes me feel as though Simon is still there, still working on the painting. It's as though he'll be right back to wipe away the tiny dot of paint.

Sometimes I just look at the two knee shapes framing the girl in the waves, and I smile. I picture Simon hidden, sitting somewhere half-hidden by a dune, watching me. *That one is a special one. I've been working on it since before we even met.* He had painted me in daylight. He'd been out there all along.

"You're very quiet," Mom murmurs, and I snap back to the present.

"Just admiring the view." I don't want Mom to think I'm feeling melancholic, even though I am, because the light is turning and if I kept walking in this direction, just walking and walking for months, I would eventually end up at Indigo Beach. But I'm also admiring the view, and I know now that these combinations of sadness and happiness are what life is all about. A melancholic, absent feeling can go hand in hand with a beautiful view that makes your heart kick. That, I think, is how it will always be. At least for me.

"Isn't the Atlantic so beautiful?" my mom asks.

"Rhetorical question," I reply. And I smile as I look out at the darkening blue stretching far away and out across forever, carrying the twinkling lights of a thousand ships, the faraway stares of a thousand lonely girls at parties looking out to sea, dreaming of something romantic, dreaming of exotic places and someone to sweep them off their feet, while I'm dreaming backward in time to a summer that has already been, the summer of my sixteenth year. A terrible summer that almost makes me want to forget. Until I remember it was also the greatest summer of my life.

about the author

Amanda Howells has always lived near the sea. She grew up on a small bay on the Atlantic Ocean and now lives in the Pacific Northwest. This is her first original young adult novel.